"Protecting you is my job. You're a material witness. I have to keep you alive."

Maria nodded. "Yes. Of course," she agreed. "I know that you're only doing your job."

Finding her had never been just a job to him. She was so much more than that… So much more than he had ever realized before meeting her. Was Maria really what everyone claimed she was? Was she really a witch?

"I could do my job more easily if you stopped lying to me and told me everything you know." He touched her again, tipping up her chin to make her meet his gaze.

Her thick black lashes fluttered as she blinked—as if trying to shield her thoughts and feelings from him. Could she sense his feelings?

Could she feel his desire for her? His madness…

CURSED

LISA CHILDS

MILLS & BOON

Published in Great Britain 2015
by Mills & Boon, an imprint of Harlequin (UK) Limited,
Eton House, 18-24 Paradise Road, Richmond, Surrey, TW9 1SR

© 2015 Lisa Childs-Theeuwes

ISBN: 978-0-263-25404-4

89-0315

Harlequin (UK) Limited's policy is to use papers that are natural, renewable and recyclable products and made from wood grown in sustainable forests. The logging and manufacturing processes conform to the legal environmental regulations of the country of origin.

Printed and bound in Spain
by CPI, Barcelona

Lisa Childs writes paranormal and contemporary romance for Mills & Boon. She lives on thirty acres in Michigan with her two daughters, a talkative Siamese and a long-haired Chihuahua who thinks she's a rottweiler. Lisa loves hearing from readers, who can contact her through her website, lisachilds.com, or snail-mail address, PO Box 139, Marne, MI 49435, USA.

With great appreciation to
Tara Gavin and Ann Leslie Tuttle
for letting me share Maria's story
and revisit The Witch Hunt series.

Thank you!

Prologue

Europe, 1655

Strong hands closed over her shoulders, shaking her awake. Elena Durikken blinked her eyes open, but the darkness remained thick, impenetrable.

"Child, awaken. Quickly."

"Mama?" She blinked again, bringing a shadow into focus. A shadow with long curly hair. "Mama."

"Rise up. Hurry. You have to go." Her mother's hands dragged back the blankets, letting the cold air steal across Elena's skin.

"Go? Where are we going?" She couldn't remember being awake in such blackness before. Usually a fire flickered in the hearth, the dying embers casting a glow over their small home. Or her mother burned candles, chanting to herself as she fixed her potions from the dried herbs and flowers strung from the rafters.

"Only you, child. You must go alone." Mama's words, the final way she spoke, chilled Elena more than the cold night air.

"Mama…" Tears stung her eyes and ran down her face.

"There's no time. They will come soon. For me. And if you are still here, they will take you, too."

"Mama, you are scaring me." It was not the first time. She had scared Elena many times before, with the things she saw, the things she *knew* were coming before they ever happened.

Like the fire.

"Is this…is this because of the fire, Mama?"

Mama didn't answer, just pulled a cape over Elena's head, lifting the hood over her hair. Then she slid Elena's feet into her boots, lacing them up as if she were a small dependent child, not a thirteen-year-old girl she was sending alone into the night. Mama pressed the neck of a satchel against Elena's palm. "Ration the food and water. Keep to the woods, child. Run. Keep running…"

"How can they blame you for the fire?" she cried. "You warned them."

Even before the sky had darkened or the wind had picked up, her mother had told them the storm was coming. That the lightning would strike in the night, while the women slept. And that they would die in a horrible fire. Mama had seen it all happen…

Elena didn't know how her mother's visions worked, but she knew that Mama was always right. More tears fell from her eyes. "You asked them to leave."

But the woman of the house, along with her sister-in-law, whose family was staying with her, had thought that with the men away for work, Mama was tricking them. That she, a desperate woman raising a child alone, would rob their deserted house. She'd been trying to save their lives.

Mama shook her head, her hair swirling around her shoulders. "The villagers think I cast a spell. That I brought the lightning."

Elena had heard the frightened murmurs and seen the downward glances as her mother walked through the village. Everyone thought her a witch because of the potions she made. But when the townspeople were sick, they came to Mama for help even though they feared her. How could they think she would do them harm? "No, Mama…"

"No. The only spell cast is upon me, child. These visions I see, I have no control over them," she said. "And I have no control over what will happen now. I need you to go. To run. And keep running, Elena. Never stop. Or they will catch you."

Elena threw her arms around her mother's neck, more scared than she had ever been. Even though she heard no one, saw no light in the blackness outside her window, she knew her mama was right. They were coming for her. The men who'd returned, who'd found their wives, sisters and daughters dead, burned.

"Come with me, Mama," Elena beseeched her, holding tight.

"No, child. 'Tis too late for me to fight my fate, but you can. You can run." She closed her arms around Elena, clutching her tight for just a moment before thrusting her away. "Now go!"

Tears blinded Elena as much as the darkness. She'd just turned toward the ladder leading down from the loft when Mama caught her hand, squeezing Elena's fingers around the soft velvet satchel. "Do not lose the charms."

Elena's heart contracted. "You gave me the charms?"

"They will keep you safe."

"How?" Elena asked in a breathless whisper.

"They hold great power, child."

"You need them." Elena did not know from where they had come, but Mama had never removed the three charms from the leather thong tied around her wrist. Until now.

Mama shook her head. "I cannot keep them. They are yours, to pass to your children. To remember who and what we are."

Witches.

Mama did not say it, but Elena knew. She shivered.

"Go now, child," Mama urged. "Go before it is too late for us both." She expelled a ragged breath of air, then pleaded, "Do not forget…"

Elena hugged her mother again, pressing her face tight against her, breathing in the scent of lavender and sandalwood incense. The paradox that was her mama, the scent by which she would always remember her. "I will never forget. Never!"

"I know, child. You have it, too. The curse. The gift. Whatever it be."

"No, Mama…" She didn't want to be what her mother was; she didn't want to be a witch.

"You have it, too," Mama insisted. "I see the power you have, much stronger than any of mine. *He* would see it as well, and want to destroy you." Before Elena could ask of whom her mother spoke, the woman pushed her away, her voice quavering with urgency as she shouted, "You have to go!"

Elena fumbled with the satchel as she scrambled down the ladder, running as much from her mother's words as her warning. She didn't want the curse, whatever the mystical power was. She didn't want to flee, either. But her mama's fear stole into her heart, forcing her to run.

Keep to the woods.

She did, cringing as twigs and underbrush snapped beneath the worn soles of her old boots. She ran for so long that her lungs burned and sweat dried on her skin, both heating and chilling her. She'd gone a long way before turning and looking back toward her house.

She knew she'd gone too far, too deep into the woods to see it clearly with her eyes. So, like Mama, she must have seen it with her mind. The fire.

Burning.

The woman in the middle of it, screaming, crying out for God to forgive them. Pain tore at Elena, burning, crippling. She dropped to her knees, wrapping her arms around her middle, trying to hold in the agony. Trying to shut out the image in her head. She crouched there for a long while, her mama's screams ringing in her ears.

Behind her, brush rustled, the blackness shattered by the glow of a lantern. Oh, God, they'd found her already.

The glow fell across her face and that of the boy who held the lantern. Thomas McGregor. He wasn't much older than she, but he'd gone to work with his father and uncles, leaving his mother, sisters, aunt and cousins behind…to burn alive.

As they'd burned her mother. "No…"

"I was sent to find you. To bring you back," he said, his voice choked as tears ran down his face. Tears for his family or for her?

Her mother had seen this, had tried to fight this fate for her daughter, the same fate that had just taken her life.

"You hate me?" she asked.

He shook his head, and something flickered in his eyes with the lantern light. Something she had seen before when she'd caught him staring at her. "No, Elena."

"But you wish me harm? I had nothing to do with your loss." Nor did her mother, but they had killed her. Smoke swept into the woods, too far from the fire to be real, and in the middle of the haze hovered a woman. Elena's mother.

"I have to bring you back," Thomas said, his hand trembling as he reached for her, his fingers closing over her arm.

The charms will keep you safe.

Had her mother's ghost spoken or was it only Elena's memory? Regardless, she reached in the pocket of her cape and held the satchel tight. Heat emanated through the thick velvet, warming her palm. As if she'd stepped into Thomas's mind, she read his thoughts and saw the daydreams he had had of the two of them. "Thomas, you do not wish me harm."

"But Papa…"

Other memories played through Elena's mind, her mother's memories. She shuddered, reeling under the impact of knowledge she was too young to understand. "Your papa is a bad man," she whispered. "Come with me, Thomas. We will run together."

He shook his head. "He would find us. He would kill us both."

Because of what she'd seen, she knew he spoke the truth. Eli McGregor would kill anyone who got between him and what he wanted.

"Thomas, please…"

His fingers tightened on her arm as if he were about to drag her off. Elena clutched the satchel so close the jagged little metal pieces cut her palm through the velvet.

He sighed as if a great battle waged inside him. "I cannot give you to him. Go, Elena. You are lost to me." But when she turned to leave, he caught her hand as her mother had, shaking as he pressed something against her bloody palm. "Take my mother's locket."

To remember him? To remember what his family had done to hers? She would want no reminders. But her fingers closed over the metal, warm from the heat of his skin. She couldn't refuse. Not when he had spared her life.

"Use it for barter, if need be, to get as far away from here as you can. My father has sworn vengeance on all your mother's relatives and descendants. He says he will let no witch live."

"I am not a witch." She whispered the lie, closing her eyes to the luminous image of her mother's ghost.

"He will kill you," Thomas whispered back.

She knew he spoke the truth. Like her mother, she could now see her fate. But unlike her mother, she wouldn't wait for Eli McGregor to come for her. She turned to leave again, then twirled back, moved closer to Thomas and pressed her lips against his cheek, cold and wet from his tears.

"Godspeed, Elena," he said as she stepped out of the circle of light from his lantern, letting the darkness and smoke swallow her as she ran.

This time she wouldn't stop… She wouldn't stop until she'd gotten as far away as she could. And even then, she wouldn't ever stop running…

From who and what she was.

Armaya, Michigan, 1986

The candlelight flickered as the wind danced through the open windows of the camper, carrying with it the scent of lavender and sandalwood incense. Myra Cooper dragged in the first breath she'd taken since she'd begun telling her family's legend; it caught in her lungs, burning, as she studied her daughters' beautiful faces.

Irina snuggled between her bigger sisters, her big dark eyes luminous in the candlelight. She *heard* everything but, at four, was too young to understand.

Elena, named for that long-ago ancestor, tightened her arm protectively around her sister's narrow shoulders. Her hair was pale and straight, a contrast to Myra's and Irina's dark curls. Her eyes were a vivid icy blue that *saw* everything. But at twelve, she was too old to believe.

Ariel kept an arm around her sister, too, while her gaze was intent on Myra's face as she waited for more of the story. The candlelight reflected in her auburn hair like flames, and her green eyes glowed. She listened. But Myra worried that she did not hear.

She worried that none of them understood that they were gifted with special abilities. The girls had never spoken of them to her or one another, but maybe that was better. Maybe they would be safer if they denied their heritage. Yet they couldn't deny what they didn't know; that was why she had shared the legend. She wanted them to know their fate so they could run from it before they were destroyed.

"We are Durikken women," she told her daughters, "like that first Elena."

"You named me after her," her eldest said, not questioning. She already knew.

Myra nodded. "And I'm named for her mother." And sometimes, when she believed in reincarnation, she was sure she was that woman, with her memories as well as her special abilities.

However, most of the time, Myra believed in nothing; it hurt too much to accept *her* reality. But tonight she had to be responsible. She had one last chance to protect her children; she'd already failed them in so many ways. They didn't have to live the hardscrabble life she had. They didn't have to be what she was—a woman whose fears had driven her to desperation.

"Our last name is Cooper," Elena reminded her.

"Papa's name," she said, referring to her own father. None of their fathers had given his child his name, either because the man had refused or she hadn't told him he was a father. "We are Durikken, and Durikken women are special. They know things are going to happen before they do."

Pain lanced through Myra, stealing her breath as images rolled through her mind like a black-and-white movie. She couldn't keep running and she couldn't make *them* keep running, either.

She forced herself to continue. "They see things or

people that no one else can see. This ability, like the charms on my bracelet—" she raised her arm, the silver jewelry absorbing the firelight as it dangled from her wrist "—has been passed from generation to generation."

But Myra was more powerful than her sisters, had inherited more abilities as a woman and a witch. That was why she had been given the bracelet—because her mother had known she would be the only one of her three daughters to continue the Durikken legacy.

Myra's fingers trembled as she unclasped the bracelet. She'd never taken it off, not once since her mother had put it on her wrist, until tonight. Her daughters had admired it many times, running their fingers over the crude pewter charms, and she knew which was each one's favorite.

Elena had always admired the star, the sharp tips now dulled with age. Irina loved the crescent moon, easily transformed—like Irina's moods—from a smile to a frown, depending on the angle from which it dangled. Ariel favored the sun, its rays circling a small smooth disk. Despite its age, this charm seemed to shine brighter than the others. Like Ariel.

Even now, in the dingy little camper, an aura surrounded the child, glowing around her head as spirits hovered close. Did Ariel know what her gift was? Did either of her sisters? Her daughters needed Myra's guidance so they could understand and use their abilities. They were too young to be without their mother, but she couldn't put them at risk. All Myra could hope was that the charms would keep them safe.

Myra knelt before her children where they huddled in their little makeshift bed in the back of the pickup camper, their home for their sporadic travels. This was all she'd been able to give them. Until now. Until she'd shared the legend.

Now she'd given them their heritage, and with the help of the charms, they would remember it always. No matter how much time passed. No matter how much they might want to forget or ignore it.

She reached for Elena's hand first. It was nearly as big as hers, strong and capable, like the girl. She could handle anything…Myra hoped. She dropped the star into Elena's palm and closed her fingers over the pewter charm. The girl's blue gaze caught hers, held. No questions filled her eyes, only knowledge. She'd already seen too much in visions like her mother's. The girl had never admitted it, but Myra knew.

She then reached for the smallest—and weakest—hand, Irina's. Myra worried most about this child. She'd had so little time with her. She closed Irina's hand around the moon. *Hang on tight, child.* She didn't say it aloud. For Irina she didn't need to—the child could hear unspoken thoughts.

Myra swallowed down a sob before reaching for Ariel. But the girl's hand was outstretched already. She was open and trusting, and because of that might be hurt the worst.

"Don't lose these," she beseeched them. Without the protection of the little pewter charms, none of them would be strong enough to survive.

"We won't, Mama," Elena answered for herself and her younger sisters as she attached her charm to her bracelet and helped Irina with hers.

Despite her trembling fingers, Myra secured the sun

charm on Ariel's bracelet, but when she pulled back, the girl caught her hand. "Mama?"

"Yes, child?"

"You called it a curse…this special ability," Ariel reminded her, her voice tremulous. She had been listening.

Myra nodded. "Yes, it is a curse, my sweetheart. People don't understand. They thought our ancestors were witches who cast evil spells."

And they had been witches, but ones who'd tried to help and heal. Her family had never been about evil; that was what had pursued them and persecuted them through the ages.

"But that was long ago," Elena said, ever practical. "People don't believe in witches anymore."

Myra knew better than to warn them, to make them aware of the dangers. She'd shown them the locket earlier, the one nestled between her breasts, the metal cold against her skin. It was the one Thomas had pressed upon Elena all those years ago. Inside were faded pictures, drawn by Thomas's young hand, of his sisters, who had died in the fire. Their deaths could have been prevented if only they'd listened and fought their fate. "Some still believe."

"Mama, I'm cursed?" Ariel asked, her turquoise eyes wide with fear. Her hand shook as she clutched the sun.

No more than I. Myra had lost so much in her life. Her one great love—Elena's father. And now…

"Mama, there are lights coming across the field!" Ariel whispered, as if thinking that if she spoke softly they wouldn't find her. Maybe she didn't hear as much as her sisters, but she understood.

Myra didn't glance out the window. She'd already seen the lights coming, in a vision, and so she'd hidden the camper in the middle of a cornfield. But still they'd found her; they'd found *them*. She stared at her children, memorizing their faces, praying for their futures. Each would know a great love as she had, and all she could hope was that theirs lasted. That they fought against their fate, against the evil stalking them, as she would have fought had she been stronger.

She just stood there next to the camper, in the middle of the cornfield, as the child protective services, who'd already declared her unfit, took her children away. The girls screamed and reached for her, tears cascading down their beautiful faces like rain against windows.

This wasn't Myra's final fate; her death would come much later. But as her heart bled and her soul withered, this was the night she really died.

But the authorities didn't take them all. Her hands clasped her swollen belly. Soon she would have another little girl. This child would need her even more than the others, for she would have more abilities than they had. She would be more powerful a witch even than Myra. But yet she would be even more cursed. The witch hunt would end for the others. But for her fourth child, whom she would call Maria, the witch hunt would never end…

Chapter 1

Energy flowed from the cards up the tips of Maria Cooper's tingling fingers. Warmth spread through her as the energy enveloped her. *This will be a clear reading...*

She had been blocking her special abilities for so long that she'd worried she might have lost them. But maybe that wouldn't have been such a bad thing. In the past they had proved more destructive than special—more curse than gift.

"What do you see?" the young woman asked, her voice quavering with excitement.

"I haven't turned the first card," Maria pointed out. Only the Significator, the fair-haired Queen of Cups, lay faceup on the table between them. The card didn't represent the young woman's physical appearance—not since the girl had dyed her hair black, tattooed a crow on her face and renamed herself Raven. But the card represented the wistfulness of the young woman's nature, so Maria had chosen it for her.

"But you see stuff—that's what people say about you," the girl continued. "That's why I wanted to learn from you—how to read the cards and how to make the potions and amulets. I know that you have a real gift."

A gift. Or a curse? She used to think it was the first and had grown up embracing her heritage. But then everything had gone so wrong, and she had begun to believe what others had—that she was cursed. That was why she had refused the girl's previous requests to learn to read. Maria had taught her about the crystals and herbs she sold in her shop but she'd resisted the cards—afraid of what she herself might see.

"I have it, too," Raven confided. "I get that sense of déjà vu all the time. I know I've already dreamed what's happening. I saw it…like you see stuff."

I hope you don't see the stuff I've seen…

"That's why I want to learn tarot," the girl said. "Because I know I'll be good at it."

Raven had been saying the same thing ever since she had first started hanging around the Magik Shoppe. The twenty-two-year-old had spent so much time there that Maria had finally given her a job, and now she had given in on teaching her tarot. She hoped like hell that she didn't come to regret caving in to the girl's pleas.

Maybe Raven had a gift. Or maybe, like so many others, she only wished she did because she had glamorized the supernatural ability into something that it wasn't. Into something powerful, when having these abilities actually made Maria feel powerless, helpless to stop what she might see.

"Thank you," Raven said, "for helping me."

I hope it helps and doesn't hurt...

"To teach you how to read the cards, I have to show you how I do a reading," Maria said. That was how her mother had taught her, having Maria watch her do readings for other people. But Mama hadn't always told the truth of the cards. Instead of telling people what she saw, she had told them what they'd wanted to see.

The old gypsy proverb that her mother had always recited echoed in Maria's head. *There are such things as false truths and honest lies.*

But there was no one but she and Raven in the old barn on Michigan's Upper Peninsula that Maria had converted into her shop. She had only the girl's cards to read. And she had already told Raven the meaning of each card, so she wouldn't be able to lie to her— even if it would be the kinder thing to do.

This is a mistake...

Her fingers stilled against the deck, which was the size of a paperback novel. She preferred the big cards because of the greater detail. She had always used them, ever since she had first started reading—at the age of four. She had read cards before she'd been able to read words.

"I've been working here almost since you opened a few months ago, but I've never seen you do a reading," Raven remarked.

And she shouldn't be doing one now. She shouldn't risk it...but it had been so long. She had missed it. Surely it couldn't happen again. The cards wouldn't come up the way they had before...

"I haven't done one in a while," she admitted. But she hadn't lost the ability. Energy continued to tingle up Maria's fingertips, spreading into her arms and chest.

Before the girl could ask her why she hadn't, Maria shuffled the cards again and eased one off the top of the deck. "This first card will represent your environment."

Maria turned over the card atop the Significator, and dread knotted her stomach as she stared down at it. The moon shone down upon snarling dogs and a deadly scorpion.

A gasp slipped through the girl's painted black lips. "That's not good."

Maria's temple throbbed, and her pulse beat heavily in her throat. "No. The moon represents hidden enemies. Danger."

The girl's eyes, heavily lined with black, widened with fear. "You're saying I'm in danger."

Not again...

"That's what that means, right?" Raven persisted, her voice rising into hysteria.

Since Maria had already taught the girl the meaning of each card, she couldn't deny what Raven already knew. So she nodded. "Danger. Deceit. A dark aura..."

Maria saw it now, enveloping Raven like a starless night sky—cold and eerie, untold dangers hiding in the darkness. Goose bumps lifted on her skin beneath her heavy knit sweater, and she shivered.

"Turn over the next card," the girl urged. "That's what's coming up—that's what's going to be my obstacle, right?"

Maria shook her head. She wouldn't do it; she wouldn't turn that card. "No. We need to stop. We can't continue." She shouldn't have even begun; she shouldn't have risked the cards coming up the way they had before. But it had been more than a year...

She had thought that she might have reversed the

curse, that her fortunes might have finally changed. She'd been using the crystals, herbs and incense that she used for healing to treat herself.

"Turn the card!" The girl's voice had gone shrill, and her face flushed with anger despite her pale pancake makeup. "Turn it!"

"No." Her heart beating fast, she could feel the girl's panic and fear as if it were her own. But she also felt her desperation and determination.

"I have to know!" Raven shouted.

Maybe she did. Maybe they both needed to know. Maria's fingers trembled as she fumbled with the next card. Then she flipped it over to reveal the skeleton knight.

Raven screamed. "That's the death card."

"It has other meanings," Maria reminded her. "You've been studying the tarot with me. You know that it might just mean the end of something."

"What is it the end of? You see more than the cards. You see the future."

As Maria stared across the table at the young woman, an image flashed through her mind. *The girl— her face pale not with makeup but with death—her fearful eyes closed forever.*

Raven demanded, "What is my future?"

You won't have one.

"I don't see anything," Maria claimed.

"You're lying!"

Maybe the girl actually had a gift—because Maria was a very good liar. Like reading the cards, she had learned at a very young age how to lie from her mother. "Raven…"

"You were looking at me, but you weren't really

looking at me. You saw something. Tell me what you saw!"

"Raven…"

"Oh, God, it's bad." The girl's breath shuddered out, and tears welled in her eyes. "It's really bad."

"It doesn't have to be," Maria assured her. "We can stop it from happening. I'll make you an amulet of special herbs and crystals…" And maybe this time it would work.

The girl shook her head, and her tears spilled over, running down her face in black streaks of eyeliner. "Even you can't change the future!" She jumped up with such force she knocked over her chair.

Maria jumped up, too, and grabbed the girl's arms. "Don't panic." But she felt it—the fear that had her heart hammering in her chest and her breathing coming fast and shallow in her lungs.

"Stay here," she implored the girl. "Stay with me, and I'll make sure nothing happens to you."

Blind with terror, Raven clawed at Maria's hands and jerked free of her grasp. Then she shoved Maria away from her, sending her stumbling back from the table.

"No. It's you," the girl said, her eyes reflecting horror. "I've seen it—the dark aura around you."

That was what Maria had been trying to remove. But she had failed. As Raven had said, even *she* couldn't change the future—no matter how hard she tried.

"It's you!" Raven shouted, her voice rising as she continued her accusation. "You're the moon!"

She hurled the table at Maria, knocking it over like the chair. The cards scattered across the old brick pavers of the barn.

Raven was right: even she, with all the knowledge of her witch ancestor, could not change what she had seen of the future. Like that witch ancestor, who had burned at the stake centuries ago, Maria was helpless to fight the evil that followed her no matter how far and how fast she had tried to outrun it.

The girl turned now and ran for the door, leaving it gaping open behind her as she fled. Just like Maria, Raven wouldn't be able to escape her fate: death.

The night breeze drifted through the bedroom window and across the bed, cooling Seth Hughes's naked skin and rousing him from sleep. He didn't know how long he'd been out. But it couldn't have been long, because his heart pounded hard yet, his chest rising and falling with harsh breaths. The breeze stirred a scent from his tangled sheets, of sandalwood and lavender, sweat and sex.

He splayed his hands, reaching across the bed. But she was gone even though he could still feel her in his arms and how he'd felt buried deep inside her body. He could taste her yet on his lips and on his tongue.

With a ragged sigh, he opened his eyes and peered around the room. Moonlight, slanting through the blinds at the window, streaked across the bed and across the naked woman sitting on the foot of it, turned away from him. She leaned forward, and her long black curls skimmed over her shoulders, leaving her back completely bare but for a silver chain and the trio of tattoos a few inches below the chain that circled her neck. There was a sun, a star and a crescent moon.

"I thought you'd left," he murmured, his voice rough with sleep and the desire that surged through him again. She was so damned beautiful with that sexy gypsy hair and all that honey-toned skin.

"I couldn't just leave," she replied as she rose from the bed.

Not after what they'd done? His pulse leaped as the desire surged harder, making him hard. Making love with her had been the most powerful experience of his life. And even though he wasn't certain he could survive it, it was an experience he wanted again. And again...

"I'm glad," he said.

She shook her head. "You won't be."

"Maria?" he asked, wondering about her ominous tone.

"You're going to be dead." Finally, she turned toward him, and the moonlight glinted off the barrel of the gun she held. He glanced toward the bedside table, where the small holster he clamped to the back of his belt lay empty. She held his gun.

"You don't want to do this," he said, holding his hand out for the weapon. But as he reached for it, it fired. The gunshot shattered the quiet of the night and...

The peal of his cell phone pulled him, fighting and kicking, from the grasp of the dark dream. Seth awoke clutching his heart, which pounded out a frantic rhythm. Pulling his hand away, he expected it to be covered with blood. His blood.

But his palm was dry. The room was too dark for him to see anything but the blinking light on his phone.

No moonlight shone through the worn blinds at the window of the motel room. The only scent was dust and the grease from the burger and fries he'd brought back from the diner down the street.

"It was just a dream," Seth said, but no relief eased the tension from his shoulders or loosened the knot in his gut. Nothing was ever just a dream with him.

Drawing a breath into his strained lungs, he reached for the persistently ringing phone. His holstered gun sat on the nightstand next to the cell. His fingers skimmed over the cold barrel before he grabbed up the phone.

Just a dream…

"Hughes," he said gruffly into the phone.

"Agent Hughes?"

"Yes."

"You were right!" The girl's voice cracked with fear as it rose with hysteria. "It's her! She's here."

"Maria Cooper?"

"I lied to you when you were here earlier. I didn't believe what you said about her, but you're right. You're right about everything!" A sob rattled the phone. "I never should have trusted her. Now I'm in danger."

"Where are you?" An image flashed into his mind of the young woman with the bird tattooed on her face. "Raven?"

"I'm at the Magik Shoppe," she replied.

The old round red barn was hardly a store. But that was another reason he'd known it was *her* shop even though he hadn't found her there, just the girl.

"Why?" he asked. He had no doubt that she was right; she was in danger. So why was she at the barn?

"I came back here to get you proof that she's the

one," Raven said. "I found it. I have the evidence you need. But you have to come quickly!"

He kicked back the tangled sheets. "I'm coming."

"How far away are you?"

"I stayed in town." Although calling Copper Creek, Michigan, a town was stretching the description since it had only a gas station, a diner, a bar and this one ramshackle motel. Despite the girl's denial, he had known the shop belonged to Maria Cooper. Finally, he'd come across one of her witchcraft stores before it—and she—was gone.

He'd stayed in Copper Creek with the intent to keep returning to the store until he caught her there. Hell, if not for the long drive up north having worn him out, he would have staked out the place until she came back. But if he had fallen asleep and she'd discovered him, the least she would have done was run again.

Maybe he should have risked staying; at least he would have been closer when Raven called and he wouldn't have to traverse the winding, rutted gravel road in the dead of night. "I'll be right there."

"You're going to be too late…"

Oh, shit. The girl must have warned her boss about him. Maria Cooper was already on the run again. "Stay there. And keep her there if you can."

Another sob rattled the phone. "No. I don't want her to find me. I don't want her to kill me, too."

Seth reached for his gun again. Maybe it would be fired tonight. "I'll protect you," he promised. "I won't let her hurt you. Just wait for me."

Her breath hitched, and he could almost see her nodding in acquiescence. "Please hurry. She read my cards. She told me I'm going to die."

He shuddered. Every time Maria Cooper had read someone's future, they had wound up not having one anymore. They'd wound up dead.

Just as he had in his *dream*…

"She's dead," Ariel Cooper-Koster said. Goose bumps of dread and cold lifted on her skin as she stood outside in the night breeze.

"You've seen her ghost, then," Elena Cooper-Dolce replied, her pale blond hair glowing in the lights spilling out of the stately house in front of which they stood. There was no surprise in Elena's voice. As she'd previously admitted to Ariel, she had already witnessed their youngest sister's murder in a vision.

Ariel stared at the ghost of a woman with big brown eyes and long curly dark hair. Caught between two worlds, her image wavered in and out of a cloud of sandalwood-and-lavender-scented smoke.

"I haven't seen her yet," she admitted. "But Mama's back…" And she hadn't seen her in years. "She wouldn't have left her if Maria were still alive." After child protective services had taken Ariel, Elena and Irina from their mother, they had been separated and hadn't been reunited until twenty years later. Once they had all found each other and saved themselves from the evil force stalking them, their mother's ghost had left them. She had stayed with the daughter who'd needed her most—the one who'd been alone. Maria, whom her sisters hadn't even known existed until those twenty years had passed. It was Irina who'd figured out that her roommate, at the time their mother had died, was actually their sister. But once they'd learned of her existence, they hadn't been able to find her.

Elena shuddered. "I hope you're wrong. For her sake and for Irina's."

"She can't know," Ariel agreed. Their younger sister was in a fragile state; eight months pregnant with twins, she had been confined to bed rest and absolutely no stress.

"She does," a raspy male voice said as Ty McIntyre opened his front door to his sisters-in-law. He was a muscular man with dark hair, dark blue eyes and a jagged scar running through one eyebrow.

"Maria is not dead," Ty said as he gestured them inside the two-story foyer of his grand house. "She knows what the two of you are thinking, though. She *hears* you."

Ariel's face heated, and Elena's flushed bright red in the glow of the chandelier hanging over their heads. "Of course…" Irina could hear the thoughts of others—especially those with whom she was connected. "We can't block her like *she* can…"

"Maria isn't blocking her right now," he said, and a muscle twitched along his clenched jaw.

"But you wish she was," Elena said as she reached out and squeezed his arm, offering support and comfort.

"Maria can't block her when she's really upset," he said. "When she's really scared. Her emotions are so strong that Irina feels them, too."

Ariel's heart rate quickened. "Maria is upset and scared?"

Maybe that was why Mama had come back to her—to get her other children to help her youngest. While Ariel had always been able to see ghosts, she couldn't always hear them. She had struggled the most with her mother's ghost—probably because of all the emotions her mother's appearance always summoned in Ariel. The pain and regret and resentment.

Ty grimly nodded. "That's why I asked you both to come over tonight," he said. "Irina wants me to go find Maria."

"You've been looking for her for eight years," Ariel said with frustration and resignation. "We all have." And with the six of them working together, they had more resources than most—financially and supernaturally.

"So you're giving up?" It wasn't Ty asking; it was Irina, standing precariously at the top of the stairwell—her legs wobbling.

Ty vaulted up the steps and caught his wife up in his arms, lifting her as easily as if she were one of their seven-year-old twins. "You're not supposed to be out of bed."

"I could hear you all," she said. But probably only in her mind, since they hadn't awakened either one of the twins.

Ariel and Elena hurried up the stairs and followed Ty down the hall as he carried Irina back to their bedroom. "We didn't mean to upset you," Ariel said.

"We came to help," Elena said, her usually soft voice heavy with guilt and regret.

Ty gently settled his wife back onto their king-size bed. Irina sat up against the pillows and stared at them all, her brown eyes even darker with hurt and accusation.

She looked so much like the ghost of their mother—so much like the picture she'd shown them of their sister Maria. The three of them looked like gypsies—like

witches—while Ariel and Elena didn't look related to
any of them or even to each other. But their abilities
united them—the Durikken blood that flowed in all
their veins. Or had once flowed in their mother's…

She hovered near Irina. Maybe she had come back
because Irina needed her more than Maria did.

"We're going to find her," Irina insisted.

Or maybe Maria would find them—after she died.

"Ty will bring her back."

It might not be possible. All they had found of their
mother's remains had been her ashes.

"She's not dead," Irina said. "I can sense her feelings. I can hear her thoughts. She's anxious and scared.
And very much alive."

For now. But if she was anxious and scared, she
must be in the danger that Elena kept envisioning. And
none of those visions had ended well for Maria…

She was gone. Maria couldn't even feel her anymore.
There had been so much panic and fear and now…

Nothing. Maybe she was just too far away. Maybe
she wasn't dead…

The wipers swished the streaks of rain from Maria's windshield, but still she could barely see—the
headlamps of her old pickup truck were not strong
enough to penetrate the thick black curtain of night in
the Upper Peninsula of Michigan. The tires bounced
over the ruts of the drive leading to Maria's little round
barn at the end of the gravel lane. No cars were parked
next to the shop.

Maria should have known that the girl wouldn't
come back here. But she'd checked for Raven's car at
the motel in town where the girl had been staying since

her move to Copper Creek. She had also checked at the house of the guy Raven sometimes dated. But his windows had been dark, the driveway empty of any cars—even his.

Maybe they'd left together. Maybe he could protect the girl since she didn't trust Maria to do that.

I don't blame her, though. I don't trust myself.

That was why she rarely stayed anywhere for long—why she kept running, as Mama had always been running. It was why Maria tried to not get too close to anyone or let *anyone* get too close to her…

She never should have hired the young woman, and she definitely never should have agreed to teach Raven to read. Her fingertips tingling from the energy from the cards, Maria regretted ever touching them again. Why hadn't she left them behind…as she had so much else in her life?

Like Raven, she needed to run now. The girl had been right about the aura of darkness hovering over Maria. But besides the cards, Maria had left something else behind in the shop—something that she couldn't leave without. Her fingers trembled as she lifted her hand to her bare neck. During her scuffle with Raven, the chain must have broken.

Her lungs burned as she breathed hard, fighting the panic at the thought of what she'd lost. It had to be here. It couldn't be gone…

The hinges of the old pickup truck squeaked in protest as she flung open the driver's door. She jerked the keys from the ignition and tried to determine by touch which one would open the door to the shop. But as she stumbled in the dark, across the gravel, she noticed the faint glow spilling out of the barn—through the open door. She had locked it behind herself when she'd left to search for Raven. And the only other person with a key to it was her employee.

"Raven!" she called out as she hurried through the door. "I'm so glad you came back!"

She reached in her pocket for the amulet of dried alyssum, rosemary and ivy, and anise and caraway seeds, eucalyptus and huckleberry leaves, and a thistle blossom. She'd cinched the sachet with a leather thong on which she'd fastened a jet stone, a piece of obsidian and a tiger's eye. "I made something for you— something to keep you safe."

Then her eyes adjusted to the faint candlelight, which wavered back and forth—not because the flames flickered but because a shadow swung back and forth in front of them. Like the herbs, Raven hung from the rafters.

Maria was too late. Again.

Or was she? She glanced around, searching the shadows for another image—an orb or mist, some field of energy that indicated Raven's ghost. But nothing manifested from the shadows.

And the girl's body swung yet. "You're still alive. Stay with me. I'll help you." *But how?*

Panic pressed on Maria's lungs, stealing her breath. She righted a chair and clamored on top of it, but then jumped down again when she realized she had nothing to cut the rope that wound tight around the girl's throat. She fumbled for a knife and scrambled onto the chair again. Summoning all her strength, she hacked at the rope until the girl fell, her body hitting the worn wood floor with a soft thud.

"Please be alive," Maria murmured as she scrambled down beside her. She'd seen others do CPR on television, so she tried breathing into Raven's mouth and pushing on her chest. But the girl didn't breathe. She didn't move. Probably because Maria didn't know what she was doing. She knew how to heal with herbs and crystals, though. But she had never pulled anyone back from the brink of death before. What could she use? What would it take?

She ran back to the table where she cut herbs and grabbed up some dried hyssop and licorice. Both were used to treat asthma because of their anti-inflammatory powers. Maybe they could reduce the swelling in the girl's throat. She added some tincture of arnica that was used for bruising. Her hands shook as she mixed it together. Then she hurried back to where the girl lay limply on the floor of the old barn.

She pressed the mixture to the girl's swollen throat and slipped some between her open lips. Then she chanted a prayer, begging the higher power to heal the wounded, to reverse her cruel fate.

"Raven?" She leaned over the girl, listening for breathing. No air emanated from the girl's black-painted lips as her mouth lay open. Maria looked to her chest to see if any breaths lifted it, but a shadow fell across the room—blocking the light from the candles.

"Don't move!" a deep voice ordered.

Maria glanced up at the hulking shadow blocking the door. Only his eyes glinted in the dark—and the metal of the gun he held. Was he who had done this to Raven? Who had killed all of the other ones?

She tightened her grip on the handle of the knife and slid it beneath the folds of her long skirt. If he came close enough…

"What the hell," he murmured, his voice a low rumble in his muscular chest. He glanced from her to the body on the floor. His brow furrowed in concern and confusion as he stared down at Raven. "What did you do to her?"

Maybe he wasn't the one who had hurt the girl.

"I tried to help her," she told him. But her herbs weren't working. "Please, do something! Save her!"

The man knelt beside Raven, and his fingers probed her wrist. "She's dead."

"No, not yet." If Raven were dead, Maria would have seen her ghost because she always saw the souls of the recently departed. And sometimes of the not-so-recently departed. "She needs a doctor."

He shook his head.

"Why won't you help her?" The answer was obvious. He had tried killing the girl; he had no intention of saving her. Or of letting Maria live...

If she had any hope of surviving—and getting help for Raven—she had to act. Just as she had swung the knife at the rope noose with all of her strength, she pulled it from beneath her skirt and swung it at the man leaning over Raven's body. She didn't want to kill him; she just wanted to hurt him badly enough that he dropped the gun.

But as she neared his body, her momentum slowed—and she hesitated before burying the blade. She closed her eyes and pushed the knife down, then gasped as strong fingers locked around her wrist. Something cold and shaped like a circle pressed against her chin.

She drew in an unsteady breath, and the gun barrel pinched her skin. Maybe she should have read her own cards. Maybe then she would have seen this—

would have seen this man. She opened her eyes to study him because his was the last face she would probably ever see.

He stared at her, his grayish-blue eyes as cold and hard as his gun. The candlelight flickered, picking up red glints in his thick brown hair. Even kneeling on the floor, he towered over her, broad shouldered and square jawed.

She tugged at her wrist, but his grasp tightened. And the knife dropped from her numb fingers onto the floor. "Let go of me…"

His mouth curved into a faint grin. "I've spent too long tracking you down to let you get away now."

Her heart slammed against her ribs. He was the *one*. The person who'd been hunting her for all these years and had taken all those other lives…

A gasp broke the eerie silence of the room. But it hadn't slipped through her lips. Or his.

She glanced down at Raven as the girl's eyes fluttered open and she stared up at them, her eyes wide with shock and horror. The girl had survived a hanging—maybe because of Maria's healing, maybe because she was stronger than she looked. But Maria doubted Raven was strong enough to survive whatever else the man had planned for her. For them.

She should have driven the knife deep in his chest while she'd had the chance. So that she wouldn't die as the others had—as Raven nearly had.

Like a witch…

Chapter 2

Red-and-blue lights flashed and sirens wailed as the ambulance pulled away from the Magik Shoppe. Rain streaked down Maria's face and soaked her sweater and skirt as she stood in the gravel drive, watching the ambulance speed away with Raven. That gasp for breath had been her only one, and then the man had done CPR on her.

Except for opening her eyes once, the young woman hadn't regained consciousness again. She hadn't been able to tell them who had hung her from the rafters.

Had it been him?

Maria turned her head to where he stood with the Copper Creek sheriff near the police cruiser. Even though he talked to the older man, his gaze was fixed on her, his steely blue eyes just as hard and cold as they'd been when he had pressed the gun to her chin.

The sheriff jerked his balding head in a couple of

quick nods, as if obeying the younger man's orders. Tall and broad shouldered, the stranger held himself with a confidence and authority born of power.

Despite the water running down his leather jacket and darkening the denim of his jeans, he seemed oblivious to the rain—focused only on her. As it had from the cards, energy flowed from him and spread through Maria so that her skin tingled with awareness and fear. She had never felt such a connection to another human being.

He had to be the one.

His conversation with the sheriff ended with the lawman hurrying back inside the open doors of the barn. So he approached her alone.

Her heart pounded with the urge to run, but before her feet could move, he was in front of her, his long legs needing only a couple of strides before he stepped close to her. So close that Maria had to tip back her head to hold his gaze as her heart continued to pound out a frantic rhythm.

"Who are you?" she asked.

His hand slipped inside his leather jacket, and she tensed, expecting him to withdraw the gun he'd put there before he'd begun CPR on Raven. But instead he took out a wallet and flashed it open to an FBI badge.

She blinked back the raindrops clinging to her lashes and read his name. Seth Hughes. And he was a special agent. But it didn't matter that he had an FBI badge; he could still be the one she'd run from in fear all these years. He could be the witch-hunter.

Anyone could be the witch-hunter.

"I've been looking for you for a long time," he said.

Tracking her down, he'd said earlier. The ominous words turned her colder than the rain that seeped through her clothes to her skin, and she shivered. "Not me." She shook her head. "You must have me confused with someone else."

"No," he said with absolute certainty. "You're Maria Cooper." He reached for her now, his big hand clasping her wrist as he turned her around.

That flow of energy between them grew more intense, her skin heating beneath his hand. Despite her empathetic gifts, she'd never reacted to anyone's touch the way she did to his. It had to be a warning…

"I'll scream," she threatened him. "Sheriff Moore is just inside the barn. He'll hear me. You won't get away with it."

"You're the one who won't get away," he said as cold metal clamped around her wrists. "Maria Cooper, you are under arrest. You have the right to remain silent—"

"Under arrest?" She jerked around to face him. "What are the charges? Assault?" She grimaced over having almost stabbed him. "You never identified yourself. You just pulled that gun on me."

A muscle twitched along his jaw. "I didn't have a chance to identify myself. I had to assess the situation."

"You can't arrest me for trying to defend myself," she pointed out.

"I'm not arresting you for trying to kill me."

"I didn't…" Until tonight she had never raised a hand, let alone a weapon, to another human being. She was all about healing—not hurting.

Had her potion or her prayer worked on Raven, bringing that gasp of breath to her lungs? Had she done enough for the girl to survive?

Agent Hughes ignored her denial and led her toward the dark SUV parked behind her pickup truck. After opening the back door, he put his hand over her head and guided her onto the seat.

Hating that even her hair tingled from his touch, she pushed against his hand. Then she twisted around on the seat, keeping her legs out so that he couldn't lock her inside the vehicle. She was afraid to get into a SUV with him, afraid of where he might take her.

Of what he might do to her…

"If not for assault, why are you arresting me?" she asked. "What are the charges?"

"Murder." That muscle twitched again along his jaw as he stared down at her.

"I didn't hurt Raven," she said. But it must not have looked like it when he walked into the barn and found her alone with the unconscious girl. "And she's going to live."

She has to…

"Your arrest has nothing to do with her," Agent Hughes said. "Yet. You're under arrest for multiple counts of first-degree murder."

She would have laughed—had he not looked so deadly serious. So instead she shook her head. "I'm not a killer."

"You're not just a killer, Maria Cooper—you're a se-rial killer. And while Michigan doesn't have the death penalty, some of the other states where you've killed do have it. You won't be able to hurt anyone else where you're going."

She didn't need any special gifts to know he was talking about sending her straight to hell.

Seth had promised to call them when he found her. But breaking his promise would probably be a bigger favor to them than keeping it. Maria Cooper was a dangerous woman.

And he had locked himself inside the tiny interrogation room at the local jail—with her. Just the two of them. The table between them was so small that every time he moved, his knees bumped against hers. That contact, however slight, sent blood rushing through his veins, roaring in his ears. What the hell was wrong with him?

Over the years, he had connected with victims… through evidence left behind at the crime scenes. And he'd had those damn vivid dreams ever since he was a kid. But never before had he had such a reaction to a suspect, as if inexplicably drawn to her no matter the atrocities she'd committed.

He pushed back his chair, but it bumped up against the cement-block wall behind him. And she was still so close he could feel her. To slow his pulse, he drew in a deep breath, and her scent filled his lungs—that sweet, smoky mixture of lavender and sandalwood that had his stomach knotting with desire…and apprehension.

He closed his eyes, but then the images from that damn dream—*that wasn't a dream*—flashed through his head. Her hair skimming across her slender shoulders. Her naked back, turned toward him, the moonlight playing across her honey skin and that trio of tattoos. She stood and faced him, the gun in her hand. The shot echoed inside his head, and he winced and opened his eyes.

"The caffeine's giving you a headache," she murmured, gesturing toward the paper cup of sludge sitting between them.

His stomach roiled at the thought of how long it

had been sitting in the bottom of the pot in the sheriff's office.

"You should drink herbal tea."

"I need the caffeine." To stay alert. To keep his wits about him. "You sure you don't want some? It's going to be a long night."

"It already has been," she remarked with a wince of her own. "You finished reading me my rights." She gestured at the paper she'd signed acknowledging that he had. "Why haven't you locked me in a cell yet?"

Because while he'd put her under arrest and read her the Miranda rights, she wasn't really under arrest. He had a warrant only to bring her in to question as a material witness in all those murders—not for committing the actual murders. Seth really didn't have enough to arrest her for murder yet, even though she was his prime—his only—suspect. He had enough only to question her involvement. Fortunately, she'd waived her right to legal representation during this interview, so whatever she said he would be able to use against her.

"I have some questions for you," he said.

"About Raven?"

"About all of them." He picked up the leather briefcase he'd taken from his car and laid it on the table between them. He unlocked it and withdrew a thick folder. "These are the people you were more successful at killing over the past eight years."

He flipped open the folder and fanned out the crime scene photos across the surface of the table as she probably did her tarot cards. He didn't need to look at the pictures. All he had to do was close his eyes, and like that dream, the images played through his mind. The first girl had been drowned. A young man had been crushed beneath a board weighted down with bricks. Another girl had been hung…as someone had tried to hang Raven tonight. And the worst, the fire…had left behind little of its victim.

Of *her* victim.

She didn't look at the photos, either. Instead she held his gaze. The color drained from her face, making her wide almond-shaped eyes look even bigger and her high cheekbones and heart-shaped chin even more delicate. "I don't know anything about any murders. I don't even know why you keep calling me Maria Cooper."

"Because that's your name. That's who you are." Now that he had found her, he had a feeling that he would never be free of her…that this eerie connection that had haunted him would always bind him to her.

She shook her head, tumbling her glossy black hair around her shoulders as she had in his dream. "No. No. I'm not her."

"Who are you, then?" he asked, humoring her. "You have no ID. No driver's license. No birth certificate."

"Is there a driver's license or birth certificate on file—anywhere—for Maria Cooper?" she asked.

"You know there's not. There is no evidence you ever existed." He tapped the photos. "But these. You're the one person every single victim had in common. You're the last person every single victim saw…when you read their tarot cards." In most of the crime scene photos, the cards were still strewn across the table.

She closed her eyes, as if trying to shut out the images before her. But was she like him? Did they live on inside her head, haunting her just as they—and she—haunted him? Then, closing her eyes would give her no reprieve. In fact, sometimes it only made the images more real for him, like those dreams that weren't just dreams.

She opened her eyes, just a little, and studied him thoughtfully. "That's why you took my fingerprints."

He glanced down at her hands, which were slightly stained on the front and slightly scratched on the back. He'd already requested that the sheriff have Raven's fingernails scraped—to see if DNA could be matched to the woman who denied she was Maria Cooper.

She narrowed her eyes more. "I may have read their cards, but that doesn't mean I killed them. You have no evidence that I hurt any of them. There's no way that a judge really issued a warrant for my arrest."

"No," he admitted.

She stood up. And so did he, reaching across the narrow table to grab her wrist again. Like every other time he'd touched her, his fingers tingled and images flashed through his mind like a slide show.

His hands cupped her shoulders, and he pulled her closer. Her chin tipped up, her lips parting on a gasp of desire. She dragged in a deep breath that lifted her breasts against his chest. His head lowered, closer and closer to hers...

He hesitated, his mouth just a breath away from her full lips. Hunger burned in his gut; he'd never wanted to kiss anyone more. Never needed to kiss anyone the way he needed to kiss her...

"Let me go!" she said, tugging at her wrist. "You have no right to keep me here."

"I have every right to keep you here," he said. Just no right—or reason—to want to kiss her. Hell, she was the last woman he should be tempted to kiss. He knew exactly how dangerous she was.

"You're a person of interest," he explained, "and I do have a warrant to pick you up for questioning." Ignoring the desire that hardened his body, he slid his hand up her arm to her shoulder and gently but firmly shoved her back into her chair. "You're going to stay here and answer all my questions."

"You have the wrong person," she said, stubbornly sticking with her lie. "I'm not Maria Cooper."

"DNA would prove who you are."

Fear widened her dark eyes. "You can't take my DNA without my permission."

"Unless I get a warrant for it," he warned her. Since he'd finally found her, he would be able to ask for one—especially since the attack on Raven. But it would be faster than waking a judge in this godforsaken county in the Upper Peninsula if she freely offered it. "If you're not her, why won't you provide a sample of your DNA to prove it? To clear yourself?"

"You forget—it's innocent until proved guilty," she said, her lips lifting in a slight smile. But it was grim—not taunting.

He had been taunted by other killers, ones who had sat across the table from him, laughing at him during the interrogation. Proud of their crimes. She didn't act that way. But then, nothing about her was completely what he had expected except for her beauty.

She was so damned beautiful.

But he reminded himself and her, "We both know you're not innocent. Your name—your description—comes up in police reports across the country going back nearly two decades. Since you were ten years old, you helped your mother run cons on desperate, gullible people."

And because of that, he doubted she was the real deal. Like so many other self-proclaimed *psychics*, she was nothing more than a con artist.

She shook her head. "You have the wrong person."

For a con artist, she wasn't a very good liar. Then again, most suspects had trouble lying to him. "So prove it."

She shook her head again.

"You won't give up your DNA, because you know it's going to be at every one of these murder scenes." He tapped the photos again as he settled back onto the chair across from her. He needed to look at those photos, to remind himself what happened to people who got too close to Maria Cooper.

The tip of her tongue slid out and flicked across her lower lip. Was she manipulating him? Did she know how that simple action had his guts constricting with desire? With *need*?

"Just—just because someone was at the crime scenes," she stammered, "*before* the crimes happened, doesn't mean they were involved in the crimes."

"Once," he allowed, "maybe even twice. But four times—five, including tonight? That's more than co-incidence. That's means and opportunity. The only person who'd be at every one of these crime scenes is the killer."

"And you," she said. "You've been at every scene."

First in his mind and then in person. He nodded. "I've been looking for you for a long time. Catching you has been my number one priority."

She shivered—maybe it was because her clothes

were wet from the rain. Maybe it was because his determination scared her.

"Number one priority?" she repeated. "Why? Nobody's died in over a year."

He cocked his head at her significant slip. "How would you know that unless…?"

"The dates on the pictures." She pointed toward the corner of one of the photos. "The most recent one is over a year old."

"Yes, no one's died in over a year," he admitted. Most of his colleagues had considered the case cold. That was why he had made the trek to the UP alone, on his own time. He'd been chasing down a lead no one else had considered worthwhile, working a case no one else cared about anymore. "Until tonight…"

She shuddered. "No. Not Raven…"

"It shouldn't have been any of them, either," he said. "No one should have died. Why? Why did you kill them?" Especially as gruesomely as she had. Was it because they'd had real gifts and she had resented them for it?

"I didn't kill anyone," she insisted. And maybe she was a better con artist than he'd thought, because she actually sounded sincere. "I would never hurt anyone."

He snorted in derision of her claim—not because of the dream but because of the reality of her swinging that knife toward his back. If the flash of the blade hadn't caught the candlelight and reflected it into his eyes… If he hadn't stopped her…

"That's not what Raven said when she called me tonight," Seth informed her. "She was afraid of you."

"She called you?" she asked, surprise flickering

through her dark eyes. "Why—how—did she contact you?"

"I gave her my card when I stopped by your shop earlier today," he said.

Her golden skin paled. "You were there earlier today? She never said…"

"That an FBI agent had tracked you down," he finished for her. "She covered for you earlier—with me, denying that you are who you are." Much as Maria herself was trying to deny her identity.

"That's because you're wrong about me," she insisted.

Seth had never been more certain of anyone's identity than he was of hers. He didn't need DNA to prove she was Maria Cooper. But he did need her DNA to link her to those other crime scenes.

"I'm not wrong," he replied. He could have added that he rarely was—because it was true and well-known in the agency. "And Raven realized I was right about you, too. She called me because you scared her."

Color returned to her face as her skin flushed. "I—I didn't mean to scare her. She shouldn't have been afraid of *me*."

"You threatened her," he reminded her. "You told her she was going to die."

Maria shook her head. "It wasn't me. It was the cards. It was what I saw."

"What you *saw*?" Did she really see things, the way he did, or was she like so many other *psychics*, a crackpot looking for money and attention? Those old police reports from people who had given up their money to her and her mother claimed that she was a fake. But maybe she'd just been faking with them…

"When I read the cards," she said, "I saw that she was in danger. I wanted to protect her. I tried to get her to stay with me—"

"She stayed," he said. "She called me from the shop. And that's where I found her—with you." If only he had been able to get there in time, the girl might not be fighting for her life at that very moment.

"She left," Maria argued, "right after I read her cards. I tried to stop her."

"Was that when you struggled?"

"Struggled?"

"The table was overturned, the cards scattered across the floor." He caught her hands in his and stroked his thumbs over the scratches on the backs of them. As if she felt the same jolt he did, she jerked her hands from his. "Is that when she scratched you, or was it when you tied the noose around her neck?"

She shook her head. "No. I found her like that... when I came back to the shop."

"So you left the shop, too? You chased after her?"

"Not right away," she said. "I made her the amulet first. Then I tried to find her—to give it to her."

"Amulet?" The dried plants hanging, like the rope, from the rafters, and the crystals and candles hadn't been just for ambiance. She used them, as witches had centuries ago, to cast spells.

"I made it of herbs and crystals to ward off the evil and protect her from harm."

"It didn't work." Harm had befallen Raven. And from the last words the girl had said to him, he had his prime suspect sitting across the table from him. Their knees touched again, his sliding between hers.

The warmth of her body emanated through their rain-damp clothes, and heat rushed through him.

Another image flashed through his mind.

Her hair tangled across his pillow. Her nails digging into his shoulders, then clawing down his back. She clutched at him, her body tensing beneath his. She cried out his name. "Seth!"

He blinked, forcing the thoughts from his brain. He had been focused on the case—and on finding her—for too long. Had he—as some of his colleagues had suggested—become obsessed? His obsession needed to be justice. Not her. He coughed, clearing the thickness of desire from his throat, and asked, "What were you saying?"

Her brow furrowed with confusion, but then she repeated, "I couldn't find her—to give the amulet to her."

"You did find her," he pointed out. "Or had you stayed at the shop the whole time, waiting for her?"

Had Maria been there already when Raven had called him? After hearing the terror in the girl's voice, he'd driven as fast as he could and also had called Sheriff Moore as he had left the motel, hoping the older lawman had been closer. Still, Seth had beaten him to the Magik Shoppe.

She shook her head again, making her wild curls cascade around the shoulders of her worn sweater. "It wasn't me. Someone else must have been there. Someone else hurt her. I tried to help her. That's why I had the knife. I cut her down." She shivered. "You'll see—when she wakes up, Raven will tell you everything."

"I hope like hell she can," he said. The girl had mentioned having evidence to prove that Maria was the one he had been looking for, the killer he was determined to stop. That was why she'd gone back to the shop, to find him that evidence. She'd risked her life for it. But what he'd found on her didn't prove that Maria was a murderer, just that she was Maria Cooper. There must have been something else…

He pulled his cell from the inside pocket of his leather jacket, checking to see if he had missed any calls. "I left a message for the hospital to call me as soon as she regained consciousness."

"And they haven't called."

Regret trapped his breath in his lungs. Had he been too late? Had his efforts at reviving her been unsuccessful? "No. They haven't."

"She's not dead."

"I wouldn't be so sure," he replied. "What the hell did you put on her throat and in her mouth?"

"Those were herbs that I use for healing," she said. "The mixture should have restored her breathing and reduced the swelling in her throat."

He held up his cell phone. "I don't think it worked," he said. "Or I would have a call by now."

Maria gazed around the small room as if searching the corners for something. For what? And she insisted, "She can't be dead."

"You better hope like hell she isn't, because I can put you at the scene. In addition to your DNA that I'm sure was under her fingernails, I'm an eyewitness." He had her. He finally had her. And now the senseless killing would stop.

"I didn't hurt her. It wasn't me." She gestured at the photos. "I didn't hurt any of them."

"You're the one. Raven confirmed it to me on the phone." Even without that confirmation, he had been certain. She was the only thing all the victims had had in common; she was the last person every one of them had seen. "Raven also said she had proof." And he needed to find out what that proof was. He needed to talk to the girl—needed her to live—so that he could officially close all those other cold-.case files. "I should call the hospital again."

But a call wouldn't be good enough. If she regained consciousness, even for just a second as she had at the barn, he needed to be there to question her. "Actually, I should go to the hospital."

She nodded and stood up again. "I want to go with you. I want to see her."

"I can't let you go," he said. "I have a material witness order for you. I don't have to release you until you answer my questions."

Or until she called a lawyer who could get her released. He could question her for only so long without charging her. And he didn't have enough to charge her. Yet.

He hoped Maria was right and that the girl wasn't dead. But he wasn't sure how anyone could have survived a hanging. He doubted that the herbs put in her mouth and on her throat had actually been a healing potion. They were more likely to have been poison.

Maria settled back onto the chair. "I'll stay," she said as if she had a choice. "Please check on her."

He slid his phone back into his pocket and reached for his keys. "I'm going to lock you in here." Because he had no doubt that if he didn't, she would be long gone by the time he returned.

But he waited for her protest. Maybe she would even ask for that lawyer now.

Instead she nodded in agreement. "That's fine with me. I want to stay until you get back anyway. I have to know how she's doing."

Seth studied her beautiful face and wished he could read her mind. Did she want the girl alive or dead? Did she really believe the girl would exonerate her? Or was she afraid that Raven would implicate her, and she wanted the young woman as dead as her other victims?

It was so much easier than he had thought it would be—easier even than killing them in Maria Cooper's little magic shops. Maybe a big-city hospital would have had better security, but here in Copper Creek he had no problem moving freely around the building, which was more urgent-care center than actual hospital. The lights low, as patients slept, he hovered in the shadows, as he had earlier that night in the barn.

He had been there when the girl had placed her hysterical phone call to the FBI agent. For him that call had confirmed that she really was a witch. How else would she have known, just as she'd told the FBI agent, that he would be too late to save her?

She had seen her future. Her fate. At *his* hands. And since she could see the future, she was definitely a witch.

But the girl hadn't seen that Maria would come back to the shop. Neither had he.

Usually when the cards came up as they had, Maria Cooper took off—leaving everything and everyone behind her. Except him. She would never be able to leave *him* behind. He always knew where she was—unlike the FBI agent who'd been trying to track her down for years.

But Seth Hughes couldn't save her—just as he hadn't been able to save the girl with that hideous tattoo painted on what must have once been a pretty face.

Maria had been the one to cut her down—just seconds after he had strung up the girl and knocked the chair from under her. He would have grabbed Maria then, but he'd known the FBI agent was on his way. He couldn't risk getting caught before he'd completed his mission.

Before he killed the most powerful witch…

And he'd thought the girl was dead—that surely her neck would have broken when she hung. But Maria had used one of her potions and some mystical spell to save her life. Or to steal her death from *him*.

Sticking to the shadows, he now crept into a room the farthest down the hall from Raven's. Then, after tripping the alarm on the machine connected to the patient in that room, he slipped deeper into the shadows. He waited for the medical staff to rush to the elderly man's aid before he stole, unseen, into Raven's room.

Acting quickly, he disconnected the air hose from the machine and poured in the water he carried in a cup. It slid down the tube and directly into the girl's airway. Her eyes opened, big with terror, and she stared up at him, a question in her gaze.

Why?

She wanted to know why he was so determined to take her life.

"Because you're a witch," he whispered. "And I'm

a witch-hunter." He didn't know if she heard him, because with one last gurgling gasp, she was gone.

Another witch dead...

But he felt none of the satisfaction of his earlier kills; his joy in the hunt was waning. Yet he couldn't leave his mission undone. He couldn't allow witches to live—to work their craft and mess with people's minds and hearts and livelihoods. He had to save the world from their evil ways.

The alarm sounded on Raven's machine now, signaling with a flat line that she was really gone this time. He disappeared again into the shadows behind a tall cart in the hall as the nurses hurried back toward the girl's room.

"What the hell happened?" one of them asked as she grabbed up the disconnected tube.

"Could she have done it?" the other nurse asked. "She's in here because she tried hanging herself."

Curses rang out, the voice deep and masculine, as the FBI agent joined the nurses at the bedside of the dead witch. He was getting close, too. Not just to Maria but to *him*.

He had been saving Maria until last, using her as bait to draw out the other witches. But she seldom shared her knowledge of witchcraft now.

While she sold the herbs and talismans and amulets, she didn't teach the craft of spells and potions. It had taken Raven a long time to get close to her, and probably no one would get that close again.

Except for him.

It was time for Maria Cooper to die.

Chapter 3

Blood and water leaked out as the scalpel sliced through the flesh and tissue of the victim's lungs. Seth didn't even flinch; he had already seen so much horror in his job.

And in his dreams.

"I don't understand it," the coroner murmured as he stared down at the water spilled on the stainless steel table.

Bright light shone onto the table and the body of the young woman lying on it. Seth stood just outside the light, in the shadows, where he felt he'd spent so much of his life.

"With the trauma to the neck and the lack of oxygen that would have caused to her brain," the doctor said, "I figured it might have been a stroke that caused her death."

"She was drowned," Seth said. He'd had the sheriff

wake up the coroner to perform the autopsy to confirm it. But he'd already known.

He had seen the water that had spilled on the floor and had condensed on the inside of her breathing tube. When he'd stepped off the elevator, he had heard the alarm beeping.

And he'd known. He was too late.

Raven had told him that he would be too late to save her. And she'd been right. He had failed her twice.

"How the hell did she drown?" the coroner asked. The older man shook his head as if befuddled. The sheriff had assured Seth that despite Dr. Kohler's age, the man was sharp. With his years of experience and the expansive county he worked, he had seen everything before.

Apparently he hadn't seen anything like this—like a woman being drowned in her hospital bed.

"I'm pretty sure someone poured water into her breathing tube," Seth said. While waiting for Sheriff Moore and the coroner to arrive at the hospital, he had investigated the scene and interviewed all the possible witnesses.

The coroner gasped but nodded his gray head. "That would have done it."

"But how?" the sheriff asked. He had joined Seth in the morgue in the basement of the county hospital, but he'd stayed even farther from that brightly lit table than Seth had. So he hadn't witnessed much of the autopsy. He wasn't asking about the medical aspects, though.

He was asking the same question that Seth had been asking himself when he'd found Raven dead. How?

Maria was in custody. Wasn't she?

"You have someone watching the suspect?" he asked Sheriff Moore. Again. It had been the first thing he had asked the man when he'd called him from Raven's bedside.

The older lawman nodded. "Yes." Now he glanced at the body on the autopsy table. "But it looks as if we should have had someone watching *her* instead."

Seth silently cursed himself. He should have had a protection detail on Raven. But he'd thought he had the right person in custody.

He could feel his suspect slipping away now, though. This death would give her reasonable doubt. A grand jury might not even indict her now. And then she would be free again.

And if Maria was free, he was certain that more people would die—since everyone around her kept dying...

If only he had been able to talk to Raven...

Frustration eating at him, Seth grumbled, "I can't believe this hospital doesn't have security."

"We've never needed it," the coroner said. "This is Copper Creek."

"But no cameras—"

"Never needed them," the doctor interjected.

"Tonight you needed them," Seth said. Because all of the nurses he'd questioned had claimed that they had seen no stranger—no one suspicious at all—lurking around the place. But they'd shivered as he'd talked to them—as if some cold spirit had crossed their paths.

Or some heartless killer...

Despite his leather jacket, goose bumps lifted on Seth's skin. Maybe it was the coldness of the morgue.

Or maybe it was something else that chilled his skin and his blood. He refused to believe in spirits.

Evil.

Hell, he knew evil existed. He had already seen so much of it. More likely what had chilled his skin was the thought that had just occurred to him.

If Maria really was at the station, then someone else was out there. Not acting instead of her but maybe in collusion with her. He should have considered before that she wasn't working alone. The gruesome ways all the other victims had died would have been hard for her to pull off alone—unless she really was a witch. Or she'd had someone stronger helping her. Probably some hapless male who had fallen for her undeniable sexy charms...

Seth swallowed nervously as he realized he could be that hapless male—that he had been distracted so much by her looks that he hadn't thought to put protective duty on Raven. His distraction had cost the girl her life. Along with the frustration, guilt ate at him, clenching his stomach into knots.

"I need to get back to the station," he said. To make certain that Maria was still there—that whoever had just killed Raven for her wasn't trying to break her out of the room in which he'd locked her.

As if he'd read his mind, the sheriff assured him, "Your suspect is still there."

Where Maria Cooper was concerned, Seth would accept no assurances. He had to see for himself. But he didn't want to just see her. He wanted to touch her, too.

"I'll drive Dr. Kohler back to his house and meet you at the station," the sheriff said.

"I have to finish up the autopsy," the doctor said.

"I can't leave her like this…" He stared grimly down at the body.

"That'll give you time to finish up the investigation here," Seth suggested to Sheriff Moore. "Maybe you'll have better luck talking to the nurses than I did."

They might talk more freely to the local lawman than the stranger he was to them. They might admit to seeing something or someone tonight that would explain how Raven had died.

And maybe now that Seth knew Maria wasn't working alone, he might have better luck getting her to talk. Maybe she would implicate her accomplice in order to save herself. If her accomplice hadn't already managed to free her…

The security at the sheriff's office wasn't much better than at the county hospital. So Seth worried that he would find her as he had found Raven: already gone.

"She's gone…"

"Who?" Elena asked as she glanced over her shoulder at her sister Ariel, who'd spoken so softly that she'd barely heard her whisper.

"Mama," Ariel murmured. She was probably being quiet so she wouldn't wake Irina. She was sleeping, finally, and hopefully so deeply that she wasn't able to *hear* them.

When they were kids, the three of them had slept together on that lumpy mattress in the camper on the back of Mama's old pickup truck. As they had then, the three of them slept together now—on the soft mattress of Irina's king-size bed, though. Elena lay in the middle, as she had all those years ago, a younger sister under each arm as if she could keep them safe from all those horrible dreams she'd had. All those horrible things she had *seen* each of them endure…

As she thought of those twenty years without her sisters, Elena's pain increased. And now she knew there was still one sister out there—still alone, as they had each been alone for so long.

Because, eventually, Mama had abandoned Maria, too.

Ariel's husband, David Koster, had discovered that as he and his best friend, Ty, had tried tracking down Maria. Elena's husband, Joseph, had other sources who had discovered other things about Maria.

Like her criminal past…

Or was it actually in the past…?

Elena closed her eyes and played out the vision she'd had days earlier.

Candlelight flickered, casting shadows about the interior of a barn. Dried herbs hung from the rafters. But they weren't the only things dangling from the worn boards. A noose swung in the cool night air blowing in through the open door.

A man crouched on the floor, leaning over a woman— trying to save her. The candlelight glinted in his auburn hair.

The first time she'd had the vision, Elena had awakened screaming. As always Joseph had comforted her, pulling her tightly against his hard chest. His strong arms had held her close, and he'd reassured her that she was safe. But she had known she wasn't the one in danger. She had thought that the woman lying lifelessly on the ground was Maria. But then she'd had the vision again and she hadn't awakened that time until later. And then she had been even more horrified.

A woman crouched behind him. Long curly black hair hung down her back. She wore an old gray sweater and a long skirt. And from the folds of the long skirt she pulled a knife. The backs of her hands were gouged, as if she'd already fought with someone. And then she swung the blade of that long knife toward the man's back...

That woman was Maria. Not the one lying on the floor. Joseph's contacts had confirmed that Elena's youngest sister had been a con artist. Elena remembered helping her mother run cons—before she, Ariel and Irina had been taken away from her. But Maria had kept running those cons—by herself—after their mother abandoned her. So she'd chosen to be a con artist. Was she now a killer?

Or had she always been?

Elena had had other visions. She had *seen* other bodies. Was Maria so damaged—so evil—that she had taken those lives?

"No…" Irina murmured the word in her sleep as she shifted restlessly on the bed.

"She can hear you," Ariel warned her. "What are you thinking?"

"I'm remembering a vision."

Ariel's turquoise eyes widened and glowed in the darkened bedroom. She knew about the visions—knew that Elena wasn't as convinced as she and Irina that it was a good idea to find Maria.

They were desperate to find the youngest Cooper sister because they were worried that Maria was in danger. Elena was worried that Maria *was* the danger.

Maybe to them all…

Ariel settled closer to Elena's side, as if seeking comfort. She softly murmured, "I hope you're wrong."

Elena shrugged so that her shoulder rubbed against Ariel's—offering comfort as she had when they were kids. "I can't help what I see."

And if Maria was what Elena was afraid she was, then they wouldn't be able to help her, either.

Maria fought to breathe as she waited in the cell, opening her mouth to suck in deep breaths—to fill her aching lungs.

Was it her fear? Or someone else's?

Shortly after Seth Hughes had locked her in the room and left, she'd felt that choking sensation. It wasn't the too-close walls that were shrinking the already small room. It was the mist that filtered in beneath the door.

"No," she murmured around the sob choking her throat. She felt as though that noose were around her neck, pulling tight, cutting off her breath. Off *her* life…

Raven had been such a sweet girl. She had never done anything wrong except for trying to be Maria's friend…and for being a witch. Raven had wanted to be a witch. That was why she'd sought out the shop. Not for the healing cures or love potions that Maria could sell her. Like learning to read the cards, Raven had wanted to learn to make the potions and cures herself.

Maria glanced down at the photos Agent Hughes had left strewn across the small table. Every one of them had wanted the same thing. To practice witchcraft…

Even the two guys. And one of them had been crushed to death, the other burned. But had becoming a witch been their real wish…or was it just because they'd wanted to be close to her?

She had been told that she was that kind of person—the kind who drew other people to her. Apparently even when she didn't want to…

Like Raven…

Her breath shuddered out with the sob that she couldn't restrain. Nobody could get close to her without losing everything.

Nobody…

She reached out for the briefcase Agent Hughes had left on the table to see what else he had inside—like maybe the keys to the door. But the case was empty; he'd only had those crime scene photos in it. No keys. She needed the keys. She had to get out of here—before she suffocated or strangled. But as soon as her fingers touched the leather, images flashed through her mind… like when she read cards or touched a crystal ball.

His smoky blue eyes stared down at her, his gaze intense. Not with anger or suspicion now but with passion. Moonlight gleamed on the bare skin of his broad shoulders and heavily muscled chest. Then his face, so handsome with his square jaw and sharp cheekbones, got closer as he lowered his body. His legs, naked but for soft hair, parted hers. And his chest covered her breasts, crushing them so that her nipples hardened and pressed against his skin.

She moaned at the exquisite sensation. But it wasn't enough. She wanted more, wanted his mouth…everywhere. On her lips, on her breasts and…

He must have read her mind because he chuckled and his chest rumbled against hers. "I can't believe this…"

She shook her head, shaking off the image. "I can't believe it, either." It couldn't be a vision; making love with Seth Hughes would *not* happen. Not just because he thought she was a killer, and she wasn't entirely convinced he wasn't one, too, but also because she would never, ever make the mistake of getting close to anyone else.

Ever again.

Even though she didn't need reminders of what happened to people who got too close to her, she tried to focus on those pictures. Maybe she could see something in the crime scene photos that would help her figure out who was doing this. Who was the dark aura following her…

But even in her visions, she never saw a person, never saw who was hurting these victims. She saw only the darkness. The evil.

And then these images that the crime scene photos had captured. She had seen them before they had even happened—in her mind as she'd read their cards. The same cards that had turned up tonight. For Raven. The mist thickened so that she couldn't see the photos. Or anything in the room.

Then the mist shifted into a human form. She expected Raven's tall thin body, so she gasped in surprise at the small stature and long curly black hair of the ghost. "No…"

She shoved back her chair, as far as the wall would allow, and jumped up. Then she turned toward the door, clawing at the handle and hammering at the wood. "Let me out! Let me out!"

"I'm not going to hurt you," that all-too-familiar soft voice assured her.

The scent of sandalwood and lavender, mixing with her own, overwhelmed her. And smoke. She always smelled smoke now whenever this ghost visited her. Tears burned her eyes. Seeing her always hurt. "I don't want to see you. I told you to leave me alone!"

Her voice cracked with so many emotions as the ghost whispered her name: "Maria…"

"Go away!" she screamed.

"I can't leave you, child."

"Why not? You had no problem leaving me before!" she lashed out.

"I did it for you," her mama's ghost insisted. "To keep you safe."

"You left a fifteen-year-old to fend for herself. How was that keeping me safe?" She had been lucky to survive on her own, driving without a license, continuing the scams so that she could put gas in the truck Mama had left her. So she could eat…

She had done it just so she could survive. But she felt sick with guilt and self-loathing as she remembered turning those cards and telling so many lies to the people who'd paid her to tell their real futures.

But that wasn't all she'd done…

There had been the fake séances her mother had taught her to run. The way of projecting her voice so the *ghost* said what the person wanted to hear. She hadn't charged as much as her mother had to summon the people's lost loved ones, but she shouldn't have charged at all for a *lie*.

Unlike her mother, most people passed from one world to the next without ever coming back. So no matter how much she had actually tried, she hadn't often been able to summon the real spirit for her mark. And then the times she had, the real spirit hadn't always said what they had wanted to hear. So she'd lied.

And people had paid more for her lies, tipping her generously as they'd cried with relief.

"My leaving you was my way of keeping you safe." Mama's reply was one that Maria had heard before. "I knew *I* was in danger."

Even though it hadn't happened until five years after she had abandoned Maria, Mama's witch-hunter had eventually caught her. He had burned her alive. And that was the first time her ghost had appeared to Maria, warning her to run for her life—that he was coming for her, too.

"I thought that no one knew about you," Mama said. "So I thought that if I left you alone, I could keep you safe…from my demons."

Maria closed her eyes, trying to shut out the ghostly image.

But Mama's voice wrapped around her, filling her head as she continued, "But you always had your own demons, hovering like that dark aura around you, putting you and anyone who would ever get close to you in danger. You were always…"

"Cursed," Maria said, bitterness filling her with the warning her mother had given her. Too many times. A child shouldn't have to grow up knowing that she would never know true happiness, that she would always be hunted.

"I should have left you sooner," Mama said, "like I did the others." The others were the sisters Maria had never known. "Or I should have given you to your father."

The father Maria hadn't even known about until

she'd read about him in the letter her mother had left her, along with the locket. She was supposed to go to him if she needed anything. She had needed her mother—not some stranger she'd never met.

"But he wasn't equipped to deal with you," Mama continued, "because I saw *this* in your future."

In the same cards Maria kept turning over for the others, Mama had seen her youngest daughter's future, too. Had seen all the tragedy and loss…

"So I had to teach you how to run," Mama explained. "How to stay ahead of the danger that surrounds you, that goes after anyone who ever gets close to you…"

Was that why Mama hadn't wanted Maria to have anything to do with her sisters? To keep *them* safe? Maria believed that Mama had always loved them more than she had the child she had actually kept.

Hurt, because Mama always hurt her, Maria opened her eyes and lashed out. "Were you the right one to teach me…when you weren't able to run fast enough yourself?"

"I always knew he would catch me one day," Mama said. "But the witch-hunter didn't know about you. No one did."

Not her mama's killer, and not even her sisters.

She turned away from the door and gestured at the pictures spread across the table over which FBI special agent Seth Hughes had interrogated her. "Your killer couldn't have done that. He's dead. My sisters worked together to end his reign of terror. They took care of him."

And he would never hurt anyone again.

Elena, Ariel and Irina hadn't known about her, but

Maria had always known about them. Mama had talked about them incessantly—about how beautiful, how smart, how sweet they were. And Maria had never felt as beautiful, as smart or as sweet. She had never felt as if she'd been worthy enough to replace everything that Mama had lost, everything that the woman had missed so much that there had been a hole in her heart. A hole that Maria had never been quite enough to fill.

"But the witch-hunter had a son." Maria remembered what she had learned from all the media coverage of the ordeal her family had barely survived eight years ago. "Could *he* be carrying on the legacy?" While Maria's family legacy was witchcraft, his was witch-hunting.

"He may not even know about it," Mama replied. "Donovan Roarke hadn't learned about the legacy until long after he lost contact with his son, when he came across the journal of his long-dead ancestor Eli McGregor, who'd begun the witch hunt centuries ago."

Eli McGregor had chased the first Elena for years. Thanks to his son, Thomas, he had never found her. But eventually Eli's descendants had found hers and killed so very many of them...

"If it's not Donovan Roarke's son, then who's after *me*, Mama?" Who hated her so much that he killed anyone who got close to her?

Sadness filled the hollow eyes of her mother's ghost. "I don't know, child."

"Then why are you here?" Maria asked. "I told you to stay away from me. I don't need you." Just as Mama hadn't needed her, hadn't loved her—not the way she had loved her three older children. "Go away! And stay away from me!"

Mama's arms reached out, as if she wanted to hold Maria. But her image faded...even as the mist thickened and took another shape: the tall thin figure of Raven.

"She led me here," the young woman explained. "When I first saw her ghost, I thought she was you. I thought he killed you, too. You look so much alike. She's your mother?"

"She's nothing to me," Maria replied. "She wasn't there for me when I needed her, like I wasn't there for you." Tears stung her eyes and filled her throat. "I didn't protect you like I promised. I am so sorry..."

Raven's ghost stepped closer, the energy of her spirit warming Maria. "I'm the one who's sorry."

"No." Maria reached out, trying to envelop the girl, but her hands and arms passed through the mist. "It's my fault. I never should have hired you. I never should have let you get close to me. Everyone who does winds up dead. It's all my fault."

"It's not you," the girl said, her eyes shimmering with tears she would never be able to shed now. "You're not the killer. I'm sorry that I thought you were. If I hadn't run from you..."

"You would probably still be dead," Maria said as regret filled her. "We would probably both be dead because we would've been together when he came to the shop. Did you see him?"

Raven's image wavered as she shook her head. "I never saw him at the Magik Shoppe. He came up behind me and started strangling me. Then I thought it might have been you. But at the hospital I saw *him*."

Maria gasped as realization struck her. "He was at

the hospital?" Why would he have gone there…unless to finish what he'd started?

"He killed me there," Raven explained. "He drowned me…"

Maria shuddered in horror. She could have asked how. But she had a more important question. "Who is he? Is it Agent Hughes?"

Raven's ghostly brow furrowed. "I don't know who he is. His face was in the shadows, but I could see the outline of his jaw and his hair. And his voice…" The ghostly image flickered, as if she was trembling with terror. "Something about him was familiar…"

So it might have been the FBI agent…

Maria wanted to ask more questions about the killer, but her heart ached over the senseless loss of her young friend. And guilt overwhelmed her. "It should have been me. I'm the one he's after. I just wish I knew why…"

Was it as simple as Mama had always said? Because she was cursed?

"Because he's a witch-hunter," Raven replied. "That's what he calls himself."

"Did you recognize his voice?"

"No, it was just this weird whisper. He said that he thought I was a witch." The ghost's lips curved into a faint smile of satisfaction.

That was all she had ever wanted—to be a witch like the older sister she had told Maria about—the older sister she had felt she would never be as smart or as beautiful as. Her sister had refused to teach Raven the craft. Maria should have refused, too, but she had identified too much with the girl.

"You are a *real* witch, Maria," Raven continued.

"Your knowledge and powers are legendary. I heard about you before I ever met you. That's why I came up here. It's why I wanted to learn from you."

Maria would never forgive herself for hiring the girl. Even though it had been a year since a murder, she should have known the hunter was still out there, still watching her.

She shivered as the girl's image grew fainter. Maria reached for her again, trying to hold her in the room. "Don't leave…"

Her voice a mere whisper, her image just a wisp, Raven warned her, "You're in the most danger from him now. He's going to try to kill you."

"Don't leave me!" she begged. She had to apologize more, had to try to make amends, to assuage the guilt that cramped her stomach in knots. "Come back!" she cried.

Keys rattled in the lock, startling her into shocked silence. She should have been relieved that the door was opening, but terror gripped her.

Even without Raven's warning, she'd known *he* would be coming for her. Soon.

The door opened, and a deep voice asked, "Who are you talking to?"

"You're back," she said, turning to where Agent Hughes filled the doorway; he was so tall, his shoulders so broad. His square jaw was clenched, his handsome face grim. Was his the face Raven had seen in the shadows of her hospital room?

"You weren't begging me to come back," he surmised. "The deputy said you were in here yelling."

"Because I wanted to get out," she said, rubbing her hands over her arms. Her sweater had dried from the rain earlier in the evening. But she was still so cold—even her blood chilled and pumped slowly and heavily through her veins. And that pressure was back in her chest, squeezing her lungs and heart with panic. "I need to get out of here."

"The deputy was watching you through the mirror and listening through the intercom," Agent Hughes divulged. "He said you were telling someone *else* to get out, that you were talking to someone in here."

She lifted her hands and gestured around the tiny room. "Do you see anyone else in here?"

"I don't see anyone," he said, glancing around the small space. "But do you?"

She drew in a ragged breath. Even without the DNA, he already knew who and what she was. She had already admitted to trying to heal Raven, so she might as well admit to the rest of her abilities. "Raven's ghost. She's dead."

That muscle twitched along his jaw. "How could you *know* that?" His gray-blue eyes narrowed with suspicion. He obviously had some ideas…

Some ideas that cast his suspicion on her again…

"I just told you that I saw her ghost." Hers wasn't the only ghost she had seen, but she wasn't about to tell him about Mama. That brought out even more pain and vulnerability than seeing Raven's ghost had.

"She was here," Maria replied honestly even though he would probably think she was lying. Or trying to con him. "Her *ghost* was here…until you came in."

Was he the reason that Raven had slipped away so quickly? Because she didn't want to see her killer again?

"Why was she here?" he asked, speaking slowly

and softly as if Maria were a young child...or mentally
unstable, which was probably what that poor deputy
thought of her, too.

"She came here to warn me. I'm in danger, too.
That's what all this is about," she said, gesturing at
those photos he'd left on the table.

He cocked his head as he continued to scrutinize
her through narrowed eyes. He was probably trying
to determine if she'd lost her mind. "What is all this?"

"All these murders," she said impatiently. Why
wasn't he following her? "*This* is about me. Someone's trying to kill *me*." Because she was the real witch.

Images flashed through her head of the murders of
everyone who'd gotten close to her. But in her mind
she was now the victim. It was her head being held
underwater, her neck the noose wound tightly around,
her body the brick-laden board crushed...her skin the
flames burned.

Not only could she see a vision of what would happen to someone, she experienced every feeling that
person did when it happened. Every moment of terror. Every stab of pain. When they died, it was as if
she died, too.

She gasped for breath, fighting to get air into her
lungs—fighting to slow her racing heart. "I need...I
need..."

She reached out and grasped his arm, digging her
fingers into the leather sleeve—afraid that she might
pass out as she had before when pummeled with all
those horrible feelings. But she couldn't count on Agent
Hughes to hold her up. She had learned long ago that
she couldn't count on anyone but herself.

So she pleaded, "Let me go..."

She could run. She could protect herself. She had been doing it for so many years…

"No," he said, his gaze dropping to her hand clutching his arm. "I can't let you go…"

She pulled back and twined her fingers together to still their trembling and that crazy tingling she felt whenever they touched.

"Just let me go to the restroom," she said. "I—I need to splash water on my face. I need a minute to…"

His brow creased, he studied her face for a long moment before finally nodding his agreement. "Okay." Maybe he'd seen that she was about to pass out, because his hand closed around her elbow.

She gasped again, at the jolt of recognition. That damn connection. His touch was familiar and exciting and frightening as hell. Who the hell was he really? She tried to pull her arm away from his grasp, but he held her easily—tightly.

"I won't run," she said. "Just show me to the door."

Instead he walked her down the hall, past the courtroom and the city hall office, to the door at the end. The town was so small that they made the most of their one city building.

"I won't run," she repeated as she stopped outside the door.

"No, you won't," he agreed. "I already checked the bathroom. No window. No other way out but this door." He turned back, but he walked only a few strides away—keeping the door in sight of his smoky blue gaze.

Dread tightened the knots in her stomach. She had hoped for a window, had hoped she would be able to find an escape route. But the splash of water on her face would have to suffice. With a sigh, she shoved open the door and stepped inside the dark room. She slapped her hand against the wall until she fumbled across the light switch and pushed it up. The fluorescent bulbs crackled and buzzed and then illuminated the small space, chasing away the shadows.

Except for one.

A noose swung from the ceiling, the rope casting a shadow on the floor. It converged with the shadow of Maria's body, as if the noose were already wound around her neck. She could feel the scratchy fibers digging into her skin, could feel the rope squeezing...

A scream tore from Maria's throat. Even before Mama's and Raven's ghostly warnings, she'd known.

She was going to be the next witch to die...

Chapter 4

The scream jerked Irina awake. But it must have been just inside her head, since her sisters slept peacefully on, their breathing deep and steady. They hadn't even stirred.

But one of her sisters wasn't with her, and she wasn't sleeping. Maria's heart was hammering, her pulse racing with fear. She was terrified. And Irina was feeling all those emotions. She reached out—not for either of her sleeping sisters. She didn't want to disturb them. She already knew what they were thinking about Maria. She reached out for her husband. Ty had left earlier—at her urging. But as always, he knew when she needed him, and he was back. His strong arms closed around her as he drew her close to his chest.

"It's okay," he murmured in that raspy voice she always found so sexy. She found everything sexy about him—his thick black hair, his eyes that were so dark a blue they were nearly black. She even loved the jagged scar that ran through one of his eyebrows. The story behind it wasn't pretty, but it had made him the man he was. The man she loved...

She shook her head. "No..."

He placed a hand on her belly. "Are they okay?"

She put her hand on the back of his big one. "They're okay."

With sudden understanding, he murmured, "Maria..."

"You need to find her now," she urged him. "She's in danger. I can feel her fear. It's more intense than it's ever been. She knows he's coming for her. He might already be there—close to her..."

Ty gestured toward a bag he'd packed and left on the bedroom floor next to the bed he usually shared with her. But tonight he had asked her sisters to stay with her while he met with his best friend and brother-in-law, David Koster. David was a computer genius; he could find out things few other people could. Maybe David had finally found something to lead them to Maria.

"I don't want to leave you," he said, "but...we have to..." They were so close, so connected that he always felt what she felt. He always knew when she needed him, and right now she needed him to find Maria before it was too late.

"Thank you," she whispered, and leaned closer to brush her lips over his. Tears leaked from her eyes and trailed down her cheeks. "You always know. You always believe..."

Her own sisters doubted Maria. But then, they didn't know her the way Irina did. She had lived with her briefly while they'd been in college; she hadn't known then that Maria was her sister. But Maria had known.

But even if Irina hadn't lived with her, she would have known her. She felt her emotions, so she knew her heart. It was good—like the witch.

But she was still a witch. And the witch hunt had resumed. Maria was the hunter's next target. Because of her powers, probably his ultimate prize.

"I know I promised you before," Ty said, "eight years ago, that I would find her. And I haven't kept that promise…"

"You will," she assured him. "You will find her." She just hoped that it would be in time. Before she died…

He nodded. "I will, and I'll be back before our babies come."

As he knew and believed in her, Irina knew and believed in her husband. He was a man of his word. A man of honor and determination.

But still she couldn't help but worry that she would be bringing her children into a world that her younger sister had just left.

Maria's scream coursed through Seth as if her terror were his. His heart hammering, he ran the few feet down the hall and shouldered open the bathroom door. While he didn't remember withdrawing it from its holster, he held his gun, his finger along the barrel, ready to squeeze the trigger should he need to fire.

Maria Cooper whirled toward him, anger replacing her fear as color flushed her beautiful face. "Did you do this? It's you, isn't it? You're the witch-hunter."

He sucked in a breath at the accusation. "Why— why would you say that?"

"You just admitted you'd been in here. If you were, you must have seen this." She raised her hand toward the ceiling. "You must have done *this*."

He glanced up at the noose hanging from a joist over her head. And he couldn't control the grimace as he remembered the marks on the pale skin of Raven's throat. But that wasn't how the girl had died. The water dripping from the unattached end of her breathing tube was how she'd died tonight. Drowned. Like a witch...

Maria Cooper couldn't have done that; she had been locked in the tiny interrogation room under the deputy's watchful gaze. She hadn't escaped him. But she hadn't escaped the killer, either.

Maybe she didn't want to, though—if she was working with him. Then, what was the noose about? Was it a diversion or a threat?

"I didn't do that," he said. "I checked out the room before I left for the hospital...in case you needed to use it when I was gone. That wasn't in here then."

She shuddered. "So he was here when you were gone..."

After killing Raven, the man had come here from the hospital. And Seth had stayed behind, waiting for the autopsy to confirm what he'd already known—that someone had disconnected the girl's breathing tube and filled it with water. He had worried that the guy would come to the police station. But he'd figured that the man was her accomplice and would try to break Maria out—not threaten her with a noose. But maybe he was threatening her not to talk.

Now Seth knew for certain that there was some sick, dangerous bastard who was still one step ahead of him.

"Son of a bitch," he murmured.

How the hell had the bastard gotten in here? He scanned the small room and noticed the displaced ceiling tiles. Reaching up, he pushed aside more of them, knocking them loose from the grids holding them up.

Then he leaned out the door. "Deputy! Search the building. Someone's been in here!"

He should have called for a helicopter and brought Maria back to the bureau tonight. Bringing her here—to this unsecured city building—had been a mistake. He was damned lucky that the man hadn't been waiting in the bathroom for her—that he hadn't pulled her up into the ceiling and helped her escape Seth.

"You should go, too, and search the building," she urged him. "You need to find him. You have to stop him…before he kills anyone else."

He stepped closer to her and touched her, just his fingers on her chin, tipping her face up so that she had to meet his gaze. But his skin tingled as if electrified. What the hell was it between them that whenever they touched, it felt so intense? So *important*…?

Her throat moved as if she was struggling to swallow—or breathe. She was scared. She hadn't faked the terror in that scream. And it was in her eyes now, dark and haunting. It was almost as if she feared him, too.

"Who is he?" he asked.

She shook her head—maybe because she didn't know. Maybe because she was trying to remove his hand. His touch…

She felt that connection between them, too. Her eyes

darkened even more with the awareness. With the undeniable attraction...

"I don't know..."

He heard the frustration in her voice, the anger and aggravation that she had no idea who had placed that noose where she would find it—as she had found that other noose just hours ago with Raven still swinging from it.

"Don't *you* know?" she asked him. "You've been chasing after me all these years, so don't you know?"

He searched his mind, his memory, for everything he knew about her—for everyone who knew her. And he shook his head. "All the people who've gotten close to you have died."

She trembled. "I know..."

There was no one left to be her accomplice. The person had to be someone else—someone who was close to her not emotionally but physically. A stalker?

Was that noose left as a threat to her life? Indicating that she would be next?

"You should go," she said. "Help them search..." Now there was desperation in her eyes along with the fear.

Seth had seen that look before—before he'd joined the bureau. Back when he'd been just a beat cop, he had seen that look in the eyes of a deer who'd accidentally crashed through a sliding door and gotten trapped inside the sunroom of a house. In that deer's eyes, he had seen sheer panic and desperation to escape—to run.

That was why Maria wanted him to leave her. So that she could run, too.

But the deer had never run again. The older cop who'd been training Seth had shot and killed the animal. He'd claimed it was so the deer wouldn't do any more damage to the house—or to itself. It had been hurt.

But Seth thought it could have survived if it had been given a chance. The old cop hadn't given it a chance. Neither could Seth...

"I'm not going anywhere," he said. "I'm not leaving you alone."

She shuddered with fear. "You don't want to be close to me. You've seen what has happened to everyone who's gotten close to me in the past. They've been murdered." Apparently her fear was for him—not for herself.

He glanced up at the noose again and barely restrained a shudder of his own. "Protecting you is my job. You're a material witness. I have to keep you alive." That was all it was; he wasn't feeling protective of her for any other reason.

She nodded. "Yes. Of course," she agreed. Too quickly, as if embarrassed over implying they might become closer than agent and witness. "I know that you're only doing your job."

Finding her had never been just a job to him. She was so much more than that...

So much more than he had ever realized before meeting her. Was she really what she claimed? What everyone else had claimed she was? Was she really a witch?

And if she was, how could she not know who was after her, who had killed all those people who had been close to her?

If Raven's ghost had really visited her, wouldn't she have told her who'd killed her?

"I could do my job more easily if you stopped lying to me and told me everything you know." He touched her again, tipping up her chin to meet his gaze.

Her thick black lashes fluttered as she blinked—as if trying to shield her thoughts and feelings from him. Could she sense what he was feeling?

Could she feel his desire for her? His madness...

He had to be crazy—after those dreams—to want anything to do with her besides arresting her. But he doubted that either of them would be safe, even with her locked up.

Her voice low and raspy, as if that noose were around her neck, tightening, she whispered, "What do you mean?"

"You told me Raven's ghost visited you," he reminded her.

"And you thought I was crazy," she accused him.

He shrugged and answered honestly, "I don't know what to think about you, Maria..."

Her lips, sensually full and tempting lips, curved into a slight smile. "You don't know if I'm crazy or..."

"Or if you're the real deal," he said. "So if you are the real deal, how can you *not* know who he is?"

Her frustration was back, knitting her brow. "I don't know..."

"Why didn't Raven's ghost tell you who he is?" he persisted. If she was telling the truth, she'd had a chance to question the ultimate eyewitness. The victim.

"She didn't see him," Maria replied. "He came up behind her at the Magik Shoppe. And his face was in the shadows at the hospital."

The room had been dark. The nurses had confirmed that. Maybe she hadn't seen him.

Or maybe Maria was making it all up.

She must have seen the skepticism on his face, because she continued, "I really saw her ghost."

"Why?" he asked. "If she didn't see him, why did she come to you?"

She looked up at that dangling noose and shivered. "To warn me that I would be next."

Instinctively he reached for her, pulling her into his arms to protect her. But instead of reassuring her or himself, touching her rattled him. His nerves jangled and his skin tingled.

Maybe it wasn't because of touching her. Maybe it was because of the threat. He couldn't imagine her hanging. Or drowning…

Or dying in any of the gruesome ways those other victims had died. He couldn't lose her.

Yet she wasn't his to lose.

He should have released her, should have stepped back. But he continued to hold her as he asked, "Why would he want to kill you? Or any of the others?"

"I don't know who he is," she replied. "But I know what he does. He kills witches, or people he thinks have special abilities."

She clutched at him, maybe in fear, maybe because she felt what he felt: that connection, that desire, that gut-wrenching *need*…

Her breath shuddered out, warming his skin even as it made it tingle. "You'll be safe, then."

If his dream was real, he wasn't safe. But it wasn't the witch-hunter he had to fear. It was *her*.

He had been so close to her. When she'd stepped inside the restroom and shut the door, he had felt the vibration in the ceiling—through which he had crawled, right above the head of the FBI agent.

Excitement pulsed in his blood, pumping hot and heavy through his body. He had outsmarted them both—the witch and the special agent. Neither of them had suspected that he was close—until she had seen the noose he had left for her and screamed in surprise and fear.

Why hadn't she known that it would be there?

She saw other people's futures, but she must not have seen her own. So then she probably had no idea what he had planned for her. The noose was only the beginning. He had wanted to torture her for years— killing everyone stupid enough to get close to her and her witchcraft ways so that he isolated her from everyone. So that she was completely alone. But the FBI agent's presence had forced him to act sooner than he'd planned.

Nevertheless, he still intended to take his time with this witch. He would use every method of witch-hunting to kill her: hanging, drowning, crushing and burning.

"Agent Hughes! Agent Hughes!" The young deputy's shout of excitement carried back from the reception area. "We've got him!"

Maria's heart thumped against her ribs. Then she rushed forward, but Seth Hughes was there, his big body blocking the doorway to the restroom.

"I have to see him." She shoved against Hughes, but the lawman was all hard muscle—like in her vision— and he didn't budge. "I have to see who he is!"

"I don't know if they've searched him. I can't let you see him until I've made certain he's not armed," Seth explained. But he led her out into the hall, to the open door of that little room where she had already spent too much time. "I want you to go back in the interrogation room and wait for me."

She shook her head as the panic pressed on her lungs again with that feeling that she would suffocate. "You're not locking me back in there."

If the man had dropped through that ceiling instead of the bathroom one with his noose…

But then the deputy who'd been behind the mirror would have seen him. And the witch-hunter was too smart to be seen. Or caught…

"It's not him," she said with sudden realization, and now disappointment settled heavily on her chest. "It's not him…"

Seth Hughes's smoky gray-blue eyes closed for a second, and his nostrils flared as he dragged in a ragged breath. "Probably not."

"Then you can't leave me alone," she pointed out. "Not if you really want to protect me."

But could she trust him to protect her and not hurt her? Was he really not the hunter? She couldn't be certain. If only she could read minds, as one of her sisters could…

Irina would know what he was thinking. Maria knew only what he was feeling—that same damn overwhelming attraction she felt for him.

"I'm not the killer," he said.

And she wondered…could *he* read minds? But if he could, he would have already known that she had not killed her friends. No, as an FBI agent, he could probably just read people's expressions, as her mother had been able to. While Seth used his abilities for interrogations, Mama had used hers to determine what her mark had wanted to hear.

Was that simply what Seth Hughes was telling her now? What she wanted to hear?

"Is that her?" a male voice asked.

The man stood next to the young deputy. While the deputy held the guy's arm with one hand, he had drawn his weapon on him with the other. "This is him, Agent Hughes."

Seth shook his head. "No, it's not."

"Is that her?" the strange man repeated, tugging free of the deputy's loose grasp. Like Seth, he was tall, but lean where the FBI agent was muscular. His features more refined where Seth's were more masculine. His hair was lighter, almost golden, and his eyes a clear green.

Maria had never seen the man before, and yet he was familiar to her. Eerily familiar. She had to have seen him before. Maybe she and Seth were wrong; maybe he was the witch-hunter and he had become so arrogant that he'd gotten sloppy.

"Mr. Waverly, you shouldn't be here," Seth said, his voice rough with an odd mixture of disapproval, irritation and sensitivity.

"You're here," Mr. Waverly said, as if Seth's presence justified his. "You're following a lead—to her."

Seth stiffened and stepped closer to her, as if he really intended to keep his promise to protect her. "How do you know that?"

"Someone in the bureau told me where you were," Mr. Waverly explained, "and what you were doing."

Seth cursed beneath his breath. "Damn, Curtis, how much did you pay for that information?"

Information could be bought from the FBI? That thought unsettled Maria even more than she had been. But then, she'd already known she couldn't trust anyone. Especially not Seth Hughes…

Mr. Waverly ignored his question and asked his own. "Is she the woman you think killed my sister?"

Maria turned to Seth, waiting for his reply, wondering if he had completely changed his mind about her involvement in the murders.

But instead of answering the question, he told the other man, "You shouldn't be here, Curtis. You're interfering in my investigation."

"I had to know—" the guy's throat rippled as he swallowed hard "—what you've found."

"And I promised that I would keep you apprised of my progress," Seth said.

"You don't think this is progress?" the man scoffed. "Finally finding the last person who saw my sister alive?"

Maria's stomach tensed at the hollow echo of loss in his deep voice. She'd never known her sisters—except for the one closest to her in age and that for only a short time—and she missed them. She couldn't imagine this man's pain.

But she didn't have to. She could *feel* it. Usually with living people, she was able to block it, and out of self-preservation she had to. But she was too exhausted to fight the feelings. His pain and regret rolled over her with his words.

"It's been so long," he said, his voice cracking, "so long with no justice for Felicia."

The name struck Maria like a hard slap. "Felicia…"

After her mother's first ghostly visit, Maria had

been forced to abandon the normal life she'd been building for herself. Going to college, sharing an off-campus apartment with the sister she'd managed to find. She'd been attending undergrad classes while Irina had been going for her doctorate. Maria'd had to leave it all behind and start over—alone. She had never felt so alone, not even when her mother had taken off in the middle of the night, leaving behind only a note and a locket.

But then she had found Felicia, and in the young woman she'd found a friend who had felt like a sister. They had been so close…until Maria had found the girl drowned—in the bathtub of the little house they had been converting into a magic shop.

She hadn't been surprised when she'd found her, though. She had already seen it—when she'd read Felicia's cards earlier that day. And she had already felt it…as it had happened…

Air caught in her lungs as she struggled to breathe. But every breath she drew brought more water into her mouth and nose, sending it down her throat so that she choked and sputtered. Her eyes burned like her lungs. She couldn't see anything, could only feel one large hand at the back of her head and the other wrapped around the nape of her neck, pushing her down—pushing her underwater.

Her arms flailed as she tried to fight him off, but her strength ebbed along with her breath. She had none left— no air. No energy…

It was easier to stop fighting. Easier to just give up. And once she stopped fighting, a strange peace settled over her, eradicating her fear and horror.

And she welcomed death...

Maybe Maria should do the same. Maybe she should just stop running and let the witch-hunter catch her. Maybe once he killed her, he would stop killing the others.

But then she saw her mother's ghost again as mist and smoke filled the hallway.

"No!" Myra Cooper yelled—so loudly that Maria was surprised the men couldn't hear her. The mist and smoke thickened as her image took shape. And she wondered why they couldn't see her. She had never been as clear to Maria as she was then.

"You can't stop running, child," Mama urged her. "You can't let him win!"

"Who is he?" she asked.

Mama had to know...

Seth knit his brows, confused, but he answered the question as if she'd asked him. "His name is Curtis Waverly. He's the brother of the first victim."

Felicia's brother. She knew who he was now and why he looked familiar. Felicia had shown her pictures of him; he'd also been on the news after her murder, offering a reward for her killer. He wasn't the witch-hunter.

Mama shook her head in response to Maria's question. "I wish I knew..."

But like Raven, she didn't know. She hadn't seen him. This witch-hunter wasn't her killer.

He would be Maria's killer, though.

"No!" Mama yelled again. Like Irina, she could hear thoughts. "You can't give up. You have to keep running..."

But what was the point of running when she was

cursed? When she would never know happiness any-way? And if she could save other lives…

"You really think he will stop?" Mama asked. "He has killed so many already."

But Maria was the one he wanted. Why else would he have killed everyone close to her?

"Not everyone," Mama reminded her. "Your sisters are alive. Your niece. Stacia is more powerful than you are. You think he'll stop if you're gone. But he won't. If he's like Eli McGregor, he won't rest until every Durikken descendant is dead…"

"I—I have to go," Maria told Seth Hughes as panic filled her. "I have to get out of here." Not just the police station. She had to get out of Copper Creek.

Now.

Mama was right. He wouldn't stop with her. He would kill the others. Elena, Ariel and Irina…

And Elena's daughter.

Did the others have daughters, too?

Would more innocent lives be lost because of her?

"You can't let her go," Mr. Waverly protested. "You need to arrest her!"

"For what?" Maria asked. "I've done nothing wrong." It wasn't her fault that she'd been born cursed. That she had been doomed to a life on the run.

The person who'd taken all those lives—he was the one responsible. The one Seth Hughes needed to catch.

If the killer wasn't Seth…

She hoped like hell it wasn't him. She wanted some-one she could trust, someone to protect her and her family. But maybe she would have to do as her sisters had—maybe she would have to take out the witch-hunter herself.

"There is no evidence to prove she committed the murders," Seth said. "There is evidence that she didn't commit the last one. So I have no reason to arrest her."

No reason to hold her. So she slipped free of his grasp. She needed to leave. Needed to put some distance between herself and that noose hanging in the restroom...

But then her throat constricted, choking off her breath, as big hands closed around her neck and squeezed. She heard a scream, but it couldn't have been hers. She couldn't speak. She couldn't breathe. So it must have been Mama's...

There was just a buzzing in her ears—the sound of her blood pumping weakly through her veins. She couldn't even see who was choking her as her vision blurred. Then everything went black as she slipped into unconsciousness.

She suspected that the next ghost she'd see would be her own...

Chapter 5

They met in darkness. The three men. And they kept their voices low as if someone might overhear them. But the person they worried about eavesdropping wasn't anywhere within normal hearing distance.

But then they weren't married to normal women. They were married to the Cooper sisters.

David Koster considered them all damn lucky. His best friend, Ty McIntyre, didn't look happy, though. He looked grim. "You sure you want to do this?" David asked him. He'd asked him the same thing when he had seen Ty earlier that night. Now the night was nearly over. "You can stay with Irina, and Joe and I can go check out this lead."

Ty shook his head. "No. I promised my wife that I would do this for *her*." He pushed his hand through his short black hair. "Hell, I promised her I would find her younger sister eight years ago."

"You've worked hard on this," David said. "We all have. But it's hard to find someone who's desperate to never be found."

"That's because she might have a damn good reason to never be found," Joseph Dolce remarked. Given his questionable past, his comment was no surprise.

"There's a statute of limitation on those cons she ran," David pointed out. And there was a damn good reason she'd had to run them: survival.

Joseph should understand that; he had grown up on the streets. But even as a kid, Joseph had probably been intimidating. Despite the fact he had as much silver as black in his hair, he was even more intimidating now. Because of everything he had seen and done...

"There's no statute of limitation on murder," Joseph said.

David had seen and done a lot in his life, too, so he used to be as cynical as Joseph. But then he had met and fallen in love with and then married Ariel Cooper. She had brought sunshine and hope and love into his life. "She's just a person of interest in those murders."

"Just?" Joseph repeated. "That's a lot. And then there're Elena's visions—"

"Which aren't always clearly interpreted until after the vision has become a reality," David reminded him. "Ariel is afraid those visions indicate that someone's after Maria. She thinks she may not live long enough to be reunited with them." And that scared her. She didn't want her first meeting with her sister to be with the woman's ghost.

David would do anything within his power to keep his wife happy. And while he had millions of dollars and contacts, he hadn't had the right kind of power to save Ariel before.

She and her sisters were the powerful ones. But even they hadn't been able to find or help Maria.

"Someone is after Maria," Ty said. "Irina feels her fear. She's scared." He turned toward Joseph. "That's why I asked you here, Joseph. You need to watch them while we're gone. You need to keep them safe."

Joseph's green eyes widened with surprise, but then he nodded in acceptance.

"You think they're in danger?" David asked, his heart beating faster.

Ty nodded. "The witch hunt has started again."

Panic and dread filled David that the nightmare had returned. He had promised that he would pilot the helicopter for Ty to follow his lead. But now he was torn. He wanted to stay. He wanted to protect his family. While his kids might be safe, since he and Ariel had adopted their children, his wife would not be safe from a witch hunt.

"I'll keep them safe," Joseph vowed.

While David hadn't known this brother-in-law as long as he'd known Ty, he trusted him. Joseph Dolce would do whatever necessary to keep the family safe from harm. But still he hesitated to leave them...

"What about that FBI agent—Seth Hughes?" he asked Ty. "Don't you trust him to keep Maria safe?" And then they could protect their wives.

"He thinks she's the prime suspect in those murders," Joseph said. "Would he protect a suspect?"

They both turned to Ty to answer the question. Ty was the former lawman among them. While he had loved his job protecting and serving the public, he loved what he did now more—finding lost loved ones. He had found everyone's but his wife's.

David understood his friend's frustration and determination. What he didn't understand now was his hesitation. And then he realized, "You don't trust Seth Hughes."

"No, I don't," Ty admitted.

He and Ty had learned at a young age to trust no one, so they had thoroughly checked out the FBI agent. "The guy doesn't need to work. He's richer than we are." And that was pretty damn rich. "He went into law enforcement because he loves it—because he wants to help people."

So why didn't Ty trust him?

Joseph snorted derisively. "You can't trust rich people." He was probably including himself. "And you can't trust that he just wants to help people. He could have another agenda entirely."

"Maria could be his agenda," Ty murmured.

"You think he's the witch-hunter?" David asked.

"He's the one who's been hunting her for almost a decade," Ty said. "And now that he's found her, she's more scared than she's ever been."

"Damn it," David said as Ty's mistrust and unease became his. "Let's get this bird in the air." He didn't want Ariel seeing her sister for the first time as a ghost. And he didn't want it to be his fault for trusting someone he shouldn't have. He turned back to Joseph, who just nodded as if David had asked his question.

He didn't need to ask. Joseph would give up his life to protect their family. But if Joseph died, then there would be no one to save the Cooper sisters from another witch hunt.

* * *

She was going to die—right before his eyes. Seth slammed his fist into Curtis Waverly's jaw. The man staggered back, but he didn't release her, his hands locked tightly around her throat.

The deputy raised the gun he held, the barrel bouncing around as his hands shook uncontrollably. The young man had probably never drawn his weapon before tonight, let alone shot someone.

Seth didn't want to be the one he shot, and he certainly didn't want Maria to get hit, either. "Put that down!" he shouted.

Then he struck Curtis again, this time driving his first hard into his throat. The man gasped as Maria gasped for breath, and he dropped to the floor, clutching at his neck.

Maria, pushed against the wall, slid down it onto the floor. Her dark eyes had already closed. Hopefully in unconsciousness—not death.

Seth dropped to his knees beside her. He didn't dare touch her neck, which was already red and swelling. He felt her wrist instead. And it was as if her pulse leaped at his touch. She was alive!

"Are you breathing?" he asked. He dipped his head close to hers. Her lips were slightly open, but he could hear no air passing through them. So he pressed his lips to hers and breathed for her. And as their mouths met, images played through his mind of other kisses. Hungry, passionate kisses…

She gasped and pushed against his shoulders, shoving him back. Her eyes were open now and wide with shock.

"You can breathe?" he asked, as he struggled for air

himself. Maybe it was nearly losing her. Maybe it was the shock of touching her lips…

She nodded, but her hands lifted to her neck. And he knew she wasn't all right.

"Call an ambulance," he told the deputy.

She grabbed his arm and in a raspy whisper protested, "No…"

But maybe the young deputy had already called in reinforcements, because a door opened and footsteps echoed from down the hall.

"What the hell's going on?" the sheriff asked as he stared down at them all. Nervous of his deputy, too, he took the gun from the kid's shaking hands.

Fortunately, he wasn't alone, since the coroner stood beside him. "Is everyone okay?" Dr. Kohler asked.

"He nearly strangled her," Seth said with a glance back at Curtis Waverly.

The man lay on the floor, his body curled into a ball of pain and misery. Sympathy tugged slightly at Seth. He knew Waverly was hurting, and not from Seth's blows.

"Then why the hell haven't you cuffed him?" Sheriff Moore asked his deputy as he shoved the kid forward.

Maria's grip on Seth's arm tightened. "No," she whispered.

She didn't want the man who had attacked her arrested?

"We should get her to the hospital," Dr. Kohler said from where he knelt on the other side of her. "If this swelling gets worse, it could cut off her breathing again."

She shook her head, then flinched and touched her neck again. "I—I need my herbs…"

"You're going to the hospital," Seth said. "Not back to that barn…" It was already a crime scene. And usually the crime scenes in this case were eventually destroyed.

That was why he'd made certain the sheriff had collected as much evidence as he could without waiting for the bureau techs to show up. Sometimes they were too late.

"I brought those herbs in," Sheriff Moore told him. "I have them in evidence."

"Are those the herbs she used on that other girl's throat?" Dr. Kohler asked his friend. When the sheriff nodded, he ordered him, "Bring them over here!"

Seth shook his head, disgusted with the other men's behavior. "She needs medical attention, not some spell…"

"Those herbs worked," Dr. Kohler said. "If someone hadn't put that water in the girl's breathing tube, she would have recovered." His voice quavered with excitement. "She would have recovered from a *hanging*! It had to be those herbs…" The doctor sounded as befuddled as Seth was.

Why would Maria have saved the girl if she'd been the one who had hurt her? None of it made sense—except that Seth had been wrong about her. Maria Cooper was not a killer. She was a healer.

Seth's dream the night before had been just that—a dream born of his suspicion and mistrust of her. Nothing more. It wouldn't come true—even though most of his other dreams had.

The sheriff hurried back with an evidence bag clenched in his hand. He handed it to the doctor, but the doctor handed it to Maria. Her hands trembled as she tore open the seal and reached into the bag.

He couldn't tell one dried weed from another. But she sorted through them quickly and pulled out a poultice. Instead of pressing it to her own throat, though, she crawled across the hall to Curtis Waverly.

He tensed when she touched him, as if he thought her touch alone could kill him. But all she did was press that poultice against his throat where Seth had slugged him.

She murmured something beneath her breath—like some weird chant. Then she told him, again in a weak whisper, "Hold that…"

Curtis's fingers trembled, but he held it. Dr. Kohler followed her across the hall and checked the man's neck. "The swelling's already going down…"

"Treat yourself," Seth implored her.

She was already reaching back into that evidence bag, already concocting another potion, which she pressed against her own throat. Only her lips moved as she chanted again. She had no voice—no breath or strength to actually utter the words.

"This is crazy," he said. "I need to take her to the hospital."

"No," she said, and now her voice was clear and loud. "I don't need medical attention."

The doctor gasped and shook his head. "I had Maurice bring me back here so I could take a look at those herbs. But I probably still wouldn't have believed it…"

If he hadn't seen it—as Seth had.

"My wife's been going to her," Sheriff Moore admitted. "She's helped Katherine with her MS." He rubbed his knuckles. "Hell, I've seen her myself. She's helped me with my arthritis."

"Have you all gone crazy?" Curtis Waverly asked. "She's a killer."

"You nearly killed her," Seth said. "Arrest him, Sheriff, for assault with intent—"

"You were going to let her go!" Curtis protested. "After all these years of looking for her, you were going to let her just walk away."

"Curtis—"

Waverly whirled toward him. "You told me that once you found her, you would lock her up for the rest of her life. That she would never get away again."

Maria turned to him, too, her eyes wide with fear. She looked the way she had when Curtis had been choking her—as if she couldn't breathe.

"You promised me justice for my sister's murder," Curtis said, his eyes hard with accusation. He obviously felt as though Seth had betrayed him.

"Justice isn't killing the wrong person," Seth admonished him as he helped the man to his feet.

"I didn't mean to…hurt her," he said, and his voice broke with sobs. "I didn't mean to… I just wanted to stop her from leaving…"

"Don't arrest him," Maria said. And her hand was on Seth's arm again, squeezing, as she stood up, too. Her strength was back.

Seth shook his head. "He has to be booked for assault."

"What about her?" Curtis asked. "Are you going to arrest her? Or are you just going to let her walk away? She'll disappear and you will never see her again. This time you'll never find her."

Seth was afraid that Curtis was right, but for the wrong reasons. He was certain that whoever had killed

Raven intended to kill Maria—just as the girl's ghost had warned her.

"I'm not letting her go," Seth vowed. "I'm going to hold her…"

Seth was holding her, all right—but not in that unsecured jail where she had nearly been killed by a man he had trusted.

Maybe Curtis hadn't meant to hurt her. Maybe he had only been overwhelmed with emotion at finally seeing her and thinking she was about to escape again. But Curtis was the one in jail now—at least until he hired an expensive lawyer to get him out on bail.

Maria was in custody, too. *His* custody. Despite her protests, he had brought her to the room he had rented at the little motel in Copper Creek.

While he stood watch near the window and door, Maria slept peacefully in his bed. Even though her potion had healed her neck so that she bore no bruises or swelling anymore, she must have been exhausted from the ordeal. The minute her curly-haired head had hit his pillow, she'd fallen asleep. The sunlight shining through the blinds and across her beautiful face hadn't bothered her at all.

But then, Curtis Waverly strangling her hadn't been her only ordeal. She had lost a friend—another one. And she'd been threatened with that noose.

Had Curtis done that?

Seth doubted it. It wasn't the man's style. Then again, Seth wouldn't have thought strangling a woman was his style, either. Was his opinion of anyone right? He'd thought Curtis harmless and he'd considered Maria Cooper a killer.

But she was a healer. She was a victim, too. Or she would be if the killer had his way. If his threat became reality…

Seth flinched at the image in his mind of her swinging from that noose. She wouldn't be able to heal herself if she was dead.

"Damn…" He pushed a hand through his hair, pulling at the strands. He welcomed the brief jolt of pain to his scalp because it helped him fight the weariness dragging down his eyelids. They were so heavy, his eyes so gritty with the sleep he'd been denied.

After Raven's call, he had checked in with the bureau and told them what had happened and that the case was now hot. But who had given up his whereabouts to Waverly? His superior hadn't mentioned the man being around the office. Curtis must have called or met his source elsewhere. Seth needed to know who among his coworkers could be bought. Because Curtis might not have been the only one who'd learned of Maria's location through this person. Instead of protecting her, as Seth had promised he would, he might be putting her in more danger. He might have led the killer right to her.

"Hell," he murmured. He should know better than to make any promises when he had never managed to keep a damn one of them.

The bedsprings creaked softly as Maria shifted beneath the blankets he had pulled over her. He stepped away from the window, closer to the bed, to check on her. Her lips parted, and a quiet moan slipped out. That damn image flashed through his mind, of her naked beneath him as he buried himself inside her. And his body ached with desire.

He bit back a curse, disgusted with himself. He was thirty-six years old, not thirteen; he should have better control over his hormones by now. He had never before been attracted to anyone involved in an investigation. His work life had never spilled over into his private life...until Maria.

He should have called for a helicopter and brought her straight back to the bureau. For questioning. And for protection. He shouldn't have brought her back to his motel room.

But he couldn't leave Copper Creek until he had thoroughly investigated Raven's murder. And he couldn't trust anyone else, including the Copper Creek sheriff, to keep Maria safe.

She moaned again, and her body wriggled under the blankets. "Seth..."

Desire jolted his heart. "I'm right here."

She lifted her arms, as if reaching for him. "I need you..."

"You're okay," he assured her, stepping closer yet to the bed.

She grabbed at his hand and tugged him toward her. "Seth..."

He sat on the edge of the bed, trying not to touch her any more. Just her hand on his had his pulse racing with that strange energy that flowed between them. "You're safe." He patted her hand before pulling his away.

Her thick lashes lifted as her eyes opened. She gasped and sat up and stared around her as if she'd never seen the room before. Or maybe as if she had seen it before...in a dream. "Where am I?"

"My motel room. I brought you here to keep you safe," he reminded her. "I should have probably brought you to the hospital, though—after Waverly attacked you." The herbs had obviously helped her. But had they really healed her completely? After she'd slept so long, he wondered. He worried.

"He got to Raven there," she said with a shiver. "And he'd nearly gotten to me at the jail. Do you really think anyplace is safe from him?"

"I won't let him get to you," he said, inwardly groaning as he heard the promise slip through his lips again. What the hell was he thinking?

"What about you?" she asked. She stared at him intensely, as if her dark eyes could see inside his heart and soul.

"It's not me," he said, trying to make her feel safe with him. If only he could feel the same with her... "I'm not a witch-hunter."

Had she really seen Raven's ghost? Had the girl really claimed that was what her killer had called himself? After watching Maria use those herbs and that indiscernible chant to heal, he was finding it harder to doubt her abilities.

"You have been hunting me," she reminded him. "You said so yourself—that you've spent the past several years tracking me down, just like he has."

"I thought you were the killer. I wanted to bring you to justice," Seth explained.

"Like you promised Curtis Waverly," she murmured. Instead of saying the man's name with anger or fear, she said it as if she pitied him. "You really shouldn't have had him arrested."

"He assaulted you," Seth said. And he felt the anger she should have over how the man had hurt her, how he might have killed her if Seth hadn't finally reacted and stopped him. "And he has enough money to hire a lawyer to reduce his charges." Or get them thrown out. He had enough money that he'd bought an informant in the bureau. "I'm not worried about Curtis Waverly. I'm worried about you."

"You said you thought I was the killer," she said. "You don't think so anymore?"

Now that he'd met her, he knew she was too petite and slender to have committed those brutal murders... alone. If she'd had help, though, the person had never turned up in his investigation. Neither had another suspect besides her, though.

"You weren't at the hospital," he said. "You couldn't have drowned Raven."

She shook her head and tumbled her hair across his pillow, making his stomach tighten with desire. "But you accused me of having an accomplice, of working with someone else..."

"You would have had to have help," he said, "to overpower the victims. You would have had to have been working with someone else." He sighed. "But in everything I've learned about you, I've found no evidence of you ever working with anyone but your mother."

"Mama..." she murmured, and so many emotions passed through her dark eyes. So much loss and regret and resentment...

It was almost as if he could feel what she felt, his heart growing heavy with it. "I know how you lost your mother," he said. "I'm sorry."

"I lost my mother years before she was killed," she said.

"It was a witch-hunter who killed her," he said with

a shudder over the horrible way she'd died. "But he's gone. He can't hurt anyone else."

"It's another one who's killing these people," she said. "Another witch-hunter."

Seth should have realized that long ago—from the horrific way all her friends had died. A witch wouldn't kill using those means. But a hunter would.

"Maybe he thinks he's doling out justice, too," she said, "by killing witches."

"You think that's his motivation?"

She lifted her slender shoulders in a slight shrug. "I don't know. I don't know what would make someone kill."

He opened his mouth, tempted to tell her about his dream—about her shooting him.

But then she continued, "When I asked about you, I wasn't asking if you were the killer. I was actually worrying about him getting to *you*. Anyone who gets close to me winds up dead."

He shook his head. "That's not going to happen."

"I just had a vision…" She drew in a shaky breath. "I saw something happening…"

Had she seen what he had—the two of them making love? Maybe that was why she'd moaned and reached for him. His body hardened as desire and tension filled him. He had to know. "What did you see?"

"You…" She reached for him now, grasping his arms with hands that trembled. The heat of her palms penetrated the thin material of his shirt.

He touched her, too, sliding closer on the bed so that his thigh rubbed up against hers. And he slid his fingertips along her jaw. "It's okay. Tell me…"

"I saw you dead," she whispered, her eyes wide with

horror. "You had been shot in the chest." She moved her hand there, pressing her palm over his heart. "There was so much blood…"

"It was just a dream." One that they'd eerily both had.

"It doesn't make sense," she said, her brow creased. "The witch-hunter has never shot anyone."

"None of the victims had gunshot wounds," he confirmed. Probably because it would have been too quick and humane for the sadistic bastard.

"Maybe he shoots you because you're not a witch and, by protecting me, you're in his way."

"Maybe it's not him."

Her lips parted on a soft gasp. "Of course. You have other cases. But…"

"But what?"

"*I* was there," she said, her hands gripping him tighter. "I saw you bleeding."

"How did you feel about that?" he wondered. Since in his dream, she had been the one who'd shot him.

"I hurt for you." Her voice cracked with emotion as her eyes shimmered. "I know we just met, but there's something between us. Something I can't explain."

"Neither can I," he admitted. Even knowing what he did, he was surprised by the inexplicable bond between them.

"You feel it, too?"

He stroked his fingers along her jaw. "I don't want to feel it."

"You don't still think I had something to do with those deaths…"

She had something to do with his death—if his dream was real. And unfortunately, she could still have something to do with the other murders—if she had someone helping her. But she was a healer. Not a killer. Or so he hoped.

"I don't know what to think right now," he admitted, wanting to blame his weariness. But with her touching him, the last thing he felt was tired. He was tense, on edge. "I need to stay focused. But you…"

"What about me?" she asked, leaning closer to him.

"You are so beautiful…"

She shook her head. "No, I'm not."

He stared into her eyes and realized she believed that; she wasn't just being coy or modest. She really had no idea how beautiful she was. "You are."

"Not enough…"

"Not enough for what?" With her honey-toned skin, curly black hair and delicate features, she was hauntingly beautiful.

"I'm just not enough…anything."

Her vulnerability hurt his heart more than the bullet from his dream. Not being able to stand her pain, he leaned forward and closed the distance between them. His lips followed the path of his fingers, along her jaw, then across her cheek until his mouth covered hers.

She kissed him back, her lips moving beneath his, parting for the exploration of his tongue. She tasted as sweet and exotic as her beauty and her sandalwood and lavender scent. Her tongue met his, boldly slipping inside his mouth.

He groaned as desire pummeled him, hitting him low in his gut so that his every muscle tensed. A car engine on the street drew his attention away from her for a moment, and he lifted his head from hers. He couldn't lose his focus. But hell, with her touching him, kissing him, he was losing his mind.

Her fingers grasped his hair, pulling him back for another kiss. A deeper kiss. She sucked his tongue into her mouth, pulling him deep—as he ached to bury himself inside her.

Her hands slid from his hair down his nape to his shoulders and she tugged him onto the bed with her, on top of her. Her curves cradled him, her hips rubbing against his erection. Her breasts pushed into his chest.

Panting for breath, he pulled back. "We can't do this," he said. She was at the most a suspect, at the least a material witness. He couldn't compromise his investigation or his integrity—no matter how much he wanted her.

Maria's eyes sparkled with desire—and something deeper—as she stared up at him. "I don't think we can *not* do this. If I read your cards, I would see this—I would see *us*. I know I can't change what I see in the cards—what I see in my head. I've seen you and me."

Me, too. But he couldn't admit that to her. She thought him safe from the witch-hunter only because she didn't realize he had the same gifts she had.

"You've seen me dead," he reminded her.

"Shot," she said. "Not dead. You'll survive. You have to survive."

He allowed a grin to lift his mouth. "And if I don't…"

"Then you may not have another chance to do this…with me."

And that was a risk he couldn't take—even if it killed him. He would rather die after making love with her than die wishing that he had.

Maria held her breath while she waited for his response. Her skin flushed with embarrassment over how brazen she had been. But she wanted him. As she'd said as she had awakened, she *needed* him.

It was too soon. He was a stranger. All those arguments ran through her head, but none of them cooled her desire for him. Because everyone who got close to her got killed, she didn't have time to form a relationship. She didn't want a relationship. She just wanted one night with this man. And he really wasn't a stranger. They had a connection she'd never had before—not with her mother, the sister she'd met or any of the friends she'd lost.

She wanted to explore this deep connection before she lost it—and him, too. She closed her eyes, unable to watch his face when he rejected her. And that image flashed behind her lids, the blood spreading across his skin from the dark hole in his chest. She swallowed the sob burning in her throat.

Kisses pressed gently against her closed lids, then slid down her cheek to her lips. She opened her eyes to his face, his smoky blue eyes dark with desire. For her.

"You're sure?" he asked.

For her response, she lifted his shirt, pulling it up over his head. Then she reached for his belt. But he pulled back and stood up, unbuckling his belt and the holster that attached to the back of it. He put aside his gun.

Maria shuddered at the sight of it and forced her focus back to him. To his heavily muscled chest. There was no hole, no blood, nothing but a dusting of reddish-brown hair. She rose from the bed and pressed a kiss to his chest, sliding her lips over a flat male nipple until it pebbled.

His fingers tangled in her hair, holding her mouth to him. His heart beat hard beneath her lips. Hard and fast and strong. He was alive.

And so was she. And for now Maria wanted to celebrate life. She skimmed her lips up his throat and over his square jaw to his ear. "I want you…"

"You have me," he said wearily, as if resigned to his fate. "You had me before we ever met…"

She shivered at his words. He felt it, too—that it was fate that they would be together. That they belonged together. But it wasn't possible for her to stay close to anyone, to keep anyone, so they had only tonight. She would have to make it enough.

She kissed him again, stroking her tongue inside his mouth. And he kissed her back—really kissed her now. But he didn't touch her with just his lips.

His hands were everywhere. They ran down her back and tugged up her sweater. As she had with his, he pulled it up and over her head. She wore only a lacy camisole beneath—for a moment. Then it was gone, too, leaving her breasts bare to his gaze.

And his mouth. It skimmed down her throat, over her collarbone to the curve of each breast. His lips closed over a taut nipple, tugging and teasing until she moaned.

He treated the other nipple to the same sweet torture, making her wriggle and squirm on the bed as a pressure built inside her. Even as his mouth stalled on her breast, his hands kept moving. He pushed her skirt and panties down over her hips, skimming his palms along the length of her legs.

It was as if they had made love before. Many times. He knew her body well. He knew exactly where to touch her and what to taste.

He bit the outer slope of her breasts, lapped the indentation of her navel, trailed his tongue down the inside of her thighs.

She gasped and moaned, clutching at his hair as he settled between her legs, making love to her with his mouth. He slid his tongue deep, then withdrew and teased the center of her femininity until her world shattered and she screamed his name. "Seth!"

It was as if her saying his name snapped his control, because he shucked off his pants and boxers. Then he was inside her, the impressive length of his erection sliding deep.

She wrapped her legs around his waist, meeting his thrusts. She grabbed his shoulders, then drew her nails down his back, holding him tight as the pressure built inside her before a deep thrust shattered it again.

As she panted for breath, he withdrew and lifted her boneless body from the mattress. He turned her over so that she knelt before him. And his cock slid inside her again, where she was wet and pulsing for him. His hands cupped her breasts, teasing the taut nipples.

She grabbed the headboard, holding it tight in shaking hands as he thrust again and again into her. Her hair fell forward and his lips skimmed across her nape—and lower across the trio of tattoos she had conned an artist into giving her when she'd been just fifteen.

All her rational thoughts vanished when one of his hands skimmed down from her breasts to touch where their bodies joined. And she came apart—this orgasm more powerful than the ones he'd already given her.

Unconsciousness threatened again, her world shattering as she wept at the intensity of their lovemaking. She had never felt anything like this—not even in her dreams.

She had never even known such passion existed.

Then he held her tight against him, and a groan tore from his throat, stirring her damp curls from her temple. His body tensed as he came, filling her. He cradled her close, rolling so that she sprawled atop him. Both gasped for breath, their hearts racing in frantic unison.

"That was…" He swallowed hard. "That was…"

"Beyond explanation." As so much of her life was, like the strange connection between them.

He didn't try to explain it or apologize or rationalize. Instead he just held her, as if he never intended to let her go. But eventually, after several moments of silence, his breathing slowed, his arms relaxed around her.

And Maria's panic grew.

What the hell have I done?

While she knew he was an FBI agent, she had no idea of his true intentions toward her. To protect her? Or kill her? She had already given him more than she ever had anyone else. She couldn't give him her life, too.

But that was the least of her worries. She didn't really believe he would hurt her, or she wouldn't have slept so peacefully in his bed for most of the day. Or at least, her sleep had been peaceful until she'd had that horrible dream…

That was her real fear—that the killer would take Seth's life. Everybody who got close to her died.

She pulled free of his arms and quickly grabbed up

her clothes from the floor. She had just put them on when mist seeped under the door. Not Mama. Not now. She didn't need to be reminded how much she was like her mother, how she never chose the right men.

"Go away," she whispered.

But the shape that formed was Raven's, the bird tattoo stark against her ghostly pale face. "You have to leave," the girl warned. "The witch-hunter is close."

Maria glanced to the bed, to where Agent Hughes slept fitfully, his muscular chest rising and falling with jerky, uneven breaths.

How close was the hunter? Was the man who'd just given her the greatest pleasure of her life the very same man who had made her life a living hell?

She turned away from him, her gaze falling on the nightstand where he had left his holster and cell phone. She reached out, but she passed over the gun and the phone in favor of his keys. No matter what he was, they would both be safer if they weren't together.

"Quickly," Raven murmured as her ghost began to fade. "He's coming for you…"

Maria opened the door, her breath held in burning lungs as the hinges creaked. But Seth didn't wake up. Hopefully, he wouldn't until she was gone. She stepped outside and drew the door shut. Cool autumn air rushed over her, chilling the skin that had been hot and flushed just moments ago.

She ached to crawl back in bed with him, to wake him with kisses and caresses so they could make love again. So she could prove to herself that it had really happened. That it had been real, because she had never believed passion that powerful was possible.

She ignored the ache and forced herself away from

the door. The motel was a two-story cement-block-and-vinyl structure with an outside stairwell. Maria hurried down the steel steps to the parking lot.

As the mist had filled the room moments ago, it now filled the lot. But it was thick and dark and close to the ground, nature's fog as night began to fall instead of supernatural beings.

She moved through it toward the vehicles, trying to distinguish which one was his. But she had made it only a few feet when a big hand reached out of the mist and wrapped tightly around her arm.

The witch-hunter was close. Very close…

Chapter 6

A scream—albeit muffled—jerked Seth awake as the terror in it reached deep inside him, squeezing his heart. "Maria!" He reached for her, but like in his dream, she wasn't lying next to him anymore.

But when he opened his eyes, he didn't find her sitting at the end of the bed. Or inside the tiny bathroom that he could see through the open door. She was gone. He jumped up and stepped into his boxers and pants while reaching for his gun.

The Glock was there, cold and heavy in its holster. He drew it out and ran from the room. Where was she?

Night was beginning to fall again and the fog that rolled in with it hid her from him, as well. Another scream, this one even more muffled, as if someone covered her mouth, drew him toward where he had parked the SUV. He moved quickly but silently, keeping low so as to not alert her attacker to his presence.

Just as he had been with Raven, would he be too late to save Maria? Damn him for losing focus, for making love with someone he'd sworn to protect. And he hadn't made that promise to just her…

As he neared where the scream had emanated from, he spied two dark shadows, taller than the cars, grappling. Maria was too delicately built to ward off the muscular man who held her tightly against his body. The fog distorted their images, overlapping their shadows; Seth didn't trust himself to take a shot.

He shouldn't have trusted her, either. She had probably just made love with him so that he would drop his guard and allow her to slip away. All those old police reports called her a con artist, but he had another, better reason than other people's claims to mistrust her. He had his dream…

Then he had her attacker, as Seth vaulted toward the shadows and knocked the man to the ground. Maria fell back against a car, out of the way of their scuffle. But she screamed his name, her fear seemingly for him now. She had reason to be afraid.

And so, probably, did Seth. The guy was strong, wrestling free of him. So Seth swung his fist, catching the guy across the jaw and knocking him down again.

The man landed with an oath. "Son of a bitch…"

"Oh, shit," Seth said with a sigh as he recognized the man's distinctively raspy voice. "I'm sorry…"

"You're apologizing to *him*?" Maria asked, her dark eyes wide with shock and anger.

He extended his hand and helped the dark-haired man to his feet. "This is Ty McIntyre," he explained. "Someone else who bribed one of your coworkers to find out where you are?" she asked. It was a fair question, given that was how Curtis Waverly had found them.

Seth shook his head. "No. I called him." Not as early as he had promised Ty that he would—the minute he'd found her. He'd thought he'd been doing the man and his family a favor—keeping them away from a killer. But after Curtis Waverly had attacked her, Seth had realized that he'd almost waited too long. He had called Ty then.

"Why? Who is he?" she asked, stepping closer and grabbing Seth's arm as if she still wanted his protection. Fear and dread radiated from her.

"Ty isn't one of the victims' family members," he assured her.

"Your partner, then?"

McIntyre laughed, either at the thought of his being an FBI agent or his working with Seth. "I'm one of *your* family members," Ty answered for himself. "I'm your brother-in-law."

Her breath audibly caught. "Irina's husband?"

"Yes," Ty replied with a big grin of husbandly pride.

"You're the knight of swords," Maria said in breathless awe.

"I'm the who?" the man asked with a deep chuckle.

"Before I left the apartment I shared with Irina, I read her cards," she explained. "I saw you coming to protect her. I knew she would be safe with you—that you'd fight for her. She could trust you."

Seth caught the wistfulness in her voice, as if she, too, yearned for someone she could trust. *He* wasn't that someone; he had too many secrets. If she learned any of them, she would never be able to trust him. In fact, she might act out his dream and shoot him dead.

Even more wistfully she added, "She could love you."

"She does," Ty said, his raspy voice cracking with emotion. "And I love her more than I had thought it possible to love anyone. That's why I had to come here first. I had to make sure you were really you. We've been looking for you for so long. We've had so many disappointments. She couldn't handle another one right now."

"Right now?" Maria asked, her beautiful face tense with concern. "Is Irina okay?"

"Great—but she's very pregnant with our second set of twins. The doctor has ordered her to bed rest. And Irina has ordered me," he said, "to bring you home—to Barrett, Michigan."

Maria shook her head, looking nearly as panicked as she had when she had seen that noose dangling from the ceiling of the restroom. "That's not my home. I can't go back there."

"You lived there—with Irina," Ty reminded her. "But it's not your home because you shared an apartment there. It's your home because of your family. All your sisters live there—and your nieces and nephews and brothers-in-law."

"They only *live*," Maria said, her voice shaking, "because I'm not there. I have to stay away from them—to keep them safe." The longing was in her voice and the pinched expression on her face. She wanted to be with her family, but she had sacrificed what she wanted for the safety of the ones she loved.

If she had anything to do with the murders, she wouldn't believe her family needed protecting. She wouldn't have had to make any sacrifices...

Ty McIntyre had been right when he'd told Seth that Maria was as much a victim as those who had died. He had been so certain that she couldn't have had anything to do with the murders. But Seth hadn't been able to put aside his suspicion. Even now he struggled more with his doubts than he had physically struggled with Ty McIntyre.

Ty's brow furrowed, and his eyes warmed with compassion. "Maria, you're wrong. You need to be with your family."

She shook her head, tangling her hair around her shoulders like the long spiral curls had tangled when she'd made love with Seth. "No," she argued. "I'm *cursed*."

She said it with the same conviction that she had insisted that she wasn't beautiful, that she wasn't enough. And, just as it had when she'd made those claims, her vulnerability reached inside Seth and squeezed his heart.

"Whoever gets close to me dies," she continued. "Ariel can see ghosts. Have her talk to Mama. She'll tell her that I'm cursed. She knew it even before I was born. She didn't want me to be around my sisters."

Seth's heart hurt even more with her pain. He understood this pain all too well. Family could hurt you the most.

"Myra said and did a lot of things she shouldn't have," Ty said. "She was wrong about you. You need to be with your sisters—with our family."

But she shook her head. "I can't—I can't come around them. I can't risk any harm coming to my family because of me."

"Maria." Ty reached out, but she shrank back and tightly clutched Seth's arm.

"Show him the pictures—the crime scene photos," she urged Seth. "Show him what happens to anyone who gets close to me."

"I already showed him," he admitted. He had shown the private investigator the photos and the case files when he'd tried to convince McIntyre that he didn't want to find Maria Cooper. Ty McIntyre had tracked him down because they'd both been looking for her—just for very different reasons.

"Then you know why I can't go with you," she told her brother-in-law. "You don't want me anywhere near your family."

"They're your family, too. We all want you to be with us, to get to know you and to keep you safe." He speared Seth with a hard stare full of his disdain and disapproval for how the FBI agent had been protecting her. Apparently he'd heard about Waverly attacking her at the police station.

"I can't release her to you," Seth said. "There's been another murder."

Ty's gaze traveled up and down him, from his bare feet to his bare chest. And Seth suspected the guy was tempted to commit one himself. "You can't still suspect that she's responsible."

No. He couldn't, but he would still be a fool to trust her, given the way she had sneaked out after making love with him. While Seth was beginning to believe she had genuine special abilities, as Ty had sworn her sisters possessed, Maria was also a con artist.

"I am responsible," she insisted, guilt quavering in

her voice and lower lip. "If those people hadn't gotten close to me, they would still be alive."

"The murders do have something to do with her," Seth told Ty. "She's involved somehow. I need to keep her here so that she can help me stop the killer. I've barely had a chance to interview her since I found her."

Ty glanced at his state of undress again. "Really? Did you get sidetracked?"

"Yes, by my friend Raven's murder," Maria said, defending him.

Seth had no defense for how he'd lost control. It was almost as if Maria had put a spell on him. Or her beauty and passion had bewitched him.

"I need to stay here and answer all his questions," she continued. "I want to help him find the killer. It's time for this to end. And when the killer's caught, I'll come home. I promise."

Ty stared hard at Seth and warned him, "You better keep her safe."

Seth nodded.

He would keep Maria safe, but who would keep him safe? He had totally lost perspective with her; he'd let her con him. Would his dream come true? Would he wind up letting her kill him, too?

Seeing Maria for the first time in person should have brought Ty McIntyre triumph. But she was so much like his wife that she made him miss Irina even more.

She was also so much like his wife that he'd known he wouldn't be able to change her mind. She was convinced that she was a danger to her family. That was why she had stayed away from them all.

To protect them…

David turned toward him as he climbed into the chopper next to him. "Are you sure you want to leave?" He had found an old airstrip to use, but they could have landed several places in the remote area.

"No," Ty admitted. "But I have to get back to my wife." Irina probably wouldn't be happy to see him. But his gut was telling him that she needed him. And he had promised that he would always be there for her. She would always come first with him.

"Of course," David said with complete understanding. He loved Ariel the way Ty loved Irina—completely. But because he loved Ariel so much, he hesitated. "What about Maria? How can we just leave her here?"

"Seth will protect her."

"What changed?" David asked. "You didn't trust him when we came up here. But now you do? Was it what the sheriff and deputy said about him?"

Ty hadn't heard much of their praise of the FBI agent firsthand. David had stayed behind at the station, talking to the local lawmen, while Ty had gone to Seth's motel alone. He hadn't wanted to overwhelm Maria.

Guilt and regret tugged at him for how he had scared her in the parking lot. But she had nearly disappeared into the fog—as she had kept disappearing into thin air anytime he had gotten close to finding her. So instinct had had him grabbing and holding on to her.

Until Seth had rescued her.

A grin tugged at his mouth, but he flinched as his slightly bruised skin stung with pain. He didn't mind that the FBI agent had struck him. Instead he respected him more for having done it.

"Oh," David said with the instant understanding

born of their years and years of friendship. "Your instincts…"

"It's more than that," Ty admitted. "Because at first my instincts were saying I shouldn't have trusted him. I had the lead she was here, and so was Seth Hughes, yet he didn't call me right away…"

David's brown eyes narrowed with renewed suspicion. "You wanted to make sure everything was all right."

"Yeah," he said. "But now we can go home."

"But everything's not all right," David said. "Another woman was killed and Maria was attacked while in police custody—while in Hughes's presence."

Ty chuckled. "And I grabbed her in the motel parking lot."

David shook his head, disgusted. "We should stay. Your earlier instincts were right. We can't trust Seth Hughes to protect her."

"He saved her from that attack," Ty reminded his friend. "And there was no way I would have gotten out of the parking lot with her. He would have killed me first."

David laughed. "And that makes you happy."

"Oh, yeah," Ty said. "There's no way Seth Hughes will let anyone hurt her. And she won't be able to run away from him again."

David nodded again with that sudden understanding. "She's not just a case to him anymore."

Ty wondered if she had ever been just a case. "She's his *Irina*."

"His *Ariel*…" David sighed. "Poor bastard. I almost feel sorry for him."

If she was in as much danger as Irina thought, then

Ty felt very sorry for him, too. Because Seth Hughes wouldn't just kill to protect her—he would die, as well.

The urge to run burned in Maria's stomach…along with her desire for the FBI agent who was insistent on keeping her in protective custody. She had almost gotten away from him. She would have if not for her brother-in-law showing up, wanting to bring her "home."

She had never had a home, just the old pickup truck with the camper on the back that was still parked in the driveway next to the Magik Shoppe. That would be home enough until the killer was caught—only then would she keep her promise to meet up with her sisters.

But she doubted she could help catch him, no matter how many of Seth's questions she had spent the night answering when he'd questioned her. She'd told him how she'd come to know each victim. She had met Felicia and one of the young men in a class on parapsychology at Barrett University. The others had sought out her.

He'd already known most of what she told him. So none of it was likely to lead him to the killer.

"Thanks for bringing me back here," Maria told Seth. She had convinced him that coming back to the Magik Shoppe just might help them find a clue to the killer.

He had refused to make the trip down the treacherous dirt road until morning. Neither of them had slept that night, though. He had stood watch at the window, and she'd lain in the bed where they had made love watching him, wanting him…

She had never felt this way about anyone—had never felt so connected. So *consumed*...

She'd had boyfriends in the past, but the relationships had been brief, and she'd never let herself get too attached because she'd known she would have to leave them and keep running. Or they would wind up leaving her...

She was already too attached to Seth. She didn't want to lose him like she had the others. She had to get away from him. For his protection and hers... The other night when she had driven back and found the barn door open and Raven swinging from that noose, Maria had left the keys in the truck ignition. Maybe if she could distract Seth, she could get away from him. Then she could do what she had after every other murder. Someday she might run far enough and fast enough that *it*, the killer and Seth wouldn't catch up with her again.

But trying to get away in the truck wasn't why she had asked to come back here. She needed to find what she had been looking for the night she had found Raven hanging. She lifted trembling fingers to her throat. It had healed from Felicia Waverly's brother strangling her. But her neck felt naked. She hadn't been without the chain and locket since Mama had left it with her...

"You shouldn't be here," he said as he pulled his SUV behind the truck. "This is a crime scene. I shouldn't let you back in there." His hands, which had done such incredible things to her body, clenched the steering wheel.

"I won't touch anything." But the locket. Even though her fingers itched to touch him again, to caress those muscles so that they rippled beneath her fingertips, she had to resist her desire for him. Because it wasn't just desire…

After they had made love, the connection between them had grown stronger; that was partly why she had run from him.

For his sake as much as hers, she needed to get away from him. She threw open the passenger's door, but he caught her arm and held her inside…with him. Her skin tingled from the heat of his palm, and she wanted him touching her the way he had. She wanted him.

"Are you conning me again?" he asked.

"Again?" She had tried conning him into thinking she wasn't Maria Cooper. But she suspected that he was talking about something else.

"Yesterday…when we…when—whatever happened in that motel room…"

Dread gripped her stomach as she worried he couldn't even acknowledge what had been the most powerful experience of her life. The connection was all on her side. She wasn't enough for him, just as she hadn't been enough for her own mother.

"*Whatever? Whatever* happened?" She tugged on her arm, trying to wrest free from his grasp. But his fingers didn't budge.

His other hand cupped her cheek, turning her face toward his. As he leaned across the console separating their bodies, his pupils dilated, swallowing the smoky blue irises. "I know *what* happened. It was amazing—unreal…"

Despite the damp air of the cold autumn morning, heat suffused Maria, and her pulse quickened. Images flashed through her mind. Not of the future but of the past. Of the two of them in bed, naked skin sliding over naked skin…as they made love frantically. Desperate for release from the feelings building inside them.

His throat rippled as he swallowed hard. "I just don't know *why* it happened."

"What do you mean?"

"I've never crossed that line before…with *anyone* involved in a case. I've never lost control like that. *Ever.*" He leaned closer, his lips just a breath away from hers. "What did you do to me?"

"You think that I…" She struggled to spit out the insult as she understood exactly how he thought she had conned him. "You think that I…purposely seduced you?"

"Didn't you?" he asked, his voice a husky whisper that raised goose bumps on her skin. "Wasn't it part of your plan to distract me so that you could escape?"

Offended that he thought she would whore herself, she lifted her chin and glared at him. "I hadn't planned that—any of *that*."

"You didn't use some of your—" he gestured toward the sign above the double doors of the barn that proclaimed it the Magik Shoppe "—special potions to make me fall under your spell?"

"My spell?" she scoffed. She'd seen his disbelief earlier. "I didn't think you believed that I am a real witch. I thought those old police reports had you convinced that I'm just a con artist."

He skimmed his fingers across her throat. "I saw you heal yourself and Curtis Waverly. There was redness and swelling and then you concocted those herbs and chanted something…"

"A prayer," she said. No one was more spiritual than a witch. "I chanted a prayer."

"I don't know what you are," he said, leaning so close now that his lips brushed across hers in a whisper-soft kiss.

Her breath caught in her lungs as desire overwhelmed her. Everything else disappeared like the mist. She saw only Seth—*wanted* only Seth. Her lips clung to his, and he deepened the kiss. As his tongue slid inside her mouth, she moaned. A kiss wasn't enough—not when she knew intimately the pleasure he could give her.

She leaned across the console, pressing her breasts into his chest—silently begging for his touch. Now she ached just for him. His heart pounded hard against hers in perfect, frantic rhythm. She reached for his shirt, wanting to open the buttons and press skin to skin. But he caught her hand, manacling his fingers around both wrists like handcuffs. His touch wasn't cold like the metal cuffs had been; it was hot, setting her aflame with desire and that curious tingling sensation that spread throughout her body every time they touched.

"Maybe you are a witch," he said with a ragged groan. "I wasn't going to do that again. I wasn't going to touch you, let alone kiss you. But every time I get close to you, I can't resist you."

"I am a witch," she admitted. But who had put the spell on whom? "But the last thing I would ever make for myself would be a *love* potion. I don't want anyone falling for me. I don't want anyone getting hurt because of me again."

She had tried other spells on herself, other cures to reverse the curse, to remove the dark aura that hung over her. But all she had ever needed to protect her from harm was the locket; she'd felt as though that had kept her safe all these years—as it had kept Elena Durikken safe from Eli McGregor. But now the locket was gone...and so was her common sense.

She had no business kissing—making *love*—with a man she couldn't trust. Despite all the promises he'd made her, or maybe because of them, she couldn't trust Seth Hughes. "I didn't plan what happened last night."

"Then why did you sneak out the minute I closed my eyes?" he asked, his distrust apparent in the question and the cooling of the passion in his eyes.

He might be beginning to believe in her special abilities, but he obviously still thought she was a con.

"I just panicked," she replied. "The witch-hunter is out there." She peered through the windshield but dark fog had wrapped around the car, blanketing it like night. Maybe a storm was coming, or maybe another spirit. "He's going to keep killing." She didn't want Seth getting killed, as she'd seen in her vision, because he had gotten too close to her.

"Your running isn't going to stop him," Seth pointed out, his hands still wrapped tight around her wrists. "Every time you run away, he finds you. Then he kills again. The only way to stop him is to turn this around. Instead of him chasing and catching you, we need to chase and catch him."

"We," she repeated. "If you mean that—if you're going to let me help—you have to let me go inside the Magik Shoppe."

He, too, peered out the window toward the fog-enshrouded barn. "Crime scene," he corrected her with a gruff murmur.

"If you let me into the *crime scene*, maybe I can

read it," she said, "like I do tarot cards. Maybe I can pick up some clues about his identity."

That muscle twitching along his jaw, he remained stoic, staring straight out the windshield as if he hadn't heard what she'd said. Or didn't care…

"You really think I'm a con," she said. He wasn't the first to call her that, but it bothered her that he didn't believe in her. Even though they had just met, she felt as if she'd known him longer—her whole life, and maybe even longer than that, maybe other lives. "Is it just me, or do you think that anyone who claims psychic abilities is lying?"

"You've conned people," he reminded her.

"There are such things as false truths and honest lies," she said, quoting her mother's favorite gypsy proverb.

"What?"

"That was what Mama always said. She believed she was making people happier by telling them what they wanted to hear rather than what she really saw." Maria sighed. "She lied so much I think the lines became blurred to her. I think she lost sight of what was real and what she'd made up."

And because she'd realized that about her mother, Maria had hoped that she wasn't really cursed. For a while she'd believed that it was just another of her mother's wild stories. That was why she'd sought out her sisters and found Irina. But then Mama's ghost had appeared to her. And she'd known then that Mama had never lied to her. Maria was cursed—to lose everyone she cared about.

"You don't tell people what they really want to hear," Seth said. "You tell them what they *least* want to hear. When you read their cards, you tell them that bad things will happen to them."

"I tell them what I see." And because of the witch-hunter, it had been bad more often than it'd been good. That was why she hadn't read in over a year—and before that, she had tried to read for only strangers. "After Mama died, I promised myself no more lies." If only that were a promise she had been able to keep. To herself. To him.

"So you're not running cons anymore?" he asked.

She shook her head.

"Then how do you get the money to set up your shops? No banks have ever loaned you money."

She had eventually taken the advice in her mother's letter. She had sought out her father. But he wasn't just her father. "I have a benefactor—someone who gives me the start-up money."

Actually, it was his creepy assistant who sent the money orders. She shivered as she thought of the intense young man.

"I've never traced a benefactor to you," he said. "And you didn't mention him when I was questioning you last night. Who is it?"

She had already brought her father enough embarrassment. She didn't want to bring him any more. "My parapsychology professor," she said. "He believes in what I do."

He narrowed his eyes in suspicion. Maybe of the professor. Or probably because he thought she'd conned or seduced the professor. But that wasn't the case at all.

"We're wasting time," she said. "I need to go inside the shop." She had to get inside the barn to search it for her locket.

Before Mama had lost them to social services, she had given each of her three older daughters an antique charm. Maria had had an image of each tattooed on her back. So Mama had had only the locket left to give when she deserted Maria. She had left it in that letter. Maybe the locket was not as powerful as the three-hundred-and-fifty-year-old charms that were rumored to have special powers, but it was the only thing Maria had left of her family. Of her heritage.

Without it, she was not a Cooper. She was nothing. The child with no birth certificate. With no driver's license. With no record that she had ever existed…

"How old were you when she took off?" he asked, his deep voice gentle with sympathy.

"Fifteen."

That muscle jumped along his jaw again. "Me, too."

"What?"

"I was fifteen the last time I saw my dad."

"I'm sorry."

"I'm not," he replied, the sympathy gone now, replaced by a coldness that raised goose bumps on Maria's skin. "My dad was a son of a bitch. And we actually left him. I never saw him again. How about you? Did you see your mom again?"

She nodded. "Like Raven, after she died, I saw her ghost. That was when I started running." Like Elena Durikken…

"And you haven't stopped for more than a few months or, at the most, a year anyplace," he said. He had done a good job of tracking down her whereabouts. Her past. "Don't you think it's time?"

"I will…once the killer is caught," she said. The promise she had made to her brother-in-law was one she intended to keep—if she lived to keep it. "You don't have to believe in what I do. Just let me do it. Let me see what I can read from the scene." She tugged on her wrists, trying to shake off his hands, but his grasp tightened. "Seth—"

"No, don't get out of the car," he warned her. "Something's not right."

She studied his face. A glaze had settled over his smoky eyes, as if he was seeing something else—something no one else could see, as the vision was only inside his head. She furrowed her brow. "Do you—?"

"The sheriff told me he would post a deputy at the scene until FBI techs could get here—to make sure nothing happens to this crime scene like it's happened to the other ones."

She hadn't realized anything had happened to the other crime scenes.

She peered through the fog and noticed a police car with a light bar on the roof parked next to the barn. "The car is there…"

"But where's the officer?" he wondered. "He should have come up to us before now."

Dread tied knots in her stomach as she noticed the empty driver's seat. "I don't see anyone…"

"Stay here. And lock the doors."

"No." Now she clutched his arm, her fingers grasping the sleeve of his leather jacket as she tried keeping him inside the car. "You can't go out there alone." That image flashed through her mind again—of his heart pumping blood through the hole in his chest. "Call the sheriff."

"There's no time," he told her. "That officer could be in trouble." He shook off her hand and stepped onto the gravel drive. Reaching beneath his jacket, he pulled his gun from its holster. "I have to make sure he's okay."

"He's probably sleeping." She glanced back to the police car, which was parked beside her old truck, which she had pulled up next to the barn that night. An eerie glow illuminated the truck interior and glinted off the metal. Uttering a gasp, she turned toward the barn just as flames burst through the roof with a whoosh of air that sounded like a clap of thunder.

Even as far away as he'd parked, the explosion rocked the SUV and sent flames and debris hurtling toward the windshield. She closed her eyes, as a reflex, to avoid any flying glass. When she opened them again, dust poured down on the SUV like rain. The police car and her mama's old truck were both ablaze—like the barn.

"Seth!" she screamed.

But he was gone.

Choking and gasping for breath, she jumped out of the car and ran toward the burning barn.

Chapter 7

Some of the most violent men Joseph Dolce had ever met—and he'd met some violent men during the course of his long and sometimes ill-spent life—surrounded the estate. They carried guns and the kind of couldn't-care-less attitude that got people killed.

The witch-hunter wouldn't get past them—not these men that Joseph had hired. They were working for his money, but they were also working for his respect. They would give up their lives to protect his family.

He and David and Ty had gathered them all at the McIntyre estate—to support Irina and so that they could keep everyone safe. Halfway home David had had to land his helicopter because of the fog; they'd sworn it was following them from Copper Creek, as if they were bringing Maria's darkness home to Barrett.

He'd once been a cynical man—a man who believed in nothing. Who had no soul...

But then he'd fallen for Elena and he'd started believing in everything. In good as well as evil. In love as well as hate. In witchcraft and spirits and things that couldn't be explained...

She had stolen his heart but given him back his soul.

He was almost relieved that David and Ty hadn't made it back yet. He didn't want Maria's darkness falling over *his* family.

Then he heard it—a scream of such terror and agony that his blood chilled. He shoved open the front door and vaulted up the stairs to the master bedroom. Irina was sitting up, as much as her swollen belly would allow, in bed. And she was screaming uncontrollably.

"Shh," Ariel said, patting her back as Elena held her tightly in her arms. "This isn't good for the babies. You have to settle down."

"It's so hot and smoky," Irina said. "So hot..."

The room was actually cold. Icy cold—which probably meant that Joseph's mother-in-law had joined them. Or maybe another ghost had. He shivered with revulsion and regret.

"It's like I'm burning," Irina said, her voice breaking into sobs. "It's like *she's* burning..."

Over her younger sister's head, Elena met his gaze. Her blue eyes were bright with unshed tears—of dread and fear.

"Ty," Irina gasped. "I need Ty."

She had no more than asked for her husband before the bedroom door opened again and he rushed through it.

"I'm here," he assured her. "I'm here!"

Elena stepped away from the bed so that Ty could

take her place. He enfolded his wife in his arms. "I'm sorry I'm late. I shouldn't have left you."

Even though Irina clung to him, she said, "You shouldn't have come back. You should have stayed with her."

Elena tugged Joseph into the hall with her and closed the bedroom door. Then she stepped into his arms, clinging as tightly to him as Irina had Ty. And her slender body trembled with silent weeping.

"What's wrong, sweetheart?" he asked. "What's going on?"

"Irina could feel her burning," Elena said, her voice cracking with emotion.

She was the strongest woman he'd ever known—usually so strong that she refused to betray a flicker of emotion.

"Maria?"

She nodded, and her silky hair brushed against his chin. "I was wrong about her," she said, her voice heavy with regret and guilt. "Just like I was once so wrong about you…"

"You weren't wrong about me," he reminded her. He held her so closely that he could feel her heart beating in his chest. "I was the man you thought I was. But loving you made me a different man—a better man."

She looked up at him, and love radiated from her eyes. "The best," she murmured.

But he hadn't always been. He'd grown up on the streets and had cared only about money and power… until he'd fallen for her and her daughter. They had brought out a side of him he hadn't known he'd possessed—a loving and tender side.

She shed her tears silently, but they streaked down

her face. He wiped them away with his thumbs, trailing them across her silky skin. As usual, her beauty had his breath catching with surprise and appreciation. She was so damn beautiful…

And he was so damn lucky that she'd taken a chance on a man like him—that she'd trusted him when half the time he barely trusted himself.

"I was wrong about Maria, though," she insisted. "She was never the danger. She was only in danger."

"Was?" He remembered that cold chill in Irina and Ty's room and wondered…

"If she's burning…"

It was too late. The witch-hunter had claimed another victim; he had burned Maria Cooper at the stake.

Smoke filled the barn with the heavy scent of sandalwood and lavender. The dried herbs hanging from the rafters caught fire, showering sparks down onto the floor of the barn. It was already burning, the fire rising higher from the source of oxygen through the hole blown into the side wall.

The hole and the fire illuminated the interior as the light flickered across the face of the unconscious deputy. At least, Seth hoped he was just unconscious. He lifted the young man into his arms and headed toward the double doors just as Maria ran inside—right past him as if she didn't even see him.

"Get out!" he yelled at her. But the crackling fire drowned out his voice.

He quickly carried the deputy away from the barn and laid him on the ground. Then he rushed back inside, shouting, "Maria! Maria!"

She had disappeared into the shower of burning herbs and rising flames—as if they'd consumed her.

His heart slammed against his ribs and panic overwhelmed him. He couldn't have lost her. Not like this…

Ignoring the heat and the flames, he stepped into the fire. "Maria!" Through the smoke he glimpsed her, kneeling on the ground near the toppled-over table and the tarot cards. Was she trying to do a reading now?

He didn't need the cards to tell him what would happen if they stayed any longer inside the fire. As the fire rose and the structure weakened, the old barn groaned and shook. And the old rafters began to give…

"Maria!" He reached for her, grabbing her up from the floor just as the roof shuddered and imploded, collapsing onto them. Holding her tightly, Seth ran through the falling rafters and crumbling plywood and burning shingles. He ran for those open doors just as the wall began to crumble, the opening closing. He ducked low, beneath the burning beam, and carried her out of the barn.

Or was he out? The smoke enveloped them yet, wrapping close around them with that overwhelming scent of sandalwood and lavender.

"Are you okay?" he asked in a raspy whisper. His throat was burning and raw from the smoke and the heat.

Maybe that was why she didn't hear it. Maybe it was because she was unconscious. Her body was limp in his arms.

Soot streaked her beautiful face and blood trickled from a small cut on her forehead. The sight of her, disheveled and hurt, reached inside Seth, squeezing his heart in a tight vise of fear. He wasn't doing a very damn good job of keeping her safe.

As he'd rushed into the barn, he'd pushed the button on his phone that connected him with the sheriff. He probably hadn't even disconnected before he shoved it back into his pocket. The sheriff would send help. An ambulance...

But Maria and the deputy needed help now. If only she were conscious...

But how would she heal herself when all her herbs were gone? Burned to ashes...

He carried her to his SUV. He would drive her and the deputy to the hospital himself.

Just as he turned back for the deputy, he heard the sirens. The sheriff had sent help. He helped them load the deputy into the ambulance, then drove Maria to the hospital himself.

And he stood watch while the ER physician cleaned her wound and affixed a butterfly bandage to the injury. His fists curled at his sides; he hated another man touching her almost as much as he hated that she'd been hurt. He had never been the possessive type, but with the killer determined to get close to her, Seth was looking at everyone as a possible suspect.

As if Seth's scrutiny made the man uneasy, he stepped back with a sigh of relief. "She's fine," he said.

At least she was conscious now. She had regained consciousness in the SUV—with a scream on her lips. She'd thought they were still in the fire. But Seth had reassured her and continued to hold her hand.

"But you should be checked out," the doctor persisted. "You inhaled a lot of smoke, and you have cuts

that appear deeper than hers. The skin on your hands
and forearms looks to be burned, too."

"I'm fine," Seth said, dismissing his own injuries.
He felt none of his own pain. Only hers. She had been
so terrified.

The young guy swallowed nervously. "Okay, then.
Well, you can get dressed now," he told Maria. He
opened the door to the private room Seth had insisted
she have, and he held it open, waiting.

Seth shook his head. He wasn't leaving her alone in
the very hospital where her friend had been murdered.
When the door finally closed behind the nervous doctor, he walked over and locked it.

"Well, this is awkward," she murmured, glancing
down at the paper gown she wore.

"I've seen you in less," he reminded her. And himself. His body tensed with a desire all the more intense
for them having made love. Now he knew the reality of
being with her, of being buried deep inside her body.
He felt closer to her than he ever had to anyone.

"He didn't have to know that," she said as she rose
from the exam table.

"You care what he thinks?"

She shook her head. "No."

"What the hell were *you* thinking?" he asked, anger
overwhelming him at the danger in which she'd put
herself. "Running into a burning building? You could
have been killed."

"You could have been, too," she replied, anger flashing in her dark eyes. "You ran in there first."

"I was looking for the deputy," he reminded her. He
suspected she had been looking for something else—

something that she wouldn't find in the ashes of her magic shop.

"I was looking for you," she said, her voice cracking with emotion as her eyes sparkled with a hint of tears. "I thought for sure you were dead..." Her breath hitched.

"I'm fine," he assured her. He stepped away from the locked door and moved closer.

"You should have let the doctor examine *you*," she said. "You could be seriously hurt."

"I'm seriously hurting," he admitted.

She gasped and reached for him, running her palms over his chest. "Where? What happened?"

"My heart stopped beating when you walked into that burning barn. And I don't think it's started back up yet." His relief that she was all right cooled his temper even while his passion caught flame. He cupped her gorgeous, soot-streaked face in his palms and lowered his mouth to hers.

Her lips parted on a soft sigh, and he deepened the kiss, sliding his tongue inside her mouth—tasting her unique flavor of sweetness and erotica. She must have put a spell on him, because he'd never wanted anyone the way he wanted her. He forgot everything else—what had happened, what he'd seen would happen—and he thought only of her and his all-consuming desire for her.

She pulled back, panting for breath. "It's beating now," she said, her palm pressed over his furiously pounding heart.

A grin tugged at his lips. "See? I don't need a doctor. I just need you." His grin fled as he realized the truth in what he'd just said. He *needed* her.

"Seth…" She wound her arms around his neck and pulled his head down to hers. She kissed him with all her passion, her lips moving voraciously over his. Then she slid her tongue inside his mouth, tasting him as he had tasted her.

Did she taste the bitterness of the secrets he kept from her? Did she know that he hadn't told her everything about himself?

She pulled back and studied his face. "Are you really all right?"

He shook his head. "No."

She uttered a wistful sigh. "I wish I had some of my herbs so I could heal your injuries."

"I'm not hurt," he said, unconcerned about whatever wounds he had.

"Then what is it?" she asked. There was tentativeness in her voice, almost as if she was afraid to know.

A lifetime of lying about who and what he was. But she was the last person he could tell the truth. She would never trust him if he did. And if she didn't trust him, he wouldn't be able to keep her safe.

Her arms around his neck, she waited for his reply, her eyes wide and vulnerable. Had she already made the mistake of beginning to trust him?

"Maria, I…" Couldn't share his secrets with her. But he had to tell her something that was true, at least. "I can't let you keep distracting me from doing my job."

Her wide mouth lifted into a sexy smile. "I really haven't put a spell on you."

"I'm bewitched all the same." He hoped like hell that was all he was.

Her teeth scraped over the full curve of her lower lip. Then she soothed the hurt with the tip of her tongue, teasing him as she stared up at him through her lashes. "Is that such a bad thing?"

Her flirting affected him, predictably, his body tensing with the need to take hers again. He released a heavy sigh. "My being distracted could have gotten us both killed."

"We're alive. We should celebrate that." She pressed her breasts against his chest. Her hardened nipples penetrated through her paper gown and his thin sweater.

He groaned as desire shot straight to his groin. As if wanting to torture him more, she arched her hips and rubbed against him. Unable to resist her, he lowered his head and kissed that sexy smile. But he pulled back before she could slip her tongue between his lips, before she could push him beyond the limits of his control.

"I need to check on the deputy and find out if he's going to make it." The explosion, or more likely a blow to the head, had knocked the young man unconscious, but Seth had managed to get him out of the fire before it had burned him too badly. The guy had been breathing when the ambulance had taken him. But then, Raven had been breathing, too, when the ambulance had taken her away from the barn.

However, if the killer was, as Maria was convinced, a witch-hunter, then he had no reason to kill the young deputy. The lawman had only been in the killer's way when he'd done what he had after each of the other murders, gone back and destroyed the crime scene.

In the past he'd thought the person had been trying to destroy evidence as well as any trace that she had even been there. Now he realized that the killer might have been trying to eradicate all trace of her—all evidence that she had ever existed.

Maria stepped away from him and nodded. "Of course. You need to go."

Seth needed to leave, and not just to check on the deputy but also to get away from her for a few minutes. He needed to shake off the spell she'd put him under before he got burned worse than he'd already been.

Seth had said he was leaving, but he didn't take a step toward the door. Instead he kept staring at her, his blue gaze intent on her face, on her body, which the paper gown did little to cover.

"You can leave me alone," she assured him. But she didn't want him to leave. His kisses had wound that pressure tight inside her so that she ached for release.

"That's the problem," he said with a ragged sigh. "I can't leave you alone…"

"The sheriff is here and all of his deputies and several state police officers," she reminded him. "I'm probably safer here than I've been anywhere else." The witch-hunter wouldn't risk trying to grab her around so much law enforcement.

"That's not what I meant. I can't leave you alone." And he dragged her against him again, his hands clenching the back of her gown as he wound his arms tight around her. The paper parted, and his palms slid down her bare back to her hips, which he pulled tight against the erection straining the fly of his jeans.

She moaned and rubbed her hips against him, seeking release. But he lifted her away from him, setting her on the edge of the exam table. He dragged the paper away from her, leaving her naked but for the flush of desire on her skin. Like the first time they'd made love, his hands caressed her with the intimate knowledge of a longtime lover.

Why was their connection so strong? As if they'd known each other forever…as if they had loved each other before?

His palms cupped her breasts, his thumbs stroking back and forth across her pebbled nipples. And he kissed her again, deeply, his tongue thrusting through her lips as it stroked over her tongue. Tunneling her fingers in his soft hair, she clutched his nape. But he pulled back, his mouth sliding down her cheek and her throat.

"I must taste awful," she murmured. Like smoke and dust and whatever else had gone up in the explosion. All of the herbs she'd spent the summer growing. All of the candles and oils she'd spent so much time making. The crystals that she'd collected over the years might have survived if the fire hadn't gotten too hot. She might be able to clean and recover their luster. But they would never be the same, their energies forever altered by the violence that had taken place in her magic shop. Maybe it was better that it was all gone.

Except the locket. Her heart ached for losing that.

"You taste sweet," he assured her. "And you still smell like sandalwood and lavender."

Her mother's scent. Like the locket, she wore it to remind herself of who and what she was. A Cooper. A witch. Now she had only the scent, as the locket was probably forever lost in the fire. But maybe it hadn't been there anymore. Maybe the witch-hunter had it. Maybe he'd found it when he'd hung Raven or when he'd set the fire.

She had no doubt that he had set it.

But she couldn't think of him now. Couldn't think of what he had done or would do. She couldn't think at all as Seth touched her...with his hands and with his mouth.

His lips traced the curve of her collarbone, and his hands skimmed from her breasts over her hips to her legs. He parted them and stroked his fingers up and down the sensitive skin of her inner thighs. His head dipped lower, his tongue laving a nipple, and his fingers slipped inside her.

She arched her neck and writhed against his hand, unable to stand the pressure building inside her. A moan burned in her throat. Then his hands and mouth switched places, his fingers teasing her nipples as his tongue stroked inside her. Pleasure rushed through her, blinding her with its intensity as she came apart. She tangled her fingers in his hair, holding him to her as he lapped and teased another orgasm from her.

Then she pulled him up, wanting him buried inside her. She reached for his belt, but he stepped back and shook his head.

His voice hoarse with passion, he said, "I can't. I can't lose my focus again." His hands shaking slightly, he grabbed up her clothes from the end of the exam table and handed them to her. "While you get dressed, I'll check on the deputy. Hopefully, he's all right and has regained consciousness. Lock the door behind me and wait for me here."

He had that look in his eyes again—that glazed-over seeing-something-else look that reminded her of Mama when the gypsy fortune-teller had really been seeing the future in her crystal ball.

"Before the explosion—how did you know something wasn't right?" she asked. "Was it really just because you didn't see the deputy?"

He nodded. "In every crime scene for these murders, the killer has come back later and set a fire."

Maria's heart tightened with fear and regret. The witch-hunter had to destroy everything and everyone that mattered to her.

If he had the locket, it was lost to her.

"That's why I had the sheriff post an officer at the scene," Seth continued. "I thought that if the killer came back, he might get caught this time. But I should have guarded it myself instead of putting some young deputy at risk."

Instead he'd been guarding her from harm. Did he resent her for that?

"You risked your life to save him," she pointed out. "I'm sure you got to him in time."

He glanced to the closed door. "I hope he's okay and has regained consciousness. He might be the only one who can give us a lead to the killer. Unless you know more than you've told me…"

She knew she was cursed to the same fate as the first witch in her family, who'd been burned at the stake over three hundred and fifty years ago. But if Seth didn't believe in her special abilities, he wasn't going to believe in legends and more-than-three-century-old curses. So she just shook her head and reached for her clothes.

He stopped at the door and turned back, his gaze holding hers. "I'm trusting you to stay here and wait for me."

She didn't lie to him or make any false promises.

She just gave a noncommittal nod. Then she finished dressing. As soon as the door closed behind him, she reached for it—but not to lock it.

Instead she held the knob while she waited for him to have walked the length of the hall. Hoping he hadn't turned back to check on her, she opened the door. She needed to leave now—before the next ghost she saw was his.

He had been lucky to escape the explosion with minor injuries. But Maria didn't count on his luck holding—not when he was getting too close to someone who had only ever had bad luck in her life.

She couldn't put him at risk again.

Growing up on the run with a paranoid mother had honed more than Maria's supernatural abilities. She had learned other things—like how to slip undetected through a crowd. So she bound her hair into a braid and slipped into some scrubs in the staff locker room. Disguised, she moved easily through the hospital and out of the employee entrance/exit doors.

As soon as she stepped out of the building, her shoes scraping against the asphalt of the parking lot, she breathed a sigh of relief.

She shivered, and wished she'd kept her sweater or had stolen someone's coat. She hurried through the parking lot.

During those years she had been on her own, she'd also learned to pickpocket. She opened her fingers, which were growing numb from the cold, to the keys she had lifted from Seth.

Guilt overwhelmed her, extinguishing that brief flicker of relief. When he found her gone, he would

be furious. He would think that she had tricked him—
that she'd seduced him just so she could escape him.

But she was the one who'd been seduced, not him.
He hadn't let her touch him—hadn't let her distract
him. But he'd given her pleasure.

And he'd promised her protection.

Should she trust him? So far he'd kept his word to
her. But in keeping his word, he was putting his life
at risk—for hers. She wasn't worth it. Even her own
mother hadn't thought so.

And Maria would never forgive herself if he died as
all the others had—violently, senselessly...

No, it was better to deceive him and run than to put
him at risk any longer.

And really, after all the years he'd been chasing her
and learning about her, he should have known better
than to trust her.

By the time he realized his mistake, hopefully she
would be gone. But she'd just neared his SUV when
strong arms wrapped around her, trapping her arms
against her sides.

It wasn't Seth. Her skin would have tingled; her
blood would have heated with desire and awareness.
While this man seemed familiar, too, he didn't set her
pulse racing with anything but fear. She opened her
mouth to scream, but his hand covered it.

"I just want to talk to you," a cultured-sounding
voice said.

It wasn't her brother-in-law who had that distinctly
raspy tone. She almost wished it had been—but then
he'd bring her back to her family and put them all in
danger.

"I'm not going to hurt you," the stranger assured her.

Yet. He didn't say it but the word hung in the air.

She stilled her struggles, and he lifted his hand from her mouth. She recognized his hands more than his voice—since those hands had recently been wound tightly around her neck.

"What do you want to know?" she asked Curtis Waverly.

"I want to know the truth about you."

She had no truths he wanted to hear. He wanted a confession that she couldn't give him.

"Were you my sister's friend like you claimed?" he asked, his already beady eyes narrowed with suspicion. "Or are you my sister's killer?"

She shook her head. "I would have never hurt Felicia. She was my friend. My very dear friend. I miss her so very much…"

His throat convulsed as if he was choking on emotion. Or as if Seth's blow had done more damage than she'd been able to heal…

Finally, he murmured, "Me, too. I miss her…"

He was suffering. That was why she hadn't wanted him arrested for attacking her. While Seth had done it anyway, he had known that Curtis Waverly would hire a lawyer to get him out.

He probably hadn't expected it to be so quickly, though.

But she was glad. She did owe this man the truth. The whole truth.

"I didn't kill her," she said, "but I am responsible for her death."

His arms tightened around her—painfully so.

Just like when he'd strangled her, she would not

easily escape him. And now she didn't have Seth to save her.

His voice eerily low and hollow, he murmured, "Then you'll have to pay…"

Chapter 8

By the time Seth had noticed his keys were gone, so was Maria. He had known he couldn't trust her. So he'd asked the sheriff to watch for her and make sure she didn't get away.

His heart pounded with fear as he ran from the building and out into the parking lot. Evening came early this far north, so the light was already fading behind the all-encompassing fog. The whole damn town seemed like the set of a horror movie—eerie and otherworldly, a place he wouldn't have thought existed outside a movie screen. A place he wished like hell he'd never had to visit.

Just like at the hotel, he spied two shadows grappling in the fog. And then her scream rang out again. Even though he'd heard it twice before, it still reached inside him—still squeezed his heart with fear.

"This is getting to be a bad habit," he murmured as

he approached them. But this man had already proved a far greater threat to her than the brother-in-law who had grabbed her in the motel parking lot. This man had already hurt her once. He drew his weapon and pointed it at him. "Curtis, let her go!"

And this time, if he didn't, Seth would shoot him. He had known the guy wasn't going to stay behind bars long. According to the sheriff, he'd been released only that morning, and he'd already come after Maria again. If only he'd been locked up longer...

"I can't." The guy shook his head, his eyes wild with grief and desperation.

"Curtis, the sheriff told me the conditions of your bail. Coming anywhere near Ms. Cooper violates the number one condition," Seth said. At least he would be going back to jail for a while. "You have to let her go!"

"I can't!" he shouted. "Just like I can't let Felicia go." Tears shimmered in those wild eyes. "She haunts me—the way she died..." His voice cracked with grief. "Someone held her down until her lungs filled with water. She was gasping. Fighting for air..."

"Stop torturing yourself," Seth told him. But Curtis wasn't torturing just himself. Tears streaked down Maria's face, almost as if she relived what her friend had endured. And maybe she did. He couldn't deny that she had supernatural abilities; he'd seen her heal herself.

So maybe she saw ghosts and the future and...

What other abilities did she have?

Ty McIntyre had said that his wife, her sister, was empathetic in addition to being telepathic. Seth didn't think Maria was telepathic, or she would have tried a lot harder to get away from him. And she never would have made love with him. But he suspected she was empathetic, that she felt what all the victims had felt.

No wonder she had left town right after the murders. She hadn't been scared just of the killer coming for her; she had been scared of the pain she'd felt when her friends had died.

"Who would do something like that?" Curtis asked between sobs, his arms constricting around Maria. His nose ran as he completely lost it. He looked nothing like the debonair sole heir to a textile fortune who regularly graced tabloid and fashion-magazine covers. He was lucky the media hadn't followed him to Copper Creek to report his current condition.

How completely had Waverly lost it? Was he beyond reason, as he'd been when he'd strangled her? Would Seth need to pull the trigger? He trained the barrel on the man's head. If it was Waverly's life or hers, it was no choice for Seth. He had promised to protect her.

"Who would do something like that to a girl as sweet and beautiful as my little sister?" Curtis asked, one of his arms sliding up and around Maria's throat.

She didn't speak or fight. She just stood perfectly still, but her eyes talked to Seth, telegraphing her fear and vulnerability. And trust. She wasn't talking or fighting, because she trusted Seth to get her out of the situation. Alive.

Waverly was a pretty big guy. A strong guy, too. If he wanted, he could easily snap her neck.

He moved his finger from the barrel of the Glock to the trigger. Then he peered down the scope, getting his target in focus. "Maria didn't do that to Felicia," he said. "She was your sister's friend."

"You told me she was your number one suspect," Curtis reminded him.

And Seth had been careless when he'd shared his suspicions with a victim's family member. But the guy's grief had gotten to him; Waverly had been blaming himself for his younger sister's death. He had been filled with guilt that he hadn't been able to protect Felicia from her killer. So Seth had assured him that there was nothing he could have done to save his sister.

"Maria is not a suspect at all anymore," he said—as he had at the police station. "She has nothing to do with any of the murders."

Her gaze had never left his face, but now her eyes widened with surprise. And relief. She was still in danger, but she was relieved that he finally believed in her. Was it too late, though?

"Why?" Curtis asked. "Did she get to you? Did she mess with your head like she did Felicia's?" His arm tightened around Maria's throat.

Finally, she made a noise, a soft gasp for breath as her almond-shaped eyes got bigger with fear.

"You don't want to hurt her," Seth said. "You need to let her go…" Or Seth would have no choice but to shoot him. He had killed before in the line of duty, but never someone with whom he'd sympathized. "C'mon, Curtis, you don't want to do this…"

The young man's arm didn't loosen, and her face began to turn red. "I have to do this. I have to stop her. She turned my sister into a witch."

If what defined a witch was having supernatural abilities, then Seth was one, too.

"Maria's innocent," he insisted. "She could not have killed the most recent victim. She was locked up in jail at the time. And there's no way she could have caused the explosion at the crime scene today. She was with me."

"Maybe she's not working alone," Curtis said. "Did you think about that? Have you considered every explanation, Agent Hughes?"

"I considered that," Seth admitted. He had even questioned her about it. But everyone she'd been close to the past eight years had died. "I wasn't certain that she would be physically capable of having killed the victims as they were killed. But I can't find anyone connected to her—anyone who would have helped her—and she couldn't have acted alone."

"If she's really a witch," Curtis said, his voice rising with his temper, "like my sister thought, she could have managed it. Maybe she puts a spell on people and forces them to do her bidding."

Seth definitely felt as though she had put a spell on him, but she hadn't forced him to do anything he hadn't really, really wanted to do. "Curtis, you must hear how ridiculous that sounds…"

"It's possible!" the man hysterically insisted. "She's a witch! You saw what she did at the jail—the herbs, the chanting. She's a witch!"

Seth couldn't deny that she was. "But she's not a killer." He stepped closer. "I don't want to have to shoot you." But he would.

Maria tried to shake her head, but Curtis held her neck too tightly. But she murmured, "No…"

"You need to let her go," Seth said. "Now." He had tried to reason with the man, but he feared that Curtis Waverly was beyond reason.

"You promised me that you would stop her," Curtis said, his voice rough with outrage and betrayal.

"I promised you that I would find and stop your sister's killer," Seth said. "And I will."

"She's right here," Curtis said, his arm squeezing harder so that Maria's face grew redder still as she fought for breath. "And I can end it now."

Seth shook his head. "I can't let you do that. You can't be jury, judge and executioner." But would he be able to stop him before the man took Maria's life?

All the stares were on her—as they had been so many times before. Back then it might have been because she'd been locked up in an observation room in some psych ward. Eventually she had learned to hide the fact that she could see what no one else could. Eventually she had learned to pass for normal.

But with these people, she didn't have to be normal. She could be who she was—especially with David's arms wrapped tightly around her, offering his unconditional support and love as he had from the minute they'd met. She had never loved or been loved as much as with her husband.

"Ariel?" Elena called her name—the way she used to when they were kids. And Ariel snapped out of it and focused again on her family.

"Can you see her?" Irina asked. "Is she dead?"

She shook her head.

"But there are ghosts here," said Joseph with such certainty and dread that she wondered if he could see, too. He shivered and said, "I can feel *her*…" He wasn't talking about Maria, whom he'd never met. Fortunately, neither had Ariel.

"Mama is here," she said. And while she might have been able to block out her ghostly voice as she often had, the other woman spoke for them both.

"But she's not alone," Irina said. "I can feel another spirit. And she's endured terrible fear and pain…and has so much guilt and regret."

Ariel leaned on her husband and focused on the other ghost. When she had first seen her hovering over Irina's bed as the pregnant woman had awakened screaming, Ariel had thought it was Maria. Her hair was black. But she was tall and thin, and when she'd turned toward the one who could see her, Ariel had seen her face—which had looked as if a bird were flying out of the side of it.

What the hell had happened to her?

"I was hung and drowned," the girl answered, almost with pride. But then, it had taken the witch-hunter two attempts to kill her; maybe that was a source of pride.

"Maria saved me from the hanging," she said.

"Maria—is she alive?" Ariel asked the spirits. "Is she okay?"

"The FBI agent saved her from the fire," Raven said.

Irina had been feeling heat and smothering from smoke—of course there had been a fire. As she'd felt that heat, she'd grabbed her charm. And Ariel and Elena had held their charms as well, praying for Maria's protection. Seth was Maria's protection.

"Seth Hughes saved Maria," Ariel told the others, who couldn't hear the ghosts. Except for Irina. She could hear, but she was completely exhausted—from her pregnancy and from her stress.

Would Ariel lose two sisters? She worried that she

might, and as if David felt her worry, he kissed her cheek and whispered, "It'll be all right…"

"We can trust Seth," Ty said. "He will protect her."

"But who will protect him?" It was Raven who asked the question. "Everyone who gets close to her dies…"

The mist began to fade as the spirit slipped from the room. But Mama turned back, her mouth open. She was speaking, or trying to—as if she was warning them again.

Were they all in danger? Or only Maria and Seth?

Maria shuddered as she wiped the blood from her face. "I can't believe you shot him!"

Waverly lay on the asphalt, writhing and groaning. Obviously he couldn't believe it, either.

"I just hit his shoulder," Seth said, as if shooting a man were of no consequence to him.

But he was an FBI agent. He had probably shot many more people than Curtis Waverly. He had probably even killed before.

His hands were gentle, though, as he wiped the blood from her face. "Are you okay?" he asked.

She jerked her head in a quick nod that had her wincing in pain. Her throat was sore from how tightly the man had held her. He could have broken her neck. Maybe he would have if Seth hadn't shot him.

But still it bothered her that he was hurting. She dropped onto the asphalt next to him. "Are you okay?" she asked.

Blood oozed from the gunshot wound in his shoulder. Her palms itched for her herbs—for the poultice she could make to press to the hole in his flesh. The bullet had probably passed through, so she could heal the wound quite easily. If she had her herbs...

"Stay away from me!" the man yelled at her. "Stay away!"

He was afraid of her?

But then, he was convinced that she was a killer— no matter that she had told him that she hadn't directly hurt his sister. Even Seth had vouched for her. Did he really believe now that she'd had nothing to do with the killings?

She had worried when she'd run *from* him that he might think she was running out of guilt. But she was really running *for* him—to protect him.

"You're the one who needs to stay away from her," Seth told Waverly. "You've violated the terms of your bail, so you'll have to go back to jail."

"I need a doctor!" the man wailed. "I need medical attention."

"I could help you," she offered. But when she reached toward him, he shrank away from her. She had healed him once. Why couldn't he trust her?

Seth shook his head and stared at her in disbelief. "Why would you want to help him after he's attacked you—twice?"

"He's Felicia's brother," she said. So he had already lost so much. She didn't blame him for wanting justice.

"See," Curtis said, "she feels guilty. She has to be her killer."

"I feel guilty because I shouldn't have let her get close to me." And that was why she shouldn't have let Seth get close, either. But he had. Too close...

"I knew I was in danger," she added.

"That's why you can't go running off alone," Seth

told her. He gestured toward the hospital, and the sheriff and two deputies rushed forward.

"We heard a gunshot," Sheriff Moore said. "Is everything all right?"

"No!" Curtis wailed. "He shot me!"

"He was about to break Ms. Cooper's neck," Seth explained.

Despite the man's injury, the sheriff grabbed his shoulders and hauled him to his feet. "You're under arrest—"

Curtis yelled and swore. "I need a doctor!"

"Please, get him medical attention," Maria implored them.

The sheriff turned to Seth, who nodded in reluctant agreement. "But don't let him slip away from you. As soon as he's treated, he needs to go back to jail. And hopefully, he won't get released on bail again."

The sheriff passed Waverly off to a couple of the deputies who'd run up behind him. "You heard Agent Hughes. Once the doctor's done with him, bring him back to the station. He violated his bail."

As the two men led him off, Curtis Waverly stared back at Maria, his eyes dark with a mixture of fear and hatred that made her shiver.

"What about you, Agent Hughes?" the sheriff asked.

"What about me?"

"Has the doctor seen you yet?"

Seth shook his head. "I'm fine."

"You should be treated, too," Maria said. Soot coated his scratches and burns, but they were still red and as angry looking as Curtis Waverly had been.

Seth snorted. "And give you a chance to run again? I'm not letting you out of my sight."

Cursed

He had defended her to Waverly, so she hadn't been able to tell if he was mad at her. But now she heard the anger in his voice. He was furious with her for taking off on him.

Why couldn't he understand that she'd done it for him?

"I brought the herbs," the sheriff said, his face reddening slightly as if he was embarrassed that he believed in her healing. "I thought you might need them."

"How is your deputy?" she asked.

"Mostly just embarrassed," the sheriff said. "He never saw who hit him."

Seth muttered a curse. "How did he not see the guy?"

The sheriff sighed and admitted, "I think he might have fallen asleep."

"If you bring me the herbs, I can put together something for the deputy's headache," Maria offered. She was grateful that not all her herbs had been lost in the fire.

The sheriff quickly retrieved the bag from his car and watched in fascination as she put together a poultice. She chanted a brief prayer over the packet and passed it to him. "Thank you, Ms. Cooper," Sheriff Moore said. "He will appreciate the help."

"Bring it to him," Seth said. "And make sure Waverly gets back to the jail."

The sheriff nodded. "Of course. What about that other matter, of Ms. Cooper's assistant? We haven't made a death notification yet."

The night that Waverly had attacked her at the police station, they had briefly discussed the death notification. "You haven't told her sister yet?" Maria asked.

The sheriff shook his head. "We only have your assistant's first name."

And Raven wasn't even her real name. The girl had rejected her given name for one she'd chosen herself.

"What about her boyfriend?" Maria asked.

"The address you gave me—nobody's lived there for years," the sheriff said.

Maria shook her head. "Maybe I got the address wrong. But I know where I dropped her off. I can show Agent Hughes."

With another thankful smile at Maria, the older lawman hurried back toward the hospital.

Maria was grateful to the sheriff for bringing her herbs. She held tightly to the evidence bag with the broken seal. Would Seth let her use any of the herbs on him?

"I can help you, too," she offered. "I can make something for your scratches and burns."

"We need to get out of here," Seth said. He reached for her, holding her arm as if worried that she might try to run off again. As he led her toward his SUV, he glanced around the hospital parking lot. His long body was tense; it was as if he felt there was someone else there.

There was.

The mist rolled in, thickening the fog. Maria already smelled the familiar scents, which now clung to her hair and her skin and hung in the air around her. Then Mama's ghostly shape became apparent—only to Maria, though.

Seth walked right through her as he opened the passenger's door for Maria. But then he shivered—as if he felt her presence. Maria couldn't step forward—she couldn't walk through her mother. It was as if Mama was blocking her from getting into the SUV with Seth.

Why are you here? Why do you keep coming back?
You're in danger, child.

Seth was angry with her, but Maria couldn't believe that he would hurt her. If he had meant her any harm, he could have let her die in the fire—or he could have let Waverly break her neck. But he kept saving her, again and again.

So Maria sucked in a breath to brace herself, and she stepped through her mother. As he had when he had arrested her after Raven's hanging, Seth covered her head with his palm and guided her down onto the seat. He was always protecting her. "Thank you…"

"Don't thank me," he said. "I'm not letting you go." He stepped back from the SUV but carefully, as if he sensed Mama there. He skirted her spectral image and then crossed around the front of the SUV, never taking his gaze from Maria. He was serious about not letting her out of his sight.

Maria wanted Mama out of her sight. She wanted to block out the ghost. But she hovered yet by her window.

He's no danger, Mama…
You're the danger, child.

That was why she'd tried to run.

Seth held out his hand for the keys she'd stolen from him. She pulled them from her pocket and dropped them into his palm. Her skin tingled at the briefest of contact with his.

"We can't leave Copper Creek yet," Seth said with a shudder as he glanced around at the thick fog. Maybe he could see Mama, still looming. "The FBI techs are coming tomorrow."

"For what? There's nothing left of the crime scene." Not even her locket.

"There could still be evidence there," Seth stubbornly insisted. "This case is hot—it's our best chance to catch him."

"What happens once it goes cold?" she asked. As all the other cases had.

A muscle twitched along his tightly clenched jaw, and he said with grim determination, "I'm not going to let that happen."

"Just like you haven't let anything happen to me." If not for Seth's interference, Curtis Waverly might have seriously hurt or even killed her. He was out of his mind with grief.

"You make it hard for me to protect you," he pointed out as he started the SUV and pulled out of the parking lot, "with the way you keep running off every time I turn my back on you."

"What happens when you're done here in Copper Creek?" she asked. "Where will you take me then? Some FBI safe house? Witness relocation?" Except that she really hadn't witnessed anything.

While she had seen the victims murdered when she'd read their cards, she had never seen their murderer. She was pretty damn certain she knew who the witch-hunter was: the son of her mother's killer, Donovan Roarke. But she had no idea what he looked like. No clue what identity he might have assumed.

Seth drew in a deep breath, as if bracing himself, and replied, "Home."

Maria tried to open the passenger's door. But it was locked. The handle wouldn't budge. She couldn't escape. But she couldn't go "home." She couldn't even call it that. "I can't go back to Barrett."

"Don't you think it's time?"

"I thought you—of all people—understood," she said. "I can't be close to my family—not when someone is determined to kill everyone who gets close to me."

"Then don't you think it's time we catch this killer and stop him?" he asked. "You told Ty that's why you wouldn't go home with him, that you intended to help me find your friends' killer. But then you tried running from me again. If not for the explosion, you probably would have taken off at your shop. Isn't that why you wanted to go back there—to try to get your truck?"

If she wanted him to believe in her, she needed to start telling him the truth. "Yes," she admitted. "But that wasn't the only reason I wanted to go back to the shop."

"You really think you would have been able to read the crime scene—that you would have been able to pick up some clue to the killer?" he asked as if he was open to the idea.

"I don't know," she admitted. "I have these visions—see bad things happen to people I care about—but I've never been able to see who the killer is."

"You can't see, or you're scared to look?" he challenged her.

"I am scared," she admitted with a shiver. Mama was gone now, but her warnings rang yet in her head. "He's a ruthless, sadistic killer."

"And you've let him control your life all these years," he said with another weary sigh of disappointment.

That disappointment stung her pride.

"You've let him keep you away from your family," Seth said. "You've let him take everything away that you've built—again and again."

Anger surged through Maria as she realized the veracity of Seth's claim. She'd been so intent on following her mother's advice to run that she hadn't realized that she had never escaped the witch-hunter. She had let this monster control her—destroy her. "Son of a bitch…"

"Yes," he agreed. "Don't you think it's time you stop running away from him and you stand and fight him?"

"You're right." She had agreed with him earlier, but now she really meant it. After seeing and feeling Waverly's despair, she understood that it wasn't just about staying ahead of the killer. Or even about stopping him. He needed to be brought to justice—for his victims and their families. "But I don't know how to stop running. It's how I grew up. It's all I've ever known."

"Why?" he asked. He reached across the console and grasped her hand, his fingers entwining with hers.

Her skin tingled at the contact between them, and her pulse quickened—as it always did—when he touched her.

"Was your mom running from the police or from social services?" he asked. "Ty told me how they took away your older sisters."

"Mama was running from the witch-hunter. She saw, in a vision, that he would come for her—that he would kill her—just as horribly as she died." A chill ran through her as she thought of the vision that had haunted her mother, the vision she'd had herself when she'd read her mother's cards. "She was burned at the stake."

He grimaced and tightened his grip on her hand. "I'm sorry."

"It happened nine years ago. You must have heard the story," she said. "If you didn't see it on the news, then Irina's husband must have told you."

He nodded. "Ty told me everything that happened. But he assured me that the witch hunt is over. That the witch-hunter died back then—eight or nine years ago—before Felicia Waverly was murdered."

"Just because that witch-hunter died doesn't mean that it's over," she pointed out. "The first witch hunt began over three hundred years ago when my witch ancestor was burned at the stake like my mother. Like my mother, she saw her fate and forced her daughter to run away." Elena, for whom Maria's eldest sister had been named, had been only thirteen when she'd lost her mother and had been forced to figure out how to survive on her own. As Maria had.

He squeezed her fingers gently, as if he understood how much the legend upset her, even though it had happened so many centuries before she was born.

Her breath hitching, she steadied her voice and continued, "The daughter got caught by the witch-hunter's son. But instead of killing her, he let her go, giving her a locket that he'd made for his mother, who'd died in a lightning strike that my ancestor had warned her about. His father swore to track down that girl and kill all her descendants."

"He wasn't very successful," Seth pointed out as he lifted her hand to his mouth. He brushed a gentle kiss across her knuckles. "You're alive. Your sisters are all alive—all their children."

"The guy who killed my mother was a descendant

of Eli McGregor," she explained. "That first witch-hunter."

"Your mother's killer is dead," Seth said again, his voice suddenly as cold as the evening air that the heat blowing out the vents had yet to dispel.

"But he had a son," she shared. Even though she'd stayed away from them, she had kept apprised of her sisters' lives. She'd read about everything that had happened to them and had learned everything she could about the man who had hunted them. "That son has to have taken over his father's witch hunt. He's the only one who can be the witch-hunter."

"The only one?" Seth asked. He released her hand and gripped the steering wheel with both of his. "Why hasn't he killed you already, then, since you're the witch he's really after? Why hasn't he gone after your sisters? They're the ones he would probably hold responsible for his father's death, aren't they?"

"I don't know. His father was crazy. He undoubtedly is, too." She shuddered at the evil inherent to the witch-hunter. "I can't imagine what goes through his mind."

"No, you can't," he said. "You may be able to see things—when you read cards—but you're not telepathic."

"No, I'm not," she admitted. "But I do have special abilities. I wish you would believe me."

"It's not that I don't believe you," he said, "but I don't believe he's the killer. I believe it's someone else, probably someone you know. A stalker who resents anyone else getting close to you. Did you jilt a lover who wouldn't leave you alone afterward?"

"Who's asking?" she wondered. "The FBI agent or the man I *seduced*?"

His intent expression cracked as a slight grin curved his lips. "The FBI agent—who's finally asking the questions he should have been asking."

"You thought you had your man—uh, woman," she said, reminding him of his suspicions. Not that he needed the reminder. No matter what he said, she was worried that Curtis Waverly had raised Seth's doubts about her again. "You were convinced I was the killer."

He reached across the console and stroked his fingers along her jaw. "I wasn't totally convinced. I had my doubts. But I wanted it to be you."

"Why?" she asked, lifting her chin away from his touch. He'd stung her pride again.

"Since you knew and had had the last known contact with every victim, it made sense that you were the killer," he pointed out.

She couldn't argue with him. Put like that, she would have suspected herself, too.

"And that makes more sense than some dead man's son coming after everyone close to you."

"You don't understand." That made perfect sense to her, but she'd had her whole life to accept and fear the witch hunt. "It's the fulfillment of that legacy, of that old curse."

"Curse?" he asked.

"I'm cursed." And because of that, she shouldn't have let Seth close, and she certainly shouldn't have begun to fall for him herself. "I'm cursed…"

The witch-hunter stayed back, far behind the FBI agent's SUV. There was something about Seth Hughes—something uncanny, something supernatural.

He hadn't just become bewitched by Maria Cooper.

It was more than that. The way he'd stared at the barn and then started toward it, he seemed to have anticipated the explosion even before the candle had burned low enough to ignite the gasoline he'd poured around the propane tanks.

How could the agent have known? Unless he saw things before they happened, as Maria did when she read the cards. But it was more than card reading with Agent Hughes, something even more instinctive and powerful.

That was probably why, even though he followed them at a distance, the agent's SUV sped up. It was as if Hughes already knew he was there. As if he sensed his presence.

Did the FBI agent have visions of the future? Did Seth Hughes know what was coming next?

His death.

The agent obviously had some special abilities, some witchcraft powers of his own. So he would have to die like the others—like a witch…

The agent wasn't heading toward town but taking a road that led away from it—away from the barn. Maybe the hunter had some psychic abilities of his own, because he realized where they were heading. They were taking the long way there, though. And he knew a shortcut that only he, in his four-wheel drive, could take. He would beat them there and set up another trap for them—like at the barn.

And hopefully, Agent Hughes wouldn't sense this one. Until it was too late…

Chapter 9

Pain throbbed in Stacia Dolce's head. It wasn't just the babysitting that was bothering her. She actually didn't mind watching her younger brother and cousins. The house was alive with emotions, and like Aunt Irina, she felt them all.

They pummeled her. Exhausted her.

Mom told her to block them.

As if...

Just as Mom couldn't block her visions, Stacia couldn't block *any* of it. She saw, heard and felt *everything*. And there was just *too much* in the house right now.

Usually she loved having the gifts she had, and she enjoyed being a witch. But then there were times, like today, that she just wanted to be a regular teenager.

The door to the attic playroom creaked open and Mom stepped inside the space. She glanced over to where the younger kids played the virtual computer game Uncle David had set up on a big screen for them. It was cool having a techie uncle.

Stacia's whole family was cool, though. Even her mom…

Most of her friends complained about their mothers. But Stacia had a bond with hers that nobody else had with theirs. She and Mom had nearly died together. But her dad had saved them. He'd been just Joseph then. But after that he had become her dad.

He called Stacia her mother's mini-me since she looked so much like her. That was cool, too, since her mom was really pretty with pale blond hair and light blue eyes. But Stacia was nearly taller than her now, so Dad wouldn't be able to call her mini-Mom much longer.

After she'd made sure the younger kids were all right, Mom walked over to Stacia. She touched her hair. "Headache, sweetheart?"

Her mom wasn't telepathic with anyone else, but it was as if she could read Stacia's mind. And Dad's.

Stacia nodded.

"I'm sorry," Mom said. "I know this must be overwhelming for you. Everyone's so scared and upset."

Stacia nodded again. "Even Grandma."

"She's here?"

"She was earlier. She's worried about Aunt Maria." She reached out and squeezed her mom's hand, which was shaking a little. "You are, too."

"Have you seen what I have?" her mom wondered.

Tears stung Stacia's eyes. "Yes." Like the tears, the vision burned her eyes. And the pain overwhelmed her. She didn't want to start crying and scare the younger kids. But Mom pulled her into her arms, and the tears slipped out. "I don't want them to die."

But she had seen death. And she worried that the only way she would ever meet her aunt Maria was as a ghost—like Grandma.

Seth glanced in the rearview mirror. If there had been a vehicle behind them, he had lost it around one of the hairpin turns in the backcountry road. Even though he couldn't see the lights anymore, he pressed harder on the accelerator.

With one hand Maria grasped the console and with the other the armrest on the passenger's door. "Slow down or you'll miss the driveway. It's coming up around the next turn."

An image flashed through Seth's mind of what could be coming up: *metal crunching, gravel flying, the car spinning end over end as it bounced down the side of a steep, dark ravine...*

He lifted his foot from the accelerator and touched the brake. But his pulse didn't slow with the SUV; it quickened to a frenetic pace.

"It's a little farther up, I think," Maria said. "It's hard to see—it's so dark."

And foggy.

The damn stuff wrapped around the SUV, hiding the edges of the road—hiding where the road ended and dropped off into that ravine. And maybe it hid the lights of the vehicle Seth suspected had followed him from the hospital parking lot. He glanced again into the rearview, but there wasn't even a glimmer of headlamps burning through the fog behind them. He hadn't actually seen a vehicle behind them. Maybe he had only imagined that someone was following them. Or maybe it was back there yet—just fully concealed by the fog.

"This is a bad idea," he murmured. "The sheriff should be the one making the death notification anyway."

"I thought that after what happened with Curtis Waverly, you understood why I want to do this," she said, her voice quavering with guilt.

"Because of what happened with Curtis Waverly, you should absolutely not be with me when I do this." In case this next of kin also blamed her for his loved one's death. Maybe he would attack her as Curtis had.

"I'm the only one who knows where Raven's boyfriend lives," she argued. "The sheriff didn't even know his name."

"Neither do you," Seth reminded her.

"No," Maria admitted. "Raven was pretty secretive about him. She had confided to me that her elder sister had always stolen her boyfriends, so she liked to keep her relationships private until she was certain she could trust the guy."

"Since she didn't introduce you to him, she must have decided not to trust the guy." Foreboding lifted the hairs on his nape. He should have listened to the instincts that had warned him this was a bad idea.

"Or she decided not to trust *me*," Maria said. "She had some special abilities. She saw the aura that hangs over me. I don't blame her for not trusting me."

"But you know where he lives," Seth pointed out. "So she trusted you with that information."

"I only know where he lives because I dropped Raven off here a couple of times." She straightened in her seat and pointed to a break in the trees lining the road. "Here. Turn here."

Seth touched the brake again and turned the wheel. The tires bounced along the ruts of a nearly overgrown driveway. "You're sure someone lives here?" he asked as his lights shone on a dark house. "The sheriff didn't think that anyone had for quite a few years."

"I probably gave him the wrong address," she said, but then insisted, "I know this is the place."

"It doesn't look like anyone's home now," he pointed out as he parked the car in front of the old log cabin. Boards had been nailed across one of the windows. "Were those boards there before?"

She nodded. "I think the glass must be broken. There wasn't anyone here when I came by looking for Raven that night I found her in the barn..."

His instincts were screaming now as his pulse quickened even more. This was it. A real lead. "Do you remember anything about him? Anything she said?"

"I told you she was really private about him."

"According to the sheriff, no one knows anything about him," Seth mused aloud. Was the mysterious boyfriend a real lead or just a story Raven—or Maria— had invented? "Hell, no one knows anything about her," Seth said. "Not even her real name. Did you get anything from her when you hired her? Her full name and Social Security number?"

"It's not as though I was going to fill out tax forms for her. I paid her cash when she worked—or in herbs and crystals," she admitted, and then sighed. "There's another crime you can arrest me for."

"Tax evasion?" He chuckled. "That is what tripped up some of the most notorious gangsters."

"I'm not a gangster."

He had known gangsters. None of them would have healed someone who'd tried to kill them. She was amazing. She was good—in a way that he hadn't realized she would be. Selfless and loving...

"No, you're not a gangster," Seth agreed. "But you're not an employer, either."

She flinched with pain. "Not now. All my employees wind up dead."

He regretted the comment. "I meant because you didn't get any emergency contact information for her. She might've given you her sister's information. Or her boyfriend's."

"I wouldn't put down a boyfriend's name as my emergency contact information," Maria replied.

"Why's that?" he asked, and then remembered something. "You never answered my question earlier about jilted lovers."

"Like Raven, I never had any boyfriends that lasted," she said.

"Why was that?" he asked. "Because you never stayed in one place for long?"

She turned to him, and the dashboard lights illuminated her beautiful face and the pain and loss in her dark eyes. "Because anyone who gets close to me dies."

That image flashed into his mind again: *the flash of gunfire as she fired his own weapon at him...hitting his heart...*

He flinched. "The two male victims..." One crushed. One burned.

She nodded, and tears glistened in her eyes. "Yes."

"They weren't witches, then. You're wrong about the witch-hunter." For so many reasons…

"They had special abilities," she said. "They wanted to learn the craft from me."

"I doubt that was all they wanted from you." He reached across the console again and traced his thumb along the line of her delicate jaw. "You're so damn beautiful." But it was more than her beauty that had him ignoring all his suspicions and doubts about her.

Had she cast a spell on him?

Just touching her face had his pulse tripping and his skin tingling. To control his desire, he turned away from her—and noticed the glimmer of light inside the deserted-looking house. "Someone's inside."

She reached for the door handle, but Seth leaned over and caught her wrist, keeping her from opening the door. "You're not going in there. It's a trap."

He didn't need the images flashing through his mind—of fire and debris blowing toward his face—to know that it was. His gut instincts were screaming at him, as they'd been on the drive here. This was definitely a trap.

The question was, who had set it? The killer? Or Maria? She was the one who had lured him out to the middle of nowhere. God, he was such a fool. Would she have to actually kill him before he was finally able to resist her?

The suspicion was back; Maria saw it in the way he studied her face, as if he were trying to read her mind.

"What's the trap?" she asked. "You going inside the house? Or you leaving me out here where he can grab me?"

"Depends on who the trap is for," Seth replied. "Me? Or you?"

"I don't know if I should be flattered or offended that you think I'd be able to trick you." Not that she hadn't given him reason, every time she'd tried to slip away from him, to doubt her.

"I wouldn't be flattered," he said. "Since I don't seem to be able to think at all around you, I'm easy to trick right now—as you know."

Her stomach flipped with regret. Did he still think she'd purposely seduced him just to try to get away? But maybe she couldn't blame him for doubting her. Given how recently they'd met, he was really a stranger but that hadn't stopped her from throwing herself at him. But then, to her, because of the connection that reached so deeply inside her, he didn't seem like a stranger. It seemed as though she'd known him her whole life and longer.

And if something happened to him, she would never forgive herself, but she would also want to know about it. She wouldn't want to be wondering where he was— if he'd just left her as her mother had.

"What if it's not a trap?" she wondered. "What if Raven's boyfriend is in there?"

And what about Raven? She hadn't seen the girl's ghost since that day she'd awakened Maria in the motel, when she'd warned her that the witch-hunter was close.

Raven...

She peered around the car, trying to discern if the fog was just fog or that eerie mist that precipitated the arrival of an apparition. The girl knew this house, knew who'd lived here. She could tell Maria if it was a trap. But none of the mist formed into her image. It remained just fog.

Mama...

Where was she now—when Maria needed her? Where she'd always been when Maria needed her.

Gone.

Of course, Maria kept ignoring her and sending her away. Ever since she had awakened alone in the camper, she had wanted nothing more from her mother but what she'd left her. Her fingers lifted, out of habit, to her neck. But it was bare, the chain broken—the locket forever gone.

Seth reached inside his leather jacket. Instead of bringing out his gun, he held his cell. "I'm going to call the sheriff. Have him send out a deputy."

"To check out the house or babysit me while *you* do it?" she asked, flinching as she remembered the barn exploding and his just being gone—running into the flames to find the missing deputy.

He glanced down at the cell phone and shook his head. "Neither."

"No signal," she guessed. "The reception is horrible up here."

"Everything's horrible up here," he said. And he reached inside his coat again, returning the cell to an inside pocket. But when he withdrew his hand, he held his gun now.

She shuddered at the sight of it as the image from her vision flitted through her mind. *Blood pumping out of the hole in his chest...*

"You're not going to go in there alone," she insisted. "I'm going with you."

"No." He peered through the windshield at the house

to where that faint light flickered through one of the windows that hadn't been boarded up. A strange look crossed his handsome face, his eyes glazed over yet intense.

"What is it?" she asked. "Do you see something that I don't?" She glanced from his face to the house, trying to figure out what had made him so tense. "Seth, what is it?"

In reply he slammed the SUV into Reverse and stomped on the accelerator. Gravel spewed from the wheel wells as he backed haphazardly down the driveway. Like earlier, when he'd been driving too fast around those sharp turns, she grasped the console and the armrest.

"What the hell are you—?" A boom louder than thunder rattled the SUV windows, and a burst of flames illuminated the woods and lifted the fog as the deserted house exploded. Fire and debris spiraled toward the windshield, but Seth turned the wheel, backing them onto the street.

"I guess we have our answer," he remarked, almost casually, as if he were nearly blown up every day. But today it had almost happened twice in less than twelve hours. "It was a trap."

"For you?" Did he think she had set it up with the partner first he and then Curtis Waverly had suggested she had? "Why would he want to kill you? You have no special abilities."

Or did he?

His broad shoulders lifted in a slight shrug. "Maybe because I'm in his way."

An engine revved and lights broke through the trees as a truck followed them out onto the road.

"And he intends to get me the hell out of his way," Seth continued. He jerked the SUV from Reverse to Drive and pressed hard on the accelerator so that it shot forward.

Her neck snapped back. "His way?"

"I'm keeping him from getting to you. And I'm going to do my damnedest to make sure he never gets to you." He reached across and squeezed her hand before returning both of his to the steering wheel.

Maria's heart constricted with fear, but she wasn't worried about the witch-hunter getting to her. She was more worried about what the witch-hunter would do to Seth so that he could get to her.

The truck's lights illuminated the SUV interior. Its engine rumbled as it drew ominously close. Then her neck snapped forward as the truck connected hard with the back bumper of their vehicle.

"Son of a bitch," Seth cursed, and gripped the wheel. Then he pressed harder on the accelerator.

"Hurry, hurry," she urged him. "You can lose him."

Seth shook his head. "No. I can't. He knows these roads. I don't—especially in this god-awful fog. I can't even tell where the road ends." The truck bumped the rear end again, sending the SUV into a tailspin. Rubber burned; gravel sprayed.

Seth yanked the wheel, steering the vehicle back to the center of the road. The headlight beams glanced off the tops of trees as the road gave way to one of the deep ravines in the Upper Peninsula.

"Where's your gun?" she asked.

He'd had it in his hand a little while ago. Now he clutched the wheel with both hands, his knuckles turning white in the dashboard lights.

"I can't shoot at him and keep the car on the road," he said, with another curse as the truck bumped them.

"Give *me* the gun," she offered. "I can shoot at him."

"No." He sped up, the wheels squealing as he steered around a sharp curve in the road.

"I can shoot," she said, then admitted, "Not well. But I might be able to get him to back off."

"He's backing off." But even as he said it, the truck closed the distance between them—the lights illuminating the interior of the SUV again. That muscle twitched along Seth's strong jaw. He maneuvered around another turn as he accelerated—too fast—and the tires squealed again.

"Give me the gun," she urged him.

"No."

And she realized why he wouldn't. He didn't trust her any more than he trusted the person who was trying to run them off the road.

"You have to let me help," she said. "Or we're both going to die."

The truck hit the SUV again. Hard. And the tires dropped off the pavement and onto the gravel shoulder, spewing loose pebbles. The vehicle began to slide down—toward the trees. And Maria screamed.

Her scream echoed inside the close interior of the car and inside Seth's mind. Outside, he saw nothing but fog and treetops, and he struggled to get the tires back on the road. Inside his head, he saw *the car turned over, lying atop its roof, the driver's side crushed, his body trapped inside as he lay unconscious. Or worse. Dead.*

But Maria wasn't dead. Blood trickled from the reopened

cut on her forehead, but her eyes were open—wide with
terror as big hands reached through the passenger's window. He dragged her from the car—dragged her up the
road to his truck.

Other images flitted through his mind.

She gasped for breath, water streaming from her face
and soaking her hair as her head popped up from a wooden
vat. Then the big hands closed over the top of her head and
pushed her under again. But she didn't drown, because
moments later—her hair still wet—she lay on a cement
floor, her wrists and ankles tethered to steel posts anchored
to the floor. Those same big hands lifted a rock onto her,
pressing it onto her chest—stealing away her breath as
the water had.

He had promised to protect her. He could not fail
her. Wrenching the wheel in sweat-dampened hands,
he steered back onto the road just as the truck drew
alongside. The driver was only a shadow in the dim
glow of the dashboard lights. As if scared that he might
be recognized, the driver turned off the headlamps. He
and the truck nearly disappeared.

But Seth knew where it was as metal crunched
against metal. The jacked-up truck was bigger than the
SUV and, with its roaring engine, faster. He couldn't
outrun it. He leaned forward slightly and directed
Maria, "Grab my gun."

If not for that damn vision—the one of her shooting
him—he would have handed it over sooner, would have
let her fire at their attacker. But his gut had tightened
at the thought of putting in her hands the gun he had
envisioned killing him.

She reached for it, her hands sliding under his jacket and over his belt to the holster. But before she could withdraw the weapon, the truck struck harder. The SUV lurched, knocking Maria away from him—against the passenger's door—as the wheels fell off the road and then the shoulder.

Metal scraped against metal, the truck catching on the driver's side of the SUV. Rubber squealed as the truck braked. Metal twisted and tore as the truck broke free. But the SUV spun out.

Seth jerked the wheel, but he couldn't regain the road. The tires slipped and metal crunched—on the passenger's side—as the vehicle began to turn. Then the wheels were in the air, spinning uselessly. The lights glanced off trees and then black sky.

And in Seth's head, everything went black.

Maria's throat burned from the screams she had uttered as the SUV had turned over and skidded on its roof down the steep ravine. With a groan of metal, it caught against the trees, its descent drawn to a shaky, tremulous stop. She drew in a deep breath, trying to refill her aching lungs.

Growing up with the horrible visions she'd had, her life hadn't been easy, but she had never screamed about anything until she'd met Agent Seth Hughes. She wasn't screaming because of him, though. She was screaming for him.

"Seth…" she murmured, struggling to turn her head in the space between the seat and the crumpled roof. He didn't answer her, not with so much as a moan. She couldn't even hear his breathing—just her own labored pants for air.

Finally, she crooked her head enough that she could peer through the gap between the roof and console toward the driver's side. But she could barely see through the moisture running in her eyes. She lifted a trembling hand to her forehead, and her fingers came away sticky with blood. Blinking back the blood that trickled into her eyes, she tried to focus. The dim glow from the dash lit some of the interior, but fog seeped eerily in through the broken windows, swirling around Seth.

He was bleeding, too. But instead of trickling, blood flowed from a gash on his head—which was jammed at a horrible angle against the post between the doors on the driver's side. Was his neck broken?

She didn't think she could heal a broken neck. But she could stop the bleeding. If she could find the bag of herbs… It had catapulted around inside the SUV as it spun over and over and could be anywhere…

"Seth!"

He didn't stir at her shout. His closed lids didn't even flicker in response. Along with the blood draining from his wound, the color drained from his skin, leaving him as ghostly pale as the apparitions that visited her.

"Seth!"

She pulled her arm from where it was trapped between the console and her seat and reached over to him. She pressed her scraped and swollen fingers to his throat, trying to detect a pulse. Her skin tingled at the contact, but his was as cold as it was pale.

"Seth, wake up." Tears rushed to her eyes, washing away the blood. "Please wake up…" She ran her fingers over his chin, over his lips, hoping to feel a breath. But his lips were cold, too.

She needed her herbs—needed to try to restore his breathing. She caught sight of the bag; it was wedged between his seat and door. She reached over him and grabbed at it. The plastic snagged and ripped, spilling herbs over him. Her hands shaking, she pulled out lavender and turmeric and licorice. Chanting a prayer, she mashed them together in her fingers and pressed them to his lips.

"Please, sweetheart, don't leave me. I need you…"

More than she had ever needed anyone.

Especially now. Branches snapped, gravel and dirt flying, as someone hurried down the steep slope. A flashlight beam danced around the ravine, then shone through the broken window, bouncing off Seth's bleeding face before shining in her eyes. She squinted, blinded, but she didn't need to see to know that the witch-hunter was coming for her.

Her heart pounded furiously with fear and dread. She moved her hand from Seth's face down his neck again to his chest. But she couldn't feel his heart beating. She twisted in her seat, trying to reach farther down his body. But his back was pressed tight against the seat, too tight for her to squeeze her hand between and pull out his gun.

The snapping noises grew louder as the hunter neared his prey. Then his feet must have slipped on the treacherous slope, because he bumped against the wreck. The SUV rocked, as if about to slip again.

Maria gasped and clutched at Seth. She couldn't let him go; she couldn't lose him. "Go away!" she screamed. "Leave us alone!"

"I can't do that," a deep voice rasped.

Shattered glass tinkled as it fell out of the metal frames. Then big hands reached through the broken window, grabbing for Maria...

Chapter 10

She welcomed the darkness—the blindness of it. And for once she saw no images—no visions. Elena breathed a deep sigh of relief—even though she knew it wouldn't last. The visions would return.

There had already been so many. So many deaths…

Elena wanted life. She wanted her sister's babies safely born. But no matter how many powers she and her sisters shared, they couldn't control their lives.

But once…they had united and killed. Could they do it again? She lifted her wrist and stared at the star-shaped charm that dangled from it. Each of the charms had powers.

They had united them to protect Maria—to save her from the danger Elena kept envisioning. But Irina was so weak that maybe uniting the charms and chanting their prayer hadn't worked.

Elena lowered her wrist—because she worried that

it was probably too late. That was why she had no more visions…

All those horrible things may have already happened. To Maria.

The gunshot jolted Seth awake, his chest burning. He clutched his hands against his heart. It pounded beneath his palm, fast and furious. He hadn't been shot; he had only dreamed it again when he'd passed out after the crash.

The crash! Remembering it cleared his mind and quickened his pulse. Had she been hurt when the vehicle went down the ravine? Or had the killer gotten to her?

"Maria!"

"I'm here," she said, the mattress shifting beneath him as she joined him on the bed.

He blinked his eyes open to find out where *here* was. His room—not at the motel in creepy Copper Creek but in his house in Barrett, Michigan. Light streaked through the wooden blinds at the windows, falling across the hardwood floor and four-poster bed.

"How…are we here?" he asked.

"You don't remember?"

Like his heart, his head pounded—with the echo of metal crunching and her screaming. "I remember the crash. He forced us off the road…"

But that was the only part of his vision that had come true…since she was here with him, instead of at the mercy of a killer.

"I thought you were dead," she said, her voice hoarse—either from screaming or with emotion. "Your head was bleeding so much, and I couldn't feel a pulse.

And your skin was cold, so cold…" She shivered as if reliving a nightmare.

It had been a nightmare…when he had awakened to those big hands reaching through the window for her, just like in his vision. Whatever she'd pressed against his lips must have revived his consciousness and his strength. He had tried to fight off the attacker despite the other man's strength. To protect her, though, Seth would have killed him. Until he had recognized him…

"Ty," he remembered. "It was Ty McIntyre who helped us out of the wreck, who got us up the ravine."

She expelled a soft sigh of relief. "Yes. He said Irina made him return to Copper Creek. They knew about the fire, so he had David fly him right to the hospital. The sheriff told him where we were going, and he happened upon the truck just as it was forcing us off the road."

"Thank God for that…" Or both Seth and Maria might have been dead by now. After the truck had raced away, Ty had helped them from the wreckage, and then, instead of waiting for an ambulance, he'd brought them to the hospital himself. Then there had been another ride, in a helicopter, that had brought them back to Barrett.

"My sisters used their special abilities to help us," Maria said as if awed by the women even though she had met only Irina. Not the others…

"Have you talked to them?" he wondered.

She shook her head. "No. Ty talked to them. He told them that we were all right. Elena had warned them about the crash. Both she and her daughter, Stacia, had seen it. They used their charms together and chanted a prayer for our protection—over the fire and the crash."

There was such longing in her voice when she talked about her family. Why wasn't she with them?

"He wanted to bring you to them." Seth remembered the argument at the hospital. And after what had happened, Seth had accepted that she would probably be safer with her family than with him, so he had willingly released his material witness into Ty McIntyre's custody. "But you're here…"

With him. In his house. In his room. In his bed. Her hair hung in damp curls around her face; she must have used his shower, because sunshine, not rain, streaked the windows. And she had helped herself to his clothes, too, because she wore one of his old T-shirts and a pair of cotton boxers that sagged low on her hips.

"I needed to stay with you," she said, her skin flushing with embarrassment. "You left the hospital against doctor's orders. You have a concussion. You needed someone to watch over you, to make sure you don't start bleeding in the brain…or swelling…"

Her sitting in bed with him, so close, had something swelling. His body tensed with desire for her. "You missed your chance," he said as he reached for her.

"What chance?" she asked, her eyes widening as his hands clasped her shoulders, pulling her close to him.

"To run away again."

"You convinced me that I need to stop running." She lifted her arms, her fingertips brushing lightly across the bandage on his forehead before sliding down his face. "I need to stay here…with you."

If she knew who he was, she wouldn't stay. She would run faster than she ever had. He needed to tell her his real identity but not now. Not yet. Not until the real killer was caught. It wasn't Curtis Waverly—he'd been either in the hospital or the jail when the truck had come after them.

But he would find out who the killer was. He had already figured out another suspect—one he should have discovered before. Once the killer was caught, maybe she would accept that Seth was no threat to her life. Only, hopefully, her heart—as she was to his. Her fingers stroked down his throat, back and forth over his leaping pulse.

"I thought you were dead," she whispered, her voice choked with emotion. "I couldn't feel you breathe. I couldn't feel your heart beating…"

"I'm alive," he said, "which I have a feeling is thanks to you and your magic potions."

She shivered. "I wasn't sure what I was doing. Or if it would work."

"It worked," he said. "I'm fine."

She pressed her hands, which trembled now, against his chest and pushed back, nearly breaking the hold of his arms around her. "I should leave."

"You just said that you need to stay with me," he reminded her.

"I need to stay with you," she repeated. "But you need me to leave. I'm putting you at risk."

"You care about me?" he asked, his heart warming with hope. If she cared enough, she might forgive him for keeping secrets from her.

Her eyes glistening with unshed tears, she nodded. "I shouldn't. I don't really even know you."

She had no idea how little she knew about him.

"But you've been there for me," she said, "saving me again and again, when no one else in my life has ever been there for me."

"Because you won't let them," he pointed out. "You keep pushing them away, like you're trying to push me away now."

"I can't be selfish," she said. "I can't stay just because I want to…"

"Then stay because I want you to." He leaned forward, closing the distance between them. He brushed his lips across hers. "Stay because I want you…"

Those tears caught on her thick lashes now, quivering before dropping onto her delicate cheekbones. He wiped them away with his thumbs.

"I can't risk your life," she said. "I can't…"

"You're not. This place is like Fort Knox." That was probably the only reason Ty had let her stay with Seth—his security system was high-tech. He also remembered something about McIntyre posting guards outside to watch the house, and probably to make sure Maria didn't try to slip away again. "No one can get in here," he assured her. "You're safe here. You're safe with me."

But she kept her palms pressed against his chest, holding him away from her. Then she pushed, forcing him to lie back down. He grimaced as pain radiated from his bruised ribs.

"I'm sorry," she said, her eyes going wide with horror and regret. "All I do is hurt you."

"You won't hurt me," he said, ignoring the image that flashed through his mind—of her firing that gun. "Unless you leave…because I ache for you."

"I can't leave you," she said, her breath catching. "I want to. I know I should, but something binds us together. Something I can't explain. I'm so connected to you."

He opened his mouth, wanting to tell her why. But then she kissed him. Not his lips but his chest, her mouth gently caressing his bruised skin.

"I'm sorry you got hurt because of me," she said, her usual guilt apparent in her throaty voice.

"It's not your fault."

"Do you believe that?" she asked, her dark eyes large with hope and vulnerability as she stared up at him. "Do you really believe I have nothing to do with the murders?"

The crash had killed whatever doubts he'd been hanging on to about her. If she'd been working with the killer, the man wouldn't have risked her life to take Seth's. "I really believe."

She released a shaky sigh. "I wish I did. But I still feel responsible for those murders and for you getting hurt."

"You're not—"

She pressed her fingers across his lips. "I want to make it up to you," she said. "I want to make you feel better." She dipped her head again, her hair brushing softly across his skin as she moved down his body. Her lips skimmed across his chest, where she teased first one nipple, then the other with the tip of her tongue. Then she trailed that tongue down his stomach.

Her fingers were unsteady as they slid beneath the waistband of his boxers and pushed them down his hips. Then she kissed him, intimately. Her lips closing around the tip of his pulsing erection, she sucked him into the moist heat of her mouth.

He tangled his hands in her hair. But instead of pulling her away, he held her against him as she continued to torture him. Her lips slid up and down as she sucked his cock even deeper. He groaned.

And she lifted her head. "Am I hurting you?"

"I'm hurting," he admitted as he sat up again.

"The doctor prescribed pain pills. Do you need one?" She reached toward the nightstand, where his holstered gun lay next to his cell phone and a brown bottle.

Ignoring the pain that pounded at the base of his skull, he shook his head. "I'm hurting for you."

Her lips quirked into a slight smile as she turned back to him. "Then let me make you feel better…"

Before she could lower her head again, he caught her shoulders, holding her back. "You didn't ask if you could borrow my clothes."

"Do you mind?" she asked, glancing down at the T-shirt and boxers. "I used your shower, too."

He minded that he hadn't been in it with her, soaping her naked skin. "Yes. I want my clothes back." He reached for his T-shirt, pulled it up and over her head. Then he eased his borrowed boxers over her hips.

He kissed all the skin he'd exposed, sliding his lips down her throat and over the curve of each breast. As she had done with him, he teased her nipples with the tip of his tongue…until she moaned. Her legs shifted restlessly, so he parted them and slid his fingers inside. She was wet and ready for him.

He pulled her astride his hips. Her fingers wrapped around his throbbing erection, and she guided him inside her as she settled on top of him. He bucked, thrusting deep, as he gripped her hips, pulling her up and pushing her back down.

She matched his rhythm, her nails digging into his

shoulders as she bobbed up and down. He leaned forward, kissing her deeply. He thrust his tongue between her lips as he thrust his cock deep inside her body.

Her inner muscles squeezed him, stroking his erection more tightly than her mouth had. He thrust harder, a groan tearing from his throat. He pulled his mouth from hers, slid it across her cheek, down her throat to the taut nipple of one breast. His teeth nipped, and then his tongue laved the sensitive point.

She threw back her head and released a keening cry as she came, her orgasm flowing hot over him. His body tensed, every muscle tight, until finally he found release, his cock pumping out an orgasm that filled her.

She collapsed onto his chest, panting for breath. "That—that was incredible…"

"You're incredible." He had never met anyone like her—so self-sacrificing, so generous. So strong…

Was it any wonder that he was falling for her…even though he knew they had no future? Because of their past, they had no future…

"I'm stupid," she berated herself as she quickly rolled off him. "I could have hurt your ribs."

"You didn't," he assured her, catching her close to his side. "You didn't hurt me."

But how badly would she be hurt when she learned the truth about him? He pressed kisses against her temple. Her lashes fluttered down, as if her lids were heavy. She had stayed awake, keeping watch over him. Now it was his turn to watch her while she slept.

But instead of seeing her delicate face in peaceful slumber, he saw her in pain—fighting to draw a breath into her lungs as the big hands continued to pile rocks onto her body, crushing her beneath the weight.

His head pounded with frustration that he couldn't see to whom those hands belonged. Who was it who was hurting the woman he loved? And why wasn't he there in this vision?

He hadn't died in the vehicle crash. So where was he? Why was he breaking his promise to protect her? Because he was already dead?

"Maria!"

The urgency in her mother's voice jolted her awake. She opened her eyes to a thick mist and the overpowering scent of smoke and sandalwood and lavender. Sunlight glowed behind the mist like flames.

"Mama…"

The mist formed into the image of her mother—the delicate-featured face with the big dark eyes that had haunted Maria since Myra Cooper's tragic, prophetic murder. Those eyes brimmed with fear. Not for herself anymore, but for her youngest daughter.

"Child," she said, her voice soft with concern and disappointment. "You are too much your mother's daughter, too much like me. Don't make the mistakes I've made."

Maria glanced to the bed, which was empty but for her, the sheets tangled around her naked body. "Seth…?" She called his name but she also questioned if her mother referred to her choice in men. Did she think Maria had made a mistake getting involved with the FBI agent?

But Seth wasn't like the men Mama had been with. Seth was honorable and protective. He didn't run from his responsibilities and try to ignore them. He took on responsibilities that weren't even his—like her.

"You need to keep running," Mama warned. "Don't stop. Don't ever stop…"

Weariness overwhelmed Maria at her mother's words so that every bone and muscle ached with it. "I can't. I can't run anymore."

"You don't want to leave *him*," Mama said, and those haunted eyes filled with disapproval.

"I can't," she repeated. "I'm not like you. I can't keep leaving the people that I…"

"The people that you what?" Mama asked. "Do you love him? You don't even know him."

"I know that he's been there for me when I needed him," Maria said. "Even when I thought he was dead, he came back to me—to keep me safe."

Relief flooded her again as she remembered him regaining consciousness and fighting off the hands reaching through the car window for her. If it hadn't been Ty, she knew that Seth would have defended her until he was really dead. She had never had anyone fight for her like that.

"Then where is he now?" Mama asked.

Maria bolted upright in bed and peered through the mist to the open door of the master bathroom with its black-and-white marble and shiny platinum fixtures. It was dark and empty. "Seth?"

"And *who* is he, child?" Mama asked.

She regretted now that she had wanted to see Mama's ghost the night before…because all Mama ever gave her was self-doubt and disappointment.

"Who is he?" the ghost prodded.

"Seth Hughes," Maria replied. "He's an FBI agent." And the only man she'd ever loved.

"With this house? With this security system?"

Mama scoffed. "He's more than you think he is." The mist began to fade, as did the smell of smoke. Only the scent remained, along with her mother's last whispered warning. "He's much more…"

Mama was right about the house, because it wasn't just a house. It was a mansion within a brick-walled estate. How could an FBI agent afford such a place?

She crawled out of the four-poster bed, leaving the warmth of its rumpled silk sheets. But she might need to drag one off the mattress to wear since she couldn't find the boxer shorts and T-shirt Seth had taken off her that morning. His cell phone and gun were gone, too. Just the bottle of prescription painkillers remained on the bedside table—unopened.

Had he left her? Naked and alone in his estate. He probably thought she would be safer here, given his security system, than wherever he had gone. But his leaving her—sneaking out while she slept—reminded her of how Mama had left her sleeping alone in that little camper they had shared for fifteen years. Her heart ached with old pain and new pain.

Then she noticed the clothes: a red sweater and dark jeans folded at the foot of the bed. She grabbed the sweater and a bra and panties dropped to the floor. He had thought of everything. But a note…

After getting dressed, she opened the bedroom door and stepped into the hall. She had helped him to his room in the early-morning hours, but she hadn't paid that much attention to the house—except for its expansive size. Now she noticed the details: the expensive oriental carpet running the length of the hardwood floor, the ornate trim and crown moldings and the antique furniture. Seth Hughes wasn't just rich; he was didn't-need-a-real-job rich. Yet he worked—not in an office or a bank but in a dangerous career that had nearly killed him more than once in the past few days.

"Who are you, Seth Hughes?" she wondered. "And why do you do what you do?"

"Maria?" His deep voice emanated from the bottom of the stairwell.

She hurried, nearly skipping steps as she rushed to the first floor. And… "Seth?"

"In here." His voice drifted through French doors that opened off the wide marble-floored foyer.

Drawn to him, as she had been since the first moment they'd met, she stepped into his den. Here was more ornate trim, more polished hardwoods, more antiques and his reason for doing what he did despite all that wealth.

A huge portable whiteboard crowded the desk, leather couch and chairs. Pictures, of every one of the witch-hunter's victims, were taped up, with notes scribbled beneath them. Her picture was there, too, with lines drawn from it to each of the victims.

She stopped in front of the board and stared up at all his evidence. Confronted with what led him to her, she remarked, "No wonder you thought it was me. I'm the one connection between all of them."

"There is another one," he said. His thick reddish-brown hair was tousled, as if he'd been running his hands through it. "The killer. We just have to find him."

A chuckle bubbled out of her with all her bitterness and anger. "We don't have to find him. He finds me. No matter how far or how fast I run, he always finds me. Even here, in this secure estate, I know he'll find me."

"Probably," Seth agreed.

And she appreciated his honesty. She didn't want the false truths and honest lies. She wanted him again—even after last night. But he was back to being the focused FBI agent—even with all his scratches and bruises, or maybe because of them.

"How does he find you?" Seth asked. "How does he always find you?"

"It's the witchcraft," she realized.

"He's not a witch-hunter," he said with a weary sigh. "You have to let that angle go. He's no descendant from some centuries-old madman."

"No. It's the witchcraft because I can't stop practicing. I always set up a shop—wherever I land. I can give up a lot, but I can't give up trying to help people." It was what kept her sane. It was what made all the running and loneliness worthwhile—if she could provide some relief for someone else. Some peace…since she would never have any of her own.

"You do always set up a shop," he murmured as he stared up at the board. "With the help of your old professor…"

Every one of her friends had died in one of her shops, after hours, after she'd left because of the cards she had read. She hadn't come across the bodies, but she'd already known what was going to happen to them…before it had happened.

"Is that how you found me?" she asked. "Through the shops?" Or through the professor?

Or had he used another method—the one that caused his eyes to glaze over while he got that blank inward stare?

He nodded again. "Of course. The witchcraft. They're drawn to it. It's the one thing that links them all. He's not the only one who's finding you. They're finding you, too. How?"

She reached out and touched Felicia's picture. "I found her," she reminded Seth. "We took that class together at Barrett University." She smiled. "A parapsychology class. Her brother made her drop it, though, and convinced her to move back home." Her lips curved. "Salem. She lived in Salem."

"Massachusetts?"

"No. Utah. It was perfect irony," she said, smiling as she remembered how much fun she and Felicia had had about that. "When...when my mother was murdered, and I started running again, I ran there. I found her."

"And the others?"

"Kevin." She touched the picture of the boy buried beneath the rocks. He had been such a sweet and funny young man. "Kevin found me. He was in that class, too."

"Two of the five victims took the class with you," he mused. "Did any of the others?"

"Not with me."

"At another time?"

She shrugged. "They didn't mention it, and neither did I. I didn't ask them about themselves." Seth had been the only one she hadn't kept at arm's length.

"Maybe it's time we find out." He glanced at his phone. "I need to stop by the bureau office and check in. I can use the computers there to find out if any of the others took that class."

"Are you going to leave me here?" she asked, nerves fluttering in her stomach. She wasn't afraid of being alone—but she was afraid that she was getting too used to being with him.

He shook his head.

"You don't think I'm safe?" Hadn't he promised her that she was?

His lips lifted into a slight grin. "I don't quite trust you to stay here and wait for me."

"I'm done running," she promised—no matter what her mother's ghost advised.

"That worries me even more," he said, "because I think that you're going to try to find him on your own."

Staring at the bandage on his head, among the other cuts and bruises, she realized that might be the safest thing for Seth—if she found the killer herself. It wouldn't be safest for the killer, though. She was still angry—so angry—over how she had let the madman control her life all these years.

"Don't even think about it," he said, pulling her into his arms.

"Can you read minds?" she wondered.

He laughed. "If only that were possible…"

"It's possible. My sister can." That was why Maria was always so careful to block her thoughts, to try to keep Irina out of her head. She hoped Seth couldn't really read minds; she didn't want him to know how she felt about him. She wasn't sure she was ready to admit it to herself yet. That she was falling for him…

Seth ignored the pounding in his head, which increased in intensity with the volume of his superior's voice.

"She should be in the interrogation room," the guy

yelled, "not sitting at your desk. She's the one link to all the victims."

"No. She's not."

Agent Ames leaned back in his chair, the metal frame creaking beneath his substantial weight. "Well, you've changed your tune. You're the one who was so convinced she's the killer that you started looking for her on your own time."

"I was wrong," he admitted with a heavy sigh of regret. "Given what's happened the past few days, I think we have proof that she can't be responsible."

"She can't be solely responsible," Special Agent Ames agreed. "But she can definitely be partially responsible. She can even be the one manipulating someone else into doing her killing."

"You've been talking to Curtis Waverly," Seth said. The man had interfered in the investigation from the beginning, throwing around his money and connections to learn what he wanted. Seth had overlooked the guy's manipulations because he'd seen his grief and loss. Now he resented it.

"He had the sheriff call me," Ames admitted. "You shouldn't have arrested him."

"He attacked Maria."

"Maria? Sounds like he's right—that she's gotten to you." The gray-haired man shook his head. "I didn't think it was possible for anyone to get you to lose focus."

Seth wouldn't have thought it possible, either. "I'm more focused than ever."

"So is Waverly. He's determined to get justice for his sister's murder. That's why I had Sheriff Moore release him."

"When?"

Ames shrugged. "Shortly after you had the sheriff arrest him the second time. They were still at the hospital. I wasn't going to be responsible for Curtis Waverly spending the night in some small hick jail."

Had Waverly paid off the bureau chief himself? Seth worried that he had, but at the moment his supervisor's integrity was the least of his concerns.

After Waverly had been released, would he have had enough time to beat them to the cabin? If he knew the area well enough, he could have. There were all kinds of back roads and snowmobile trails around the cabin. Had Waverly been staying in Copper Creek all that time, plotting Raven's murder? "Are you sure that justice is all he wants?"

"What else could he want that the rich kid doesn't already have?" Ames asked.

"Vengeance," Seth said, anger coursing through him as he remembered the man's arm wound so tightly around Maria's delicate throat that she'd gasped for breath. "Curtis Waverly could have been the one driving the truck that ran us off the road last night."

"The sheriff is investigating the accident," Ames said.

"It was no accident."

"According to the sheriff, it was foggy out and you were unfamiliar with the roads," Ames said with a faint twinkle in his eyes. He knew Seth was a better driver than to let weather and road conditions get the best of him.

"And a truck drove me off the road. You'll find its paint on the wreckage of my SUV, and you'll probably find the truck burned out somewhere. That's what this guy does to whatever evidence might be left behind to link him to his crimes. It could be Curtis Waverly."

Ames shook his head. "Doubtful. I think he really just wants justice."

Seth snorted.

"What do *you* want, Hughes?" his boss asked. "You've gotten too personally involved with this case. If you didn't have…whatever the hell it is that you have, I'd take you off it. But you're the one hope we have of finally catching this killer as long as you aren't falling for the number one suspect."

He wasn't falling for Maria, not anymore. He had already fallen—deeply in love with her self-sacrificing nature and her beauty and sensitivity. Now he could only hope like hell that he was right—that she had nothing to do with the murders.

Maria twirled the chair, which creaked beneath her weight. She leaned back and scanned the walls of Seth's small office. It was half the size of the den at his estate, the chair painfully underpadded and uncomfortable. "Why would you work here, Seth?" she mused aloud.

"I ask myself that," a male voice replied.

But it wasn't Seth. He'd gone inside another office with a gray-haired man. This guy had thin hair and a cheap suit that barely contained the belly that spilled over his belt as he leaned against the open jamb of Seth's door.

"You ask yourself why you're here?" she asked, wanting clarification of his comment.

"I ask myself why moneybags Hughes wants to work here," the man explained.

She gestured to the framed awards and certificates that covered the walls and sat atop Seth's cluttered desk. Maybe those answered her question. "Because of those?"

Seth's coworker snorted in derision. "Who the hell knows why he does anything? Do you?" he asked. "Have you known Hughes long?"

It felt like her whole life…and inexplicably longer. She shook her head. "I didn't even know the FBI had an office in Barrett."

"Some important people live in this town," he replied, his voice sharp with envy. "That computer guy— you know, Michigan's answer to Bill Gates—David Koster."

Her middle sister's husband.

"Elena and Joseph Dolce. They own most of the town."

Her oldest sister and her husband. That witch hunt eight years ago had been all over the news—even national media outlets had picked it up and ran coverage on it.

"And Ty McIntyre and his wife, Dr. Irina Cooper-McIntyre. They own a lot of properties around here, too."

Ty hadn't been mentioned as much in the news since he hadn't had as high a profile as David Koster and Joseph Dolce. That was why Maria hadn't recognized him at the motel in Copper Creek. He'd always been the Knight of Swords to her, though.

She barely suppressed a smile of pride. These wildly successful, influential people were her family. But they were also strangers to her. She didn't know them the way she knew Seth. Or did she know Seth?

Lisa Childs

"Of course, compared to Hughes," the man continued, "they seem about as poor as I am."

"Why is he so rich?" she asked, curiosity getting the better of her. Was it inherited money? From his family?

She hadn't noticed any family portraits or photographs hanging around his house. But then, she had been too concerned about him to really check out the place. He had mentioned his father being a bastard, though, so he wasn't likely to have his picture in his house. Would he have accepted an inheritance from the man, or had he made his own money?

"He probably got his money the same way he got those," the man replied, gesturing at the awards. "With his damn psychobabble voodoo shit."

"Voodoo?" Her breath caught in her lungs. "What do you mean?"

"That psychic mumbo jumbo he spews." He put his hand to his balding head in what must have been an imitation of Seth. "Oh, he's seen this—he's seen that. And it always breaks the damn case."

"He has visions…"

"He probably got so rich because he sees what numbers are going to hit for the lottery. Or what stocks will skyrocket. But will he share that information with anyone else? Hell, no." Bitterness twisted the man's face into a grotesque grimace. "Not ethical or some other garbage…"

And now she knew whom Curtis Waverly had paid to learn Seth's whereabouts. She also knew why she and Seth had had such an immediate and deep connection. They were more alike than she had ever imagined. He was psychic.

He had as many special abilities as she had—or maybe more. And if the witch-hunter realized that, he would have a motive to kill Seth other than just to get to her. He had another witch to kill…

Chapter 11

Seth stared at the computer screen, but he didn't see the college transcripts. Instead he saw that image in his head: *those big hands holding Maria's head underwater as bubbles rushed to the surface, where her hair billowed like a wet black cloud.*

"What do you see?" she asked.

He shook his head, clearing away the image. "I can only verify that you, Felicia and Kevin took the para-psychology class at Barrett University."

"I don't want to know what you see on the computer," she said, her hands gripping his shoulders as she leaned over the back of his chair. Her face was so close, her gaze so watchful. She had been studying him intently ever since he had come back from his meeting with Ames. "I want to know what you just saw inside your head."

Nothing she wanted to see.

He groaned with sudden realization. "Culpepper was in here. He talked to you."

"Yes. He told me what you didn't," she said, hurt flashing in her dark eyes. "That you have psychic powers, too."

He shrugged, unwilling to accept any labels. "I don't know what I have."

"You see things."

He nodded but clarified, "Not all the time. But sometimes I see...things."

"Bad things? That's why you do this, why you work in law enforcement," she surmised, "even though you're rich."

Rich. He didn't think about the money anymore, which was funny given how much it had meant to him when he and his mom had been trying to make ends meet. Then they had met his stepfather. He had been rich, but more important than that, he had been kind. And that had meant much more to Seth than his money.

"I want to stop the bad things from happening," he admitted. Especially to her.

"Do you?" she asked. "Can you...once you've seen it happen? Are you able to interfere and change the future?"

"It's the future," he pointed out. "So it hasn't happened yet. Sometimes I can interfere. Sometimes I can change what I've seen."

"Often?" she asked, her voice breathless with hope.

"No," he said, hating that he had to dash her hopes. "Not often enough." But this time he would have to change pretty much every vision he'd had since meeting her. Or he would lose her and his own life.

She expelled a shaky sigh of disappointment. "I was afraid you'd say that."

"But I have interfered," he said. "I saved a boy that I saw die. I found him in time. He's still alive."

"Anyone else?" she asked, narrowing her eyes as if skeptical now of his claims.

He probably deserved her doubt, since he had doubted her abilities and had called her a con artist. "I stopped a killer before he claimed three more victims that I watched him kill in a vision."

"You see more than I do," she said with a wistful trace of envy. "I can read the cards. I can see people's fate through the cards."

"You see ghosts, too," he reminded her with a shudder of gratitude that he couldn't.

"But it's too late then," she said. "I can't help them. I can't do what you can."

"Your herbs have healed—I've seen that myself. Then I've heard and read that your amulets have protected. Your talismans have brought good fortune." He brought up the blog he'd found, the one that had helped lead him to her. "They talk about you—the healing witch. A lot of people want your sachets and amulets, your candles and potions. A few of those people want to be you. That's how you're found no matter where you go. You're a legend."

She shivered. "The only legends I've known are of killing and curses. I don't want to be a legend."

"Maria…"

She sniffled and shook her head. "I need a minute. Where's the restroom?"

The memory of the noose hanging from the ceiling flashed through his mind. And from the way the color drained from her face, she remembered, too. "You're safe here, Maria. No one will hurt you."

"No?"

Then he realized that he already had. By not telling her about his visions, he had hurt her. She would never forgive what other secrets he kept from her.

Pain struck sharply, low and deep in her back—as if someone had shoved in the blade of a knife. This time the pain Irina felt was hers. Not anyone else's.

She sucked in a breath. She couldn't be in labor. It was too early. She covered her belly with her hands and felt the strong kicks of little feet.

"Are you all right?" Ty asked as he settled onto the bed next to her. His hand covered hers on her belly. "Are they all right?"

She waited, but no other pain stabbed her. "Yes, I'm fine," she said, "now that you've brought Maria home."

"She's not home," Ty said with regret in his raspy voice.

"She's home," Irina said as she leaned closer and kissed Ty—right on his scarred eyebrow. He was still the sexiest man she'd ever met. So she skimmed her lips down the side of his face to his chin. Then his lips...

He chuckled—that deep, throaty chuckle that made her weak in the knees. "You are supposed to be taking it easy, Mrs. McIntyre."

"I will," she promised. "Everything's going to be fine now."

His brow furrowed, buckling that scarred eyebrow she loved so much. "The new witch-hunter is still out there," he warned her. "We haven't caught him."

"But Maria isn't scared anymore." Irina smiled as

her younger sister's emotions washed over her. "She's in love."

"With Seth Hughes?" Ty asked, and his raspy voice was even gruffer with concern.

Irina nodded. "Must be—since she's with him." And from the feelings of Maria's that Irina had felt, she had really been with him. Intimately. "She loves him."

Ty blew out a ragged breath.

"Why does that worry you?" she asked. "You left her with him. You must trust him."

"David's going to check him out more thoroughly," he said. "We don't think he's exactly who or what he says he is."

Irina shivered as fear rushed over her. Again that feeling was her own. Maria was blissfully unaware and would remain blissfully unaware until it was too late. Given that she loved him, it already was too late.

He would never forgive her for running away again. But she had no choice—not if she wanted to keep him safe. She didn't need Irina's telepathic gift to know that his visions were not any better than hers. The way he had clenched his jaw so tightly that a muscle twitched in his cheek betrayed his tension and his fear.

Her hand trembling, she pushed the button for the elevator, then gasped as the doors opened to Raven.

But there was no forewarning mist, no raspy whispers. No tattoo on her face. Instead of dyed black hair, hers looked naturally black—even the streaks of violet in it looked natural as they matched her eerie violet-colored eyes. And her name: Violet.

Maria remembered now what Raven had said about her sister: she had respected her as much as she'd resented her. She had wanted to be exactly like her. That was how she'd gotten to Maria, because Maria had been able to identify with the young woman's envy and admiration. Commiserating over older, better sisters had drawn them close, closer than Maria should have allowed anyone to get.

"I'm supposed to meet with Special Agent Seth Hughes," the woman said. "But I think you're the one I really need to talk to about my sister. You're Maria."

She nodded. Guilt and regret overwhelming her, she could only whisper, "I'm sorry."

"It wasn't your fault," the young woman assured her. "It was hers. She knows that now."

"You can see her ghost?"

Tears glittered in those mysterious violet eyes as Violet nodded. Maria identified with the woman and the history Raven had given of her. Violet had been gifted since childhood, able to see things no one else had. Like Maria, she had embraced her witchcraft and made the most of it. But she hadn't wanted Raven to be part of the life that had chosen her.

"I can't see her anymore," Maria admitted, feeling the loss of Raven's ghost almost as acutely as she had felt the loss of the girl herself.

"She's embarrassed and regretful. She thinks that she brought him to you," Violet explained. "She feels it's all her fault."

"It's mine," Maria insisted. "He's been after me all this time. I never should have let her close to me. I never should have agreed to teach her."

"You wouldn't have had to...if I had. I saw that something bad would happen to her," Violet explained.

"I saw that she would be murdered if she became what I am. What *you* are…"

"A witch," Maria murmured. But she knew who and what she was. She asked the girl what she really wanted to know. "Who's the witch-hunter? Did she tell you?"

The woman's gaze shifted away from Maria, beyond her. She turned, expecting the mist and maybe Raven's image. Instead she saw Seth leaning against the doorjamb of his office as if he had been there for a while.

Had he been watching her ever since she'd left him? Had he known she was going to break her promise and run again? Of course he knew… Even if he couldn't read other people's minds, he could read hers because of that connection between them.

The woman spoke to them both now. "Raven hasn't told me who the man is. She doesn't know his real name."

"I need to talk to her," Maria said. "She needs to come to me again. I'm not mad at her."

Violet shook her head as more tears glistened in her eyes. "She's passed over. She's gone now."

And so were whatever leads Raven's ghost might have given them to the witch-hunter.

The hunter watched as they walked from the building. The agent kept his hand on the witch's arm, as if he didn't trust her not to run away again. He was a fool to try to hang on to her. His chivalry in trying to protect her was just going to get him killed.

He would do it now, with the gun he'd purchased off the street, but he wasn't the only one who watched them. He was more patient than the others knew. He had been watching Maria Cooper for years; he could watch her awhile longer...until he found his opportunity to kill her.

He'd had other opportunities over the years. But he hadn't been ready to end it then. He hadn't been ready to end her.

Instead he had used her—her ability to draw people to her—to draw out the other witches. She had already drawn out another one, the one with the purple eyes and streaks in her hair.

Then there were her sisters and nieces. They were all witches, too.

So much killing to do...

So little time...

He had to get busy. But first he had to get rid of Special Agent Seth Hughes, and not just because the guy stood between him and Maria. He had to get rid of Hughes because, just like the others, Hughes was a witch, too.

Seth watched her—as he had at the bureau. Maybe he had more abilities than just seeing the future. Maybe he could read minds, because he'd known that the moment she had learned what he had kept secret from her, she would take off. And she didn't even know it all. But realizing that he had kept one secret from her had shattered that fragile trust she'd begun to feel for him.

When she learned the rest, he would never be able to rebuild what he'd just destroyed. "I'm sorry," he said, because he should have told her but couldn't. Sorry, too, because he couldn't let her go.

He had spent too long looking for her to let her slip easily away from him. Especially as a killer waited somewhere out there, probably close by, to get her alone, waited to kill her.

"You should have told me," she said as she hesitated outside the door he held open for her.

To his bedroom. Would she share it with him again? Or had he destroyed not only her trust but also whatever else she had begun to feel for him?

"I don't tell people," he said.

"You're embarrassed?" she asked, her voice sharp with accusation. Apparently it offended her if he denied his abilities.

"I would feel like a fraud if I claimed to be a psychic," he explained. "I'm not sure it's even real. It comes and goes. I can't do it on command, like other people think. I'm not a psychic. I just have…psychic moments."

She glanced to the bed and then to his face. "Have you had any about us?"

"Yes." He couldn't tell her about the shooting, not without making her even angrier with him. "I knew you and I would make love."

She stepped farther into the room, closer to the bed. "It was inevitable."

"It was incredible," he said as he followed her, moving close enough that his chest brushed her back. Then he lowered his head so his lips brushed across her ear when he added, "I knew it would be…from the dream. But yet, it—you—surpassed whatever I could have envisioned."

"What do you envision now?"

Horrible things. Her drowning. Her being crushed. He flinched and shut out the images. "You forgiving me for not telling you," he said.

She chuckled, recognizing his lie. "Why should I forgive you?" she challenged him. "What are you going to do for me?"

"I got that box of stuff you wanted," he told her. "It's in my den."

She nodded. "That's a start."

"But it's not enough?"

Hurt flashed through her eyes, and he remembered that she had once referred to herself as that—as not enough. Instead of waiting for a reply, he turned her in his arms and pressed his lips to hers. Determined to prove to her that she was more than enough for him, more than he deserved, he deepened the kiss. His tongue stroked in and out of her mouth, driving deep.

Her fingers tunneled into the hair at his nape. Instead of tugging him away, she clutched him closer. She tangled her tongue with his, sucking it deeper into her mouth.

At least she still wanted him—even if she couldn't trust him. He wanted her trust, too. But he had no way of earning it—not with the secret he was keeping.

She pulled back from him and stared up into his eyes, as if she knew he was keeping more from her and she searched for the secret. "Why do I react this way to your touch?"

"What way?" he asked.

"I tingle," she replied, "all over."

"Here?" he asked, sliding his lips across her cheek to her ear. He blew lightly on her lobe and she shivered. He moved his mouth down her throat, flicking his tongue across the point where her pulse pounded quickly beneath her skin. "Here?"

She moaned and leaned against him, as if her knees

had weakened. Instead of supporting her, he pushed her back—onto his bed. Then he unsnapped and dragged her jeans down her legs and pulled her sweater over her head.

"I didn't thank you for the clothes," she murmured, her face flushing with embarrassment.

"You lost everything last night," he reminded her. "I bought you some other things." Actually he'd ordered them from a nearby boutique and had them delivered. "They're in the closet." Hanging next to his clothes, lying in drawers next to his. He had never lived with anyone before, always more focused on his professional life than his personal one. But he liked the idea of her living with him.

"I didn't lose everything," she said.

"No," he agreed as he stood up and shrugged out of his own clothes. "You still have your family."

"I still have you," she said, her eyes wide with awe as she stared at him.

She had seen him naked before, so he doubted his nudity accounted for her reaction. Was she just surprised that he'd stuck around?

"I'm not going anywhere," he assured her as he joined her on the bed. "Except here…" He kissed her shoulder, then skimmed his lips down her arm to the curve of her elbow. "And here…" He ran his tongue along the crease. Then lower to her hand, where he licked her fingers.

Her breath shuddered out. "Seth…" She tried to sit up, but he pushed her back onto the pillows, as she had pushed him last night.

And as she had made love to him, he made love to her. Kissing every inch of her, stroking his tongue and then his thumbs across her nipples. Then he moved down her body, licking his way across her navel, through the curls between her legs. And he buried his tongue inside her, lapping and thrusting, until she tensed and screamed his name.

Unlike at the hospital, he couldn't hang on to control and think only of her pleasure. He had to take his own, so he thrust his throbbing erection into her wet heat. She locked her legs around his waist and her arms around his shoulders, and she arched her hips, meeting his every thrust. Her fingers dug into his shoulders and her inner muscles clenched him, pulling him deep, and she came again.

And so did he. A groan tore from his soul as pleasure shattered his world. He wanted her clothes in his closet and her body in his bed—every night. But she was already wriggling free of his arms and out of his bed.

He relaxed when water ran in the bathroom, but then moments later another door opened. He opened his eyes as she was stepping into the hall. "Where are you going?"

"You said that box is in your den," she replied as if that were answer enough.

He didn't really think she was running, but still he hurriedly dressed and followed her downstairs. "What are you doing?" he asked as she opened that box of things he'd had one of his staff purchase for her.

She lifted out some candles and sat them on his desk. Crystals and sachets of herbs joined the candles. And then, her hand shaking, she lifted out the package of tarot cards. "I didn't ask for these," she said, her gaze going to his face. "I won't read anymore."

"You will," he said, "once the killer is caught. You'll be able to read again."

She dropped the cards back into the box. "I don't want to read."

Given what she saw when she did, he didn't blame her. But he also knew from experience that it was impossible to ignore a psychic ability. "What do you intend to do with all this stuff?"

"I'm going to hold a séance," she replied matter-of-factly, as if he should have known.

"Raven's sister said it was too late," he reminded her. "That Raven is gone. She's passed over." He hoped that the sister was wrong, though, because Raven could give them information no one else could—if she could speak from beyond the grave.

Maria turned toward his whiteboard and the photos taped to it. "Not all of them have passed over, not with the violent ways they died. I'll be able to bring at least one of them back to talk to me."

He shuddered at the thought of a ghost in his house. But he knew it wouldn't be the first time. He had felt other presences; he just wasn't able to see them clearly as Maria and Raven's sister were able.

"You don't see ghosts," she said.

"Sometimes when I handle a victim's personal effects, I see what they saw…when they died." Too bad it wasn't admissible in court or grounds for a search warrant that could lead him to evidence that would be admissible.

"Did you do that with them?" she asked as she stared up at the whiteboard.

He nodded, swallowed the lump in his throat and replied, "Yes."

"And what did you see?"

"You."

She whirled back to him. "What?"

"Not killing them," he clarified. "But you were the one person they all saw before they died." Just as he had in his dream.

Chapter 12

McGregor...

David Koster grimaced as the name came up on the screen of his tablet. Unable to sleep in the guest suite of Ty's house, he'd resumed his online investigation.

"What is it?" Ariel asked as she leaned over his shoulder, her breasts soft and full and naked against his back. She gasped as she saw the name, too, and her warm breath tickled his neck.

He shivered—more at her closeness than at what he saw. The woman excited him as no one and nothing else ever had.

"You found him," she said. "You found Donovan Roarke's son."

He had done what Donovan Roarke had been unable to do. The crazy private investigator had tracked down Myra Cooper and three of her daughters. But he hadn't been able to find the wife and the son who had been hiding from him.

David shook his head. "I didn't find him. He found us."

"Why?" Ariel asked. "Do you think he wants vengeance for what Elena, Irina and I did to his father?"

David shrugged. He knew about abusive fathers. His own hadn't been, but Ty's father had—until David had stopped him. "Or maybe he wants to thank you…"

Maybe that was what motivated him. Or maybe it was what Irina had told Ty…

"We need to tell everyone else," Ariel said. "We need to warn them."

David hesitated.

"You don't think we should tell them?"

"We will," he said. In their family it was impossible to keep a secret. But he wanted to do a little more digging first—into the past of Donovan Roarke's son.

And he wanted to make love to his wife. He set the tablet down and turned toward her. Her hair, so red and vibrant, was tousled around her naked shoulders. Her skin shimmered in the faint light of the bedside lamp.

He pushed her back onto the pillows and covered her mouth with his—her body with his. She shifted beneath him, arching into him, taking him deep into her body as she had already taken him deep into her heart.

Passion and love burned between them with an intensity that humbled and awed David. He wasn't worried about McGregor having found them. He wouldn't let anyone hurt his family. He had killed once to protect someone he loved; he would have no qualms about killing again.

***

Maria stared into the flickering flame of the sandal-wood candle. Seth had stepped out of his den to take a call on his cell, leaving her alone with the candles and incense and the ghosts. He might have been skeptical about the séance, but it was working. Along with the scent of sandalwood, the den filled with mist.

"I'm so sorry," she murmured. For all their deaths.

"It wasn't your fault," a soft voice whispered.

"Raven?" Maybe her sister had been wrong; maybe she hadn't passed over.

The mist formed into a tall, athletic shape. But the wispy hair was blond and short. The spirit was of Felicia Waverly. "No, my friend…"

"Licia." She reached out, wanting to wrap her arms around the girl she had loved like a sister. "I'm sorry." Most sorry about her death because, after her mother's ghost had warned her to run, Maria had sought out Felicia, tracking down her former classmate at her home in Utah. "I never should have gone to see you."

"I still would have died."

Maria squinted, trying to see Felicia's image more clearly. "Why?"

"Because this is all about me," Felicia said. "I'm the reason for the killing, not you."

"Felicia, is that why I never saw your ghost?" Not as she had seen the others. She had figured that Felicia had been mad at her, that she had blamed her for bringing the danger—the evil—with her and hadn't wanted to see her again.

"I wanted to warn you," the girl replied. "But I didn't know how to explain…what I can't understand myself."

Excitement quickened Maria's pulse. "You know who killed you?"

The ghostly image wavered as she nodded. "I didn't actually see him. He came up behind me. But I know who he is."

"Who?" Maria asked.

"My brother. My brother killed me."

"What?" Maria asked. He had seemed so grief stricken, so determined to find justice for Felicia's murder.

"Actually, he's not my real brother—only a step-brother," she explained with a shudder of revulsion, as if she couldn't stand anyone thinking they might have been really related. "He's my stepmother's eldest child. He's an evil, violent man…just like his father was. That was why he took my father's name instead of his own."

Maybe that was why Curtis Waverly had seemed so familiar to Maria. He had changed his name to hide his identity. But she knew who he was now. He was the witch-hunter—the son of the man who had killed her mother and had tried to kill her sisters and niece.

"He killed me for the inheritance," Felicia said. "All that money he uses to get what he wants—that was *my* money. He never would have gotten his hands on it if I had lived." The ghost began to fade. "He only wanted to kill me. But he keeps killing to cover his tracks…"

"No," Maria assured her friend, but the ghost was gone. "He keeps killing because of who he is…" A McGregor—he had to be a McGregor.

"Who's who?" a deep voice asked.

"Curtis Waverly," she answered Seth. "That's not his real name. He took his stepfather's name—Felicia's dad's name. He's the son of the witch-hunter. He's taken over and is witch-hunting now."

"No, he's not." But Seth couldn't explain how he knew it. "None of these murders have to do with that legend. I think it has more to do with the professor of that class you took."

"But only three of us took it here at Barrett University," she argued. "You couldn't even find out if the other victims had ever been in Barrett."

"It doesn't matter if they came here," Seth said. "Professor Chandler teaches it online and travels around the country lecturing about his novel on parapsychology. Every one of the victims has had contact with him. That phone call just confirmed it. Raven's sister confirmed Raven attended one of his lectures and had an autographed copy of his book."

"But why would he do it?" Maria asked. "He teaches parapsychology. He believes in—even reveres—psychic abilities. That's why he gives me money for the magic shops."

"Exactly," he said. "He gives you money so he knows where you are—before anyone else does." Resentment gripped him.

"He's not the only one," she said. "His assistant sends me the money orders."

"Then we need to talk to them both," he said. "The professor first, though."

"He wouldn't be a witch-hunter," she said, dismissing his suspicions. "It doesn't make sense."

"But it makes more sense that the estranged son of some guy your sisters killed would be killing everyone close to *you*?"

"Yes," she stubbornly persisted. "You have to admit that he has the most motive. Vengeance. And if he's half as crazy as his father…" She shuddered.

"Then wouldn't he be going after your sisters? Or their kids? Why you? You haven't had any contact with them. Why go after the people close to you?"

She shrugged. "Maybe it's like how lions take down the zebra that gets separated from the herd. I'm an easier target than they are. They're together. They're strong."

"Why do you think it's Curtis?" He glanced around the room. The air in it was heavy with her scent and smoke from the candles. He squinted his eyes as he peered around, but he could make out no celestial images.

"The ghost is gone."

"Who was it?" One of the boys who had loved her and died for her? Inexplicably, jealousy coursed through him. But those guys were gone—physically and spiritually. Yet they had a better chance of being with her again than he did…once she learned the truth about him.

"Felicia Waverly," she replied. "She told me that Curtis is the killer."

"She saw him?" How the hell would he bring this new information to his supervisor? Or a judge? He couldn't—without risking his career and his freedom. They would probably commit him. There were already too many rumors flying around the bureau about him.

With a sigh of disappointment, she replied, "No. But that's the only way he inherited his money—by killing her."

"He had an alibi for her murder," Seth pointed out. "And no reason to commit the other murders."

"You don't think he could have bought the alibi—like he bought your whereabouts?"

"He could have," he admitted. Initially he had suspected Curtis of the murder, so he had thoroughly investigated the man. But several people had seen Curtis the night his sister had drowned.

Or so they had claimed...

A shiver of unease raced down his spine as he remembered that, on the bureau chief's orders, the sheriff had released Curtis. He was free again—free to attack Maria again as he had already.

"But why would he kill the others? To cover his tracks? It's been years since Felicia died." He shook his head. "It doesn't make sense that he would keep killing." That he would keep torturing Maria, cutting her off from everyone she cared about.

If he had killed his stepsister, he had gotten away with murder. Why would he have kept risking getting caught?

But then, why had he attacked Maria not once but twice in front of a federal agent?

Maybe he was just so arrogant that he thought no one would catch him. Or that if he was caught, he could buy his way out of trouble—as he'd been buying his way out of the arrest for attacking Maria.

Was the bureau chief the one who'd given him Seth's whereabouts? Could he trust anyone but himself?

Maria's fingers touched her throat—as if she was remembering those attacks. "Curtis Waverly makes more sense than Professor Chandler killing anyone."

"He's another link between the victims," Seth

pointed out. A link he probably would have discovered earlier if he hadn't been so convinced Maria was the killer. "So I'm going to talk to him."

She leaned over his desk and blew out the flames, sending spirals of smoke into the air. "I'm going with you."

"No, you're going to your sisters," he said. "Ty keeps calling. They're dying to see you."

"They'll be dying if they do see me," she insisted. "It's bad enough that I'm here."

"In my house?" Did she regret coming home with him—regret forgiving him for keeping the visions from her?

"In Barrett. I swore I was never coming back here. I was never even going to return to Michigan again, but Copper Creek called to me."

As she had called to him before they had ever met, beckoning him to fall for her. "I can't leave you alone here," he said. "I can't trust you to not take off again." And probably confront Curtis Waverly with the allegations of his sister's ghost.

"So take me with you."

"I can't do that, either." He shook his head. "If Chandler is the killer, then I would be delivering you right to him."

"He's not the killer." She uttered a ragged sigh of resignation and reluctantly admitted, "He's my father…"

"I see your mother from time to time," Dr. Chandler said as he led them through the foyer of his Tudor house, which was just off the campus of Barrett University. "Even in death, she's beautiful."

"You loved her." And that was probably why he had

convinced himself that he saw her, even though Mama had said that the self-proclaimed expert of parapsychology actually had no psychic abilities himself.

In only his early fifties, the professor was a handsome man with his black hair and unlined face. His mouth lifted in a self-deprecating grin. "I was a besotted kid when I met your mom."

Maria turned to Seth, who stood protectively next to her in the professor's living room, as if he was ready to defend her should her father try to hurt her. "Dr. Chandler was working on his thesis when he met my mother," she explained. "He interviewed her and included her in his research."

"That was thirty years ago," the professor added. "She was raising three daughters alone. She was an amazing woman. I couldn't help but fall for her." He winked at Seth. "You understand…"

Heat flushed Maria's face. "No, it's not like that," she said. She had fallen for Seth, but she knew better than to think he had fallen for her, too. Sure, he was attracted to her, but as he'd told her before, he was just doing his job. "Agent Hughes is investigating the murders."

"Your mother's murder was solved eight years ago." The professor shivered despite the thick cardigan sweater he wore. "It happened just as she had seen it. At the hands of the man she knew was coming for her."

Because she had always known how she would die, Mama had lived in fear, taking little pleasure in life. Maria didn't want to live her life the way her mother had. She wanted to stay with Seth, but until the witch-hunter was caught, it wasn't possible for her to stay anywhere.

"It happened—" Maria turned to Seth and held his gaze, trying to make him understand that it was the curse "—just as the legacy foretold, with one of the McGregor descendants determined to kill all the descendants of that first witch, Myra Durikken."

"That has nothing to do with this," Seth said. "It has to do with you, Professor. Over the past eight years, there have been five murders—"

Maria interrupted to detail how they had died. "Drowning, hanging, crushing, burning…"

"Witch-trial murders." The professor sucked in a breath of surprise and nodded. "There must be another witch-hunter."

"Yes," Maria said, relieved that someone else agreed with her. Maybe now Seth would realize that it wasn't just a silly legend. This was her reality.

"These murders have more in common than the way the victims were murdered," Seth persisted. "Dr. Chandler, they have you in common. Every one of these victims took one of your classes, here in Barrett or online, or they listened to your lecture or had a copy of your book."

The professor, whose face had grown pale and whose eyes had widened behind his glasses, was clearly shocked—as Maria had been when Seth had told her. Even though he had been protecting and making love with her, he hadn't become as distracted as he'd claimed he was. He had been working the case, trying to find a link between the victims other than just her.

But given the interest in witchcraft of each of the victims, and her reading their deaths in their cards, she was still the stronger link.

"They also have me in common," Maria assured her

father. "I doubt their deaths have anything to do with you. They were all interested in the supernatural, so of course they might have attended one of your classes or lectures or bought your books. It doesn't implicate you. You're not the one responsible." Too old to be Donovan Roarke's son, he was not the witch-hunter.

Dr. Chandler lifted a shaking hand to his face and rubbed it along his jaw. "Their deaths might have everything to do with me."

Maria gasped. "That can't be…"

"What do you mean?" Seth asked, his smoky blue gaze intense as he studied the professor.

"During my lectures I've been going into great detail about the witch hunts, about the ways that witches are killed," he explained.

"But why?" Maria asked. "The class I took from you focused on psychic abilities. So did your book. You've never talked about witches or witchcraft."

"I'm working on another book," he replied, "about your mother dying at the hands of a witch-hunter." He reached out to her, caught her hands in his and squeezed. "I'm sorry, honey, if this brings up all the pain again. But there were so many reports about what happened eight years ago. I wanted to go into more detail than those sound bites on the evening news. Your mother deserved having her story told in its entirety."

Maria squeezed his hands back as emotion rushed over her. "Thank you." He had loved her mother so much, maybe more than Maria had. "Thank you for honoring her this way."

"Honoring or taking advantage?" Seth asked, his voice heavy with cynicism. "Given the sensationalism of the story, you're sure to make a lot of money off the book and the lectures you're apparently already giving about it."

"Seth!" she admonished him.

But Dr. Chandler nodded. "Agent Hughes is right," her father admitted. "I do stand to make a lot of money off your mother's tragedy. At least, that's what my agent and editor think after reading the draft."

"I'll need their names," Seth said, ever the FBI agent. "And besides them, who else might have seen this book?"

The professor lifted his shoulders in a shrug. "I don't know who else at their offices might have read it."

"What about your office? Did you give anyone else a copy of it?" Seth asked.

He shook his head. "I should have given you a copy," he told Maria. "Or at least discussed it with you before I sold the book."

She smiled. "It's fine. I haven't been in contact with you all that often over the years." Her face flushed with embarrassment when she realized it had usually been only when she'd needed something from him. Not support or comfort. They didn't have that kind of relationship, since they hadn't even known about each other until Maria had brought her mother's last letter to him. Despite the DNA they shared, she had never felt the connection with him that she had with any of her other family members.

Or with Seth.

But Dr. Chandler had promised he would make it up to her that he hadn't been in her life. But his way of doing that had been to write checks. Without his financial support, Maria wouldn't have been able to set up her magic shops every time she started over.

"So no one else has seen the book?" Seth asked.

"Nobody that I know about," the professor replied.

"What about your assistant?" Maria asked. "Does Ethan still work for you?"

He shook his head. "He left me a few months ago. He needed some time off. But he'll be back." He grinned. "He always comes back."

Goose bumps lifted on Maria's skin as she remembered the creepy young man. "He does?"

"He'll be gone for a few months. Then he comes back—helps me with my correspondence and my research—before he needs to leave again." A sad smile lifted his handsome face. "It reminds me of your mother. Of you…"

"Have you seen him recently?" Seth asked.

"No," her father replied. "But he called, sounded as though he was working on something important. But he said he was almost done and then he would come by and talk to me."

"Don't meet with him," she warned, worried about her father's safety. While he wasn't a witch, and his young assistant had always seemed to idolize him, he was closer to her than anyone else right now. Except Seth. "Don't let him anywhere near you!"

Seth was already on the phone, giving orders to the police officers who had followed them to her father's home. It hadn't mattered to him that Dr. Chandler was her biological dad; he had still suspected the man was capable of killing everyone she had cared about.

Maria hadn't believed it. She hadn't believed, either, when her mother had told her the professor was her dad. But after Mama had taken off, Maria had struggled alone for a few years before eventually seeking him out. Then he, and a DNA test, had confirmed the claim her mother had made in her goodbye letter. He hadn't resented finding out that he had a daughter. He had wanted to make up for the years they had missed. He had wanted to take care of her, had given her money and a scholarship to the school where he taught. But Maria had always felt more like a science experiment he wanted to study than a daughter to him.

When Seth hung up his call, he turned to her father. "I need to know everything about your assistant, including where we might be able to find him."

Near. Maria was certain of it. If Ethan O'Donnell was the witch-hunter, then he was close. Always watching her. Always waiting to kill those she cared about before, eventually, he killed her.

Ethan O'Donnell was not the witch-hunter that Maria thought he was. Given everything Seth had learned about the young man, the professor's assistant was probably the killer who had been stalking Maria. But he wasn't the descendant of the first witch-hunter from over three hundred and fifty years ago. He wasn't the son of the man who had killed Maria's mother and aunts and had tried to kill her sisters.

Seth stood back in the foyer near the door as she and the professor hugged. They didn't look like father and daughter, but they had a connection—one that had compelled Maria to let him know where she was when she had finally stopped running long enough to set up one of her magic shops.

But Ethan O'Donnell had also seen the postcards she had sent to her father, so he had also learned where she was. And he had sent other people to her—to learn her ways of witchcraft.

Then he killed them.

Seth knew now *how* the murders had happened. He just didn't know why. He waited until he and Maria were in the car, driving back toward his estate, before he asked, "What made you think about your father's assistant?"

She shivered despite the warm air blowing from the SUV vents with such force that it stirred her curls, tangling them around her shoulders. "He was my father's teaching aide at the time Felicia, Kevin and I attended that class. And he was just always—" she shivered again "—a little too intense."

"But what made you think he might be the killer?" he wondered. Maybe it was investigative curiosity or maybe it was jealousy that had him asking, "Had you ever had a relationship with him?"

Now she shuddered with disgust. "God, no!"

Her admission gave him some relief. "Then he's not a jilted lover who might be stalking you."

"Definitely not," she replied.

"He could still be obsessed with you. Maybe he wanted something to happen between you and him." Seth couldn't blame the guy for that, but he could blame him for how he had handled her rejection.

"He never even talked to me," Maria said.

Seth sighed. "Then I don't understand why he would have become a killer."

"There's only one explanation," Maria replied. "He's a descendant of that first witch-hunter. He must be the son of the man who killed my mother."

"You don't know that." But Seth did. And maybe

it was time he finally told her the truth, no matter the consequences. "Maria…"

But before he could say more, the wheel jerked, rubber slapping against asphalt. He had been vigilant about other cars on the road and had made certain the same one hadn't stayed near them—on the way to the professor's brick-and-stucco Tudor and since they had left the college campus. Had he just driven over something that had blown the tire?

Then the windshield shattered, glass spiraling out from a hole in the middle. He reached across and grabbed the back of Maria's head and pushed her lower than the dashboard. "Get down!"

Then he ducked himself and gripped the wheel, keeping the SUV on the road. There were no steep ravines here, but he didn't want to swerve out of control. Even though the bare rim rumbled against the road, he couldn't stop the SUV. That was what the shooter wanted. He was out there somewhere, determined to kill Seth.

So determined to get to Maria that he would kill an FBI agent to get to her. Could it be Ethan O'Donnell? Had he been watching the professor's house, waiting for them to show up?

"He's going to kill you," she said, her voice shaking with horror. "He's going to kill you just to get to me."

"He's not going to get you," Seth vowed. But even as he made the promise, those images flashed through his head.

Her being drowned, sputtering and choking for breath as the water filled her nose and mouth and slid down her throat to her lungs. And once she had passed out, he tied her to the stakes anchored in the cement floor. And he began piling those rocks atop her body, snapping her bones, crushing her organs until she breathed her last...

"I'll die before I let him hurt you," he swore, cursing as the driver's-side window shattered, too.

"I'm afraid that's what's going to happen," she murmured, tears of fear streaking down her face. "Right now..."

Chapter 13

Ty had been a good cop. But he was an even better private investigator. He was good at finding people who didn't want to be found—well, good with everyone but Maria. And he was damn good at following someone without their being aware that he followed them.

Apparently even an FBI agent…

He'd been trailing Seth Hughes since he and Maria had left Hughes's impressive estate. While they had been visiting with the professor, he'd noticed someone else parked outside Chandler's house. Maybe the person had noticed him, because he'd taken off. But it was clear now he'd been leaving only so he could ambush the FBI agent.

Ty flinched as each shot rang out. One struck the tire. Another bullet shattered the windshield and the last one the driver's-side window as Seth drove past where the other car had been waiting for him—pulled off into a tree-lined driveway.

The SUV rolled to a stop against the curb across from the driveway, the horn blaring as a body slumped over the wheel.

"Damn it!" Ty cursed as he braked hard and threw his vehicle into Park. He should have reacted faster. Seth was hurt, but maybe he could protect Maria. The passenger's door of the SUV opened. But it wasn't her who dropped to the ground. As the horn continued to blare, Seth slipped from the vehicle and sneaked around it, his gun drawn.

Ty expelled a breath of relief. He was alive. And if he'd been hurt, he wasn't seriously injured—because he moved quickly. He circled around to that vehicle concealed in the driveway.

Ty hurried across the street to back him up, his gun drawn, too. Seth, blood trailing from cuts on his face, nodded at him, and Ty pulled open the passenger's door as the FBI agent dragged open the driver's door. "Drop the gun! Drop the gun!" he shouted.

The man's hands trembled on the gun he held, but he didn't drop it. He continued to hold it, but he didn't point it at either Seth or Ty. He pointed it through the windshield at the woman who hurried up to the vehicle.

"I told you to stay put," Seth told Maria.

"And let him kill you when it's me he wants?" She shook her head. "No…"

And Ty realized that his wife was right. It was too late for Maria. She already loved the FBI agent.

Seth ignored her and shouted again at the man in the car, "Put the damn gun down!"

Ty cocked his gun, too. "Do as the agent says."

"I saw Felicia," Maria told the man. "Her ghost came to me."

The gun trembled more in the man's hands—so much that Seth reached out and easily snapped it out of his grasp. Then he dragged the suspect from the car and hooked him up. "Curtis Waverly, you're under arrest for attempted murder. Again…"

"For murder," Maria corrected him. "Arrest him for murder. He killed Felicia. She told me you killed her."

Curtis shook his head. "No. No, I would never kill her. I *loved* her."

"You love her money—money you wouldn't have gotten if you hadn't killed her," Maria accused him. "You only inherited it because she's dead."

The cuffed man began to sob, his muscular body shaking with grief. "I would give up all that money for her—to bring her back. I loved her. She wasn't really my sister, you know. We could have been together. We could have been…if she hadn't died."

Maybe loving Irina as long and as deeply as Ty had had given him some of her power of empathy. Because he felt the other man's pain and inconsolable loss.

Ty met Maria's gaze and realized she felt it, too. While this man had just tried to kill her and Seth, he wasn't the killer. He wasn't the witch-hunter.

"We should have gone to the hospital," Maria said as she lifted her fingertips to Seth's handsome face. She gently applied some lavender oil to the scratches on his skin. "You're cut again." Hurt again—because of her.

"I'm fine," he assured her, and he stepped back so that her hand fell to her side.

She couldn't blame him if he didn't want her to

touch him—if he didn't want her healing. Cursed as she was, she was bad luck for anyone who got close to her.

He paced around his bedroom, as if the adrenaline had yet to leave his system. "I should have let Ty McIntyre take you to your sisters, though—where you would be safe."

That was why Ty had been following them—to protect her. To make sure she stayed safe. But as usual, Seth had kept her safe. He had also been right about Curtis Waverly; he wasn't the witch-hunter.

Ty had confirmed that he and David Koster had searched for Donovan Roarke's son, and it wasn't Curtis Waverly. He was a few years too young and not the same coloring as either Roarke or his wife. So it had to be Ethan O'Donnell.

"You should have gone with Ty," Seth repeated.

She couldn't blame him if he didn't want her anywhere near him anymore. She had brought him nothing but danger and pain. "If you want me to leave…"

She would, even though it would be the hardest thing she had ever done, harder even than when she had left the apartment she had shared with her sister Irina. As much as she had loved her sister, she loved Seth so much more.

"No!" He rubbed his hand over his face, wiping away traces of blood. "No. I should take you to your family, but I don't want you to leave." His throat rippled as he swallowed hard. *"Ever…"*

She shivered at his intensity even as his admission warmed her, chasing away her doubts and fears. Maybe he wouldn't reject her. Maybe she was enough for him. "Seth…"

He wrapped his arms around her. "You're cold. I'm

sorry that we had to stay at the scene so long. That's another reason you should have left with Ty."

"He had to stay, too. We both had to talk to the police," she reminded him. "We were eyewitnesses to the shooting." But that shooting and those earlier attacks on her were all that Curtis Waverly had done. He hadn't killed his stepsister. He had loved her, and his grief had driven him to insanity.

She could understand love driving one beyond reason. She was afraid that she loved Seth like that. And if something happened to him…

Seth shook his head. "I didn't think he killed her or the others. But he kept trying to kill you."

"You saved my life." And had nearly lost his own. She wrapped her arms around his waist, the holster at the small of his back digging into her forearm. "You saved my life again."

"Always," he said. "I will always keep you safe. Please believe that—that you're safe with me."

Growing up as she had, always on the run, always knowing she was cursed, she had never felt safe. Until now, until Seth Hughes held her tight.

Her heart shifted in her chest, warming and swelling, as love for him filled her. She had never felt like this. None of anyone else's emotions or even her own had been as intense as what she felt for Special Agent Seth Hughes. She opened her mouth, wanting to share her feelings with him as their intensity overwhelmed her.

But he lowered his head and took her open lips in a deep kiss. His tongue slid over hers, tasting—teasing.

She slid her hands up his back to his broad shoulders. Then she pushed off his jacket. He released her—

just long enough to strip the sleeves from his arms. Then he grabbed her again, clutching her close to him.

But she pressed her hands against his chest and pulled free. Just long enough to drag off her sweater and kick off her jeans…until she stood before him naked. It wasn't just her body she bared to him, though. She bared her heart, too, as she made love with him, kissing every bruised and scratched inch of his skin she exposed as she stripped off his clothes. She stroked her fingertips over every sculpted muscle, which rippled beneath her touch.

He made love to her, too, kissing and touching her everywhere she loved: her lips, the side of her neck, the curve of her collarbone. Then his mouth closed over a nipple, his teeth scraping gently across the point before he stroked his tongue over it.

She moaned and lifted her legs, wrapping them around his waist, holding tight as he carried her to the bed. He laid her on the edge of the mattress. Then he kissed her some more, his mouth skimming down her body. His tongue stroked over her clit now, back and forth before dipping inside her.

"Seth!" She came, her body trembling.

But before the pleasure ebbed away, he was there— thrusting inside her. The pressure built again, winding tighter and tighter. She locked her legs around his waist once more, matching his every thrust.

He leaned down, kissing her deeply. His tongue stroked in and out of her mouth, across hers. Then his lips skimmed down her throat, his tongue teasing her pulse—making it jump wildly as the pressure broke free.

She clutched at him, holding him close as the orgasm slammed through her. Overwhelmed with pleasure, Maria could not hold in her feelings any longer. "I love you! I love you, Seth!"

He didn't return the declaration. He just held her closely, wrapping her tightly in his arms, as if he had meant what he'd said, as if he never intended to let her go.

Maybe that would have to be enough for her—since she had never been enough for anyone else. She hadn't actually expected him to return her feelings. She hadn't actually expected him to love her when no one else had.

Once he fell asleep beside her, she tugged free of his arms. She pulled on his shirt and buttoned just a couple of buttons, then headed down to his den.

Instead of turning on the lights, she lit the candles that sat on his desk. And in the flickering glow, she studied the whiteboard and the pictures of all those poor victims.

"I know who killed you all," she said. If it wasn't Curtis Waverly, it had to be Ethan O'Donnell. "It's time to stop him. To make sure he doesn't kill anyone else."

Especially not Seth.

"Help me," she implored their spirits. "Tell me where your killer is."

But no mist formed. It was so late that even the spirits must be tired. Restlessness filled Maria so that she couldn't relax. She couldn't sleep. Now that she knew who the killer was, she just wanted him stopped. Before he killed again...

Before he killed Seth.

She settled into the chair behind his desk. Unlike the one at the bureau, the leather was supple, the cushions thick and comfortable. But she couldn't relax, not even in the chair. Maybe Seth had something she could drink, something to ease her tension.

She opened a drawer and peered inside. Something glinted in the dim light, but it wasn't a bottle. It was metal—ancient pewter—from a locket.

Her heart slammed into her ribs. Her fingers shaking, she fumbled around for the chain and pulled it from the drawer. The big oval locket dangled from the chain. The clasp had been replaced.

He'd fixed her chain. Why did he have it?

When had he found it?

And what else did he have? A book lay beneath the locket, the leather cover probably as old as the locket. Why wasn't it on the shelves in here or in the library, which was next to his den? Why was it hidden away like the locket?

She lifted it out. And as she did, an envelope slipped from between the cover and the brittle pages. The letter wasn't that old, maybe just a few years. The sender was a law firm, the addressee, Seth McGregor Roarke.

Dread clenched her stomach, so tightly that she doubled over with pain. She didn't even need to open the book to know to whom it belonged. It was the journal of Eli McGregor—the first witch-hunter. The man who had started all the killing over three hundred years ago.

Her fingers trembling, she pulled the letter from the envelope. The first sheet was from the law firm; it discussed his inheritance as the only heir of Donovan Roarke. The next sheet was from his father:

Mac,
If you're receiving this letter, it's because my vision came true and the witches killed me, burn-

ing me at the stake like I burned their mother.
I haven't seen you in many years, but no matter
how your mother tried to change you, I know that
you are a McGregor through and through. You
have the special abilities—the visions.

You won't be like Thomas, who let the witch
go instead of making certain her lineage ended
by killing her. You will be like Eli, like me.
You'll avenge my death. You won't rest until all
the witches are gone.

Seth awoke with a start, angry that he had fallen
asleep. Again. He reached across the bed. The sheets
were still warm from her body. The scent of sandalwood and lavender hung yet in the air, filling his
senses. But she was gone.

He jerked upright. He had to find her—before Ethan
O'Donnell did. The image flashed through his mind—
that first one.

Maria sat at the foot of his bed, her naked back
to him. She leaned down, her hair falling forward—
swirling around her shoulders. Leaving her back completely bare but for that trio of tattoos. And the thin
chain of her locket.

Or was the image inside his head? It seemed so
real—as though he could reach out and stroke his fingers across her silky soft skin. "Maria?"

She stood up then and turned toward him…and just
like in his vision, she held his gun. Instead of staring
down the barrel of the gun, he stared at the locket nestled between her naked breasts.

"You found it." He had intended to give it back to her.
Eventually. After he had explained everything to her.

"How did you get it?" she asked.

"It was in Raven's hand," he replied. "I found it when I gave her CPR at the barn."

"And you took it?" she asked. "Why did you take it?"

"I thought it was evidence," he explained. "More proof that the two of you had struggled before her death."

"But you didn't put it in an evidence bag."

He had wanted to, but he hadn't been able to seal the locket away in plastic. To him it wasn't just a piece of jewelry. It was a piece of history—his history as much as or more than Maria's—and proof that all his descendants hadn't been as evil as Eli McGregor or his father.

"You brought it home with you," she pointed out. "You fixed the clasp. Why?" Her voice shook with anger and fear, and the gun shook in her hands.

He glanced at it, then met her gaze. "I brought it home for me," he admitted. "Because it belonged to my family."

The pictures still inside had been drawn by Thomas McGregor, of his little sisters, who had died in the lightning fire of which Maria's ancestor had warned them. "But then, after getting to know you and realizing you weren't responsible for the murders, I accepted that it's yours. That's why I fixed the clasp, so you could wear it again. I wanted to give it back to you."

"Why?" she asked. "Like you said, it belongs to your family. It's yours, Mac."

His gut tensed with dread and regret. She had found the journal, too. His sad and sinister inheritance from his father. "Don't call me that," he snapped, and he

began to shake, as he had every time his father had
called him that—usually after he'd beat the crap out of
him or his mother. "Don't *ever* call me that."

"Where did the *Hughes* come from?"

"My stepfather—my *real* father, the man who protected and hid us from the madman who used to abuse
my mother and me."

She nodded. "That was how you knew the witch-
hunter wasn't Curtis Waverly. That's probably also why
you identified with Curtis—you shared similar pasts
and both took your stepfathers' names."

"You were right about my biological father," he said.
"He was crazy." Seth leaned forward, tempted to reach
for the gun. But that other image flashed through his
mind, of her firing the weapon. "You're wrong about
me, though. I want nothing to do with that sick legacy.
I am *not* my father's son. I'm not a McGregor."

"You're the last one."

"Your eldest sister is one, too. She's a descendant
somehow. So are your niece and your four-year-old
nephew. They're McGregors," he reminded her. "Do
you think they'll automatically become witch-hunters
just because of their genetics? It doesn't work that
way."

"Why not? We're all witches just because we're
Durikken descendants. You are what you are." She
raised that gun, pointing the barrel directly at his heart.
"And I can never trust you because of it, but most of
all because you lied to me about it!"

He shook his head. "I didn't lie." He was not a liar.
"I just didn't tell you."

"Because you knew I would never trust you if you

told me the truth," she said. "You knew I would never fall in love with you."

His heart ached with the intensity of his love for her, the love he had known he couldn't declare until she knew his true identity. He held out his hand—not for the gun but for her. "Maria…"

"Was that all part of your plan?" she asked as tears streaked down her face.

"Plan?" he asked, his head pounding with confusion.

"Are you working with Ethan O'Donnell? Or maybe even Curtis Waverly—you two share a common past. Maybe you convinced him that I'm the one who killed his sister so that he would kill me," she said, her eyes dark with mistrust.

If she had been falling in love with him, it wasn't apparent now. She stared at him, her expression hard with hatred.

"Neither of them is smart enough or evil enough to pull this off on their own. As I suspected all along, there had to be a McGregor behind it."

He sucked in a breath of pain. After all they had shared, how could she think him evil just because of who his father had been?

"You might as well shoot me," he suggested, pointing toward the gun, "just like I saw in my vision. It would probably hurt less than hearing your opinion of me." And having all his fears confirmed—she would never trust him. Never love him as he loved her.

The barrel trembled, the gun shaking in her grasp. "What? It was me? You saw *me* shoot you?"

"I saw this," he confirmed. "You with the gun, you firing that gun into my chest when you found out who I was." He swallowed hard. "Was. I got rid of his name. I wanted nothing to do with him and nothing to do with that damn legend."

She shook her head. "I'm not going to shoot you," she said, "unless you try to stop me."

"Stop you? From killing me?"

Since she was so fixated on the past, she probably thought that was the only way to end the witch hunt— kill the witch-hunter's son, no matter that he'd had nothing to do with the killing.

"From leaving," she clarified. She held the gun with one hand while she grabbed up her clothes from the floor.

He lurched forward, hoping to disarm her. But she lifted the barrel to his chest again, to the heart that ached with fear over the thought of her out there without him, at the mercy of the real killer. "You can't leave."

"I swear I'll shoot you," she threatened. "You saw it, so you know that I will."

"I saw other things, too," he shared. "I saw you being drowned."

"You saw my death?"

Maybe if he told her what he'd seen, she wouldn't leave him; she would understand that the danger she was in wasn't from him.

"You don't die by drowning," he said. "He only holds you underwater until you pass out. Then he ties you up, holding you down while he piles rocks on top of you." She gasped, but he forced himself to continue— for her sake. "That's how you die—he crushes you to death."

Tears ran down her cheeks; he wasn't even sure she knew she was crying, though. She was so focused—on hating him. "You only saw that because it's you. That's what you want to do to me."

"I want to protect you, Maria." He swallowed hard, choking on the emotion overwhelming him. Now that she knew all his secrets, he could give her the words he had struggled to contain earlier.

When she'd told him she loved him, he had wanted to declare his feelings. But it wouldn't have been fair…until he'd told her the truth. Now, staring down the barrel of his own damn gun, he didn't care about fair.

"I love you, Maria," he said. "And I want to love you, Maria, for the rest of our lives."

"That'll be short if you try to stop me," she warned him, clutching her clothes to her chest with one hand while she held the gun with the other. She moved around the bed, her gaze trained on him.

"And it'll be short if you leave me," he said. "We've fought him off because we've been together. You won't be able to fight him alone."

"I won't be alone," she assured him, "because I'm keeping your gun." She ducked into the bathroom, the lock snapping behind her.

He followed her and pounded lightly on the door. He might have considered kicking it open, but then she would no doubt believe he was trying to hurt her—and she would hurt him by firing the gun.

"Maria, you have to know I would never hurt you. I'm not the monster my father was. You have to know that." He had struggled with his own doubts growing up, and so had his mother. When he'd started having visions, she had been so frightened that he was going to be like his father. That was why he'd wanted to become an FBI agent, to use his gift for good—not to hurt people as his father had.

"We have this connection," he reminded her. "I feel as though I've known you forever. You have to feel the same way about me. You wouldn't have made love with me if you really believed I was a killer."

The door opened again, and he drew in a breath, hopeful that he'd gotten through to her. But, dressed now, she still held the gun. He would have grabbed it from her if not for the vision taunting him. He had seen her fire it, and from the cold glare she directed at him, she no longer had any feelings for him.

"I don't know you at all," she said. "You made sure of that—with all the secrets you've kept from me. Secrets I should have known…"

"You told me you loved me," he reminded her.

"I was wrong," she said. "I didn't even know who you were. Now that I know, there's no way I could ever love you. The hatred between our families runs too deep."

"It wasn't all hate," he reminded her. "Thomas gave Elena that locket. He loved her."

She glanced down at the locket. "He did love her, and he wanted to protect her. That's why he let her go."

"I can't let you go," he said, holding his hand out for the gun.

She shook her head, her eyes glistening with more tears and disappointment. "Then you don't love me, either."

He looked down the barrel. And he had no doubt now that she would shoot him.

But if he let her leave and something happened to her, he would die anyway. So he grabbed for the gun, and just like in his vision, it went off…

Chapter 14

She moved like a criminal—like Joseph used to move. He had once been able to go invisible—able to move around the most dangerous area of the city undetected. How did his men not notice her?

Was she real?

Or maybe he and his daughter Stacia were so close that he was getting like her, and he had begun to see ghosts, too. The two-way radio he held crackled in his hand. Finally they'd noticed her.

"Joe," Shorty said. "There's some scary chick coming up to your front door—dressed in some cape thing. And she's armed, man."

"She has a gun?" he asked with surprise. From everything her sisters had told him, Maria wasn't the type to go for weapons. With her powers, she didn't need them.

"Sorry, man, that she got past the guys," Shorty said. "You want me to send up some guards—"

"No," Joseph said as Ty headed down the stairs to the foyer. "We've been expecting her."

They had been anticipating her, actually, and for a long time.

Maria couldn't stop shaking, and it had nothing to do with the cold autumn air of the predawn hours. She had fired a gun—a gun she had stolen from an FBI agent. That wasn't all she'd taken from him, though.

She clasped the McGregor journal under one arm as she stood outside the door to her sister's estate. She had slipped past security and made it through the gates surrounding the estate, but not inside the mammoth stone-and-clapboard house. She waited on the porch, in the shadows, her heart pounding with fear and adrenaline.

What if Seth had chased her here? What if she had led the witch-hunter right to her family?

But he already knew Ty, so he probably knew where her sisters were. Why hadn't he tried to hurt them, then? They were the ones who'd killed his father, the ones on whom his father had asked that Seth—that *Mac*—seek vengeance.

Could she have been wrong about him?

She wished she was, but then his voice echoed inside her head, emotionlessly recounting his gruesome visions of her death. She shuddered and then gasped when the door finally drew open.

"Maria, are you okay?" Ty McIntyre asked as he ushered her inside and peered out into the darkness beyond her. "Where's Hughes?"

She glanced back into the darkness, too, in case he'd followed her. There were other men out there—

security guards. But he wasn't there. If he were close, she would have felt it. She would have felt *him*.

"Hughes is not his name," she said, clasping the book even tighter. She had kept the gun, too, in the pocket of the cape she'd pulled from his closet on her way out his door. He'd had the clothes she'd worn in the fire cleaned. "I need to warn my sisters. I know it's late—or early—but I need you to bring them together for me."

"They're all here," he said as he shut the door behind her.

Had they known she would need them?

"Ariel and Elena are staying to help out Irina while she's confined to bed rest." He led her to a wide stairwell. "They're all together in our room."

"And you don't mind?"

He grinned. "I'm a lucky man to have an amazing wife and the support of her incredible sisters. With seven-year-old twins, I could never manage on my own."

"You're busy," she said. "Maybe I shouldn't be here." Especially as there were children in the house, children she might be putting in danger.

"I'm glad you're here," he assured her. "Your sisters are, too."

"They already know?"

His grin widened. "They probably knew you were coming before you did." He led the way up the stairwell and to an open door off a wide hall. His arm extended, he waited for her to cross over the threshold.

But she hesitated, her stomach tight with nerves, and panic overwhelmed her. "I—I shouldn't be here." Her presence might still put them at risk. "It's not safe to be around me." She turned back to the stairs. "I need to leave…"

"No!" Ty's raspy voice wasn't the one that uttered the protest. This voice was soft and feminine yet strong and certain, too. "You're where you belong."

She didn't belong here; she had never belonged anywhere. Although for a little while, she had felt as though she'd belonged…with Seth. But he wasn't who she'd thought he was. And she needed to warn her family that he was the witch-hunter. She drew in a breath, bracing herself, before she turned back to that bedroom doorway.

A redhead stood next to Ty, her fingers gripping his forearm. "It's her—it's really her…" She blinked back a shimmer of tears and gazed intently at Maria. "You look so much like Mama…even more than Irina does. You look so much like her."

"You do," agreed the blonde who stood behind the taller redhead. She was petite with flaxen blond hair and pale blue eyes. "I'm so glad you're here." She stepped forward and stared at Maria, as if unable to believe that she was real. "I keep seeing horrible things."

Things like Seth had claimed he'd seen? But he probably saw those things only because he was doing them to her. It was his hands drowning her until she lost consciousness, his hands piling rocks on top of her until she lost her life.

"Don't torture the fat chick," a voice murmured from inside the room. "I can't get out of bed without these babies falling out. Please bring Maria in here."

Ariel and Elena laughed. Then they reached for Maria, each taking one of her arms. They pulled her into the bedroom with them. Tiffany lamps brightened the large master bedroom and shone across the face of the woman lying on the sleigh bed. Her palms cradled her belly, as if she were already holding her unborn children.

Since she could read minds, she probably knew that she needed to protect them from Maria, from the dark aura that always hung over her.

Irina lifted her hands from her belly and held out her arms. "I'm so glad you're here."

From the first moment she had met Irina, Maria had felt the deep connection with her. Deeper than any connection she'd had with anyone...until she had met Seth Hughes. But that one hadn't been real, because he wasn't real.

"Maria," her sister called to her as if from a distance, bringing her back to them from her maudlin thoughts.

She moved closer to the bed, which Ariel and Elena had already settled onto, but she didn't embrace her sister. Irina was the one who looked like Mama, eerily so.

"We've been looking for you for so long," the dark-haired woman said.

"We've been so worried about you," Ariel added.

"There's no reason to worry anymore," she assured them. She had her life even though she'd lost her heart. "I know who the witch-hunter is."

"You don't," Irina said with a sad shake of her head. "You think you know, but you're wrong."

Maria had been so upset over what she'd learned that she must have stopped blocking her thoughts from her telepathic sister. But the others couldn't hear, so she had to explain. "I'm not wrong. And I have the proof right here."

She handed the journal and the letter over to her oldest sister. Elena's father had been a McGregor descendant, but like Thomas, he had fallen in love with their mother and hadn't been able to hurt her. So Elena's grandmother had carried on the McGregor curse, hurting Mama by having her children taken away. Well, all the children she'd known about; she hadn't known about Maria.

"It's Eli McGregor's journal," Maria explained. "And that letter is from Mama's killer to his son. FBI Agent Seth Hughes is his son. He's the witch-hunter."

She waited for a reaction, for the shock and betrayal she had felt when she'd discovered her locket and the journal in his desk drawer. But they just stared at her. All of them—even Ty, who stood by the open door.

And the shock and betrayal was all hers again. "You knew!" she exclaimed as she backed away from the bed. "You all knew who he was!"

"My husband just found out," Ariel said. "Seth and his mother had changed all their records to hide from Roarke. They'd done a good job of changing his identity."

"So no one would know who and what he is," she said. "A killer. He intends to kill me." Instead he had made love with her and had made her fall in love with him. If only she had known the truth…

"No," Ty insisted. "He really thought *you* were the killer. That was why he's been chasing you all these years—to arrest you. Not to kill you. He would never hurt you."

Her brother-in-law was wrong about that. By keeping the truth from her, Seth had hurt her. The pain and betrayal she felt was worse than when Mama had left her.

Maria shook her head in denial of Ty's claim. "No…"

"I can *feel* his feelings," Irina said. "He's a good man. And he loves you."

Seth had claimed that he did, but Maria couldn't believe that he could love her. She couldn't believe that *anyone* could love her.

"We love you, too," Irina said, speaking again to Maria's thoughts.

Maria shook her head again, unable to accept their love. "You don't even know me."

Elena laughed. "I've had so many visions that I feel as if I've lived your life with you. And Irina has felt all your emotions. We know you."

"And we love you," Ariel added. Her heart shone from her eyes, the turquoise glowing. She was one of those women—one of those generous, loving women.

Maria had wanted to be that kind of woman, but she'd been too busy running all these years. From Seth?

"You can trust him," Irina assured her. "He's not his father."

"He's not the danger," Elena said, her pale eyes glazing over as she slipped into another vision. "He's the one in danger."

"What do you see?" Ariel asked, wrapping her arm around her older sister's tiny waist. "What do you see?"

Elena shook her head. "I don't know. The vision isn't clear…"

Ariel lifted the blonde's delicate wrist, adorned with a charm bracelet with only one charm. A star. And she pressed her own wrist, her own charm—a sun—

against it. Irina reached over and joined her hand with theirs, metal glinting off her wrist and the tiny crescent moon that dangled from a bracelet.

The room warmed, alive with energy. Mama hadn't been lying or even exaggerating about the charms. They did have special powers.

And so did Maria's sisters.

That was how they'd stopped Seth's father. Forever. It was how they'd saved her. They were powerful women. Women she could trust...

Elena slipped into a trancelike state, her eyes locked in a blank inward stare. "He's bleeding," she murmured.

"I didn't shoot him," Maria said as she withdrew his gun from the pocket of the cape she had found in his closet. "I shot in the air—so that he would back off and let me leave. I didn't want him following me. I didn't want to lead him to all of you."

"He knows where we live," Ty said. "I've given him my address. I've invited him here."

"He loves you," Irina repeated insistently. "That's why he didn't dare tell you who his father was. He hated the man, too. His father abused him and his mother. They ran from him, hid from him. He grew up like you and Mama did, running from place to place. You were all running from the same monster."

He had told her the truth, then—about his childhood, about his hatred for his father.

"But the book." Her fingers trembling, she reached for her locket. "And the locket. He had the locket, too. He took it from Raven." She turned to Ty. "The girl who died in Copper Creek. I think he killed her."

"No." Ty shook his head. "You know he didn't. Look

what he's done to protect you. He got run off the road. He nearly died. He's not the killer. And you know he's not."

She wrapped her fingers tightly around the locket. "No, he's not…"

And she had threatened him with a gun despite everything he had done for her. But she had been so stunned and so hurt to learn that he'd been keeping secrets from her—secrets that he knew would affect her. All those times she had brought up the witch-hunter, he should have told her the truth. But he'd kept silent.

Finding out the truth as she had, on her own by accident, had devastated her. And she had been too emotional to think rationally. She had reacted like a wounded animal, lashing out at the person closest to her. And no one had ever been as close as Seth.

Elena grasped her sisters' hands and squeezed her eyes shut, focusing on the images in her head. "He's in danger. Extreme danger."

"Because of me?" Maria asked, her heart heavy with dread.

"He's found the real killer," Elena replied.

"He found Ethan O'Donnell?" And because of her, Seth didn't have his gun to defend himself from the madman.

Ariel shook her head. "No. It won't be possible for Seth to find O'Donnell."

"Why not?" Was Seth already dead?

Ariel could see ghosts, too. Maybe after the way Maria had treated him, he had gone to her sister instead of her. Tears stung her eyes. Had she lost the man she loved…forever?

"Ethan O'Donnell is dead," Ariel said. "Can't you see him?"

Maria blinked, trying to clear her eyes. When had the mist swept into the room?

"Mama brought him," Ariel murmured, her voice sounding far away. "She guided him here—to us."

"Ethan?" The mist shifted into a male form—tall, gawky, with slicked-back hair. "Ethan. What happened? Did Seth do this to you?" Maybe Ariel was wrong and the two men had already had a confrontation. Seth had promised to protect her—always.

"Seth?" the young man asked. "Who's Seth?"

"The FBI agent," she said. "Isn't that who killed you?"

The ghost's image blurred as he shook his head. "No. I don't know the FBI agent. I know my killer. So do you."

"Oh, my God…" She closed her eyes on a wave of dread and fear. And an image flashed behind her lids.

Seth, clutching his chest, blood spurting between his splayed fingers. All the color draining from his face as his life ebbed away…

She hadn't shot Seth but someone else would—or already had. Had the killer confronted Seth at his house, or had Seth stumbled across the man when he had gone looking for her?

"Maria, do you know who the killer is?" Ty asked, his brows drawn together in confusion. He couldn't see or hear ghosts; he had no idea what Ethan had said. He must have just noticed the horror that gripped her.

She nodded and tightened her grasp around the gun. "I have to go. I have to get there before it's too late. Seth thinks Ethan is the killer. He won't realize he's in danger…"

Until he was dying.

"Send Seth a message," Irina suggested. "Warn him."

"He has visions, but he's not telepathic," Maria replied. "He's had visions of my death. He warned me. But I didn't listen to him. I didn't trust him. I told him that I would never trust him—that I would never love him." And now it might be too late for her to take those words back, for her to profess her love again.

"Tell him," Irina said. "You don't have to be telepathic. Not when you have the connection the two of you have. Ty has no special powers, but he can hear me…without my having to say a word. He can hear me because of our love."

Ty tensed, as if he was listening now. "You're going into labor."

"Tell him you love him—" A grimace twisted Irina's face as the labor pains began.

But she didn't need to finish what she had been about to say. *Tell him you love him…before it's too late.*

"I have to go," Maria said. "I have to save him." She headed toward the door, stopped and turned back. "I'm sorry. I want to be part of this family. But I'll be nothing if Seth dies. I'll be nothing…"

"You can't go alone. Wait for me," Ty said, but even as he said the words, he stepped closer to his wife, his arms reaching for her.

"I—I can't wait…"

Because Seth couldn't wait for help; he would be dead soon—because of her.

"I'm sorry to come by at this hour," Seth said as Professor Chandler opened the door. He glanced over his shoulder, looking for the police cars that were supposed to be stationed out front. "Where are the officers?"

The professor shook his head. "I sent them away. I'm fine. Perfectly safe. Ethan O'Donnell would never come after me."

"What about Maria?" he asked, his pulse racing with fear. "Has she been here?"

"She left your protection?"

"Yes." Because he'd lied to her, he had destroyed whatever trust she'd had in him. "This is the only place I could think that she would come."

"Really?" Dr. Chandler asked. "Doesn't she have sisters who live here in Barrett, too?"

"Yes, but she hasn't wanted to see them." Because she had thought Seth—the witch-hunter—would try to kill them, too. "You're the only person she's kept in touch with over the years. You're the only person she trusts."

"The only?" The professor lifted a dark brow. "When you were here earlier this evening, you two seemed quite close."

Seth flinched, remembering how close they had been—his body entwined with hers, buried deep inside her. Their hearts beating the same frantic rhythm.

"Maria doesn't let anyone close to her. Not anymore."

And certainly not him. Never again would Seth get close to her.

"She doesn't trust you? Why wouldn't she trust you?"

"I kept something from her," he admitted. "Something I should have told her when we first met."

"That you're a McGregor descendant."

Shock jarred Seth. "You know that?"

How? He and his mother had been careful to erase their past and any connection to Donovan Roarke. They'd wanted to make sure that he would never find them again. And that no one would ever associate them with the monster the man had been. But their new identity hadn't been foolproof, since Roarke's lawyer and executor had eventually tracked him down.

The professor nodded. "I've been researching that book, you know. About the Durikkens and the McGregors and the Coopers and the Roarkes. I tracked everyone down."

"I'm not a witch-hunter, like she believes," Seth assured her father. "I want nothing to do with that crazy legacy."

"I know. She will, too," the professor said. "Just like her sisters aren't really witches."

"No, they're not," he agreed with a sigh of relief. At least her father understood. "They have some special abilities, though."

"But they don't practice witchcraft," Dr. Chandler said. "They don't cast spells and concoct magic potions. Not like Maria does. She's a real witch, like her long-dead ancestor. Your father shouldn't have gone after the other women at all."

"He was a crazy, sadistic bastard." And no one knew that better than Seth…except for Maria's mother, whom he had so brutally murdered.

How could Maria think, after all the times they had made love, that Seth was anything like his father?

I love you…

The thought popped into his head just as the visions

usually did. Those horrifying visions…of Maria suffering. He had to find her.

I love you…

He flinched, his head pounding as if someone were knocking on it—trying to get inside, trying to read his mind.

"Uh, uh…" He pushed a hand through his hair. "So you never answered my question," he said. "Have you seen Maria tonight?"

"I was asleep," he said, gesturing at the robe he wore over flannel pajamas.

"And I'm sorry I woke you," Seth said. "I just really need to find her." Before any of those horrible visions became reality.

"She has her own key, you know," the professor remarked as if just now remembering. "Maybe we should check the house to see if she came in while I was sleeping."

"Thank you," Seth said. "I appreciate you letting me look around."

The professor nodded. "Sure. I want to make sure she's all right, too. I can check upstairs. I doubt she's up there, though. I would have heard her."

Seth nodded. "I'll look around down here. Thanks again." He hurried around the house, throwing open doors and turning on lights since the fog had come down with him from Copper Creek. The thick mist clung around the house, darkening the windows despite dawn's arrival.

"Professor." He paused at the bottom of the stairs. "Professor? Is she up there?"

"No," the older man called down. "Did you check the basement?"

He hadn't, but the door was there, just around the back of the steps that led up. It stood open, a bare bulb swinging over the stairs leading down. Each step creaked beneath his weight as Seth descended to the dimly lit cellar. When his foot hit the cement floor, he paused and listened.

Something shifted and dropped onto and then rolled across the floor. And someone moaned.

His heart slammed into his ribs, and he shouted her name. "Maria!"

Water stained the floor, overflowed from a wooden vat in the middle of the partial cellar. In front of a stone foundation wall, he saw another mound of rocks.

"Oh, my God! Maria!" Everything from his vision had happened just as he'd imagined it.

And just like in his vision, he couldn't see her face; her head was turned away, her long wet hair soaking the floor beneath her. He ran to her and began to lift the rocks from her body. She hadn't been completely covered yet. Maybe she wasn't crushed, just unconscious from the water in her lungs.

"Get away from her," a deep voice warned.

Seth reached for his gun, but the holster was not at the back of his belt. It was sitting empty on his bedside table. Still crouched next to her body, he lifted off another rock, his hands wrapped tightly around it.

"Put it down," the professor ordered, as authoritatively as he might have commanded one of his students to follow directions in class. He cocked the gun in his hand and trained the barrel right at Seth's chest.

If Maria was dead, it didn't matter if the madman shot him in the heart. He had already lost it…to her.

"You're going to have to shoot me," he told the professor, "because I'm not going to let her die."

"She's a witch," her father said. "She needs to die."

"She's your daughter."

"Maria Cooper is an evil sorceress," Professor Chandler insisted, "just like her mother. Myra Cooper tricked me and seduced me—with her magic potions and mind control."

"You can't blame Maria for what her mother did," Seth said. If only she hadn't held against him what his father had done…however horrible it had been.

"Maria tries to do the same," Chandler said. "She uses me for money—to open those little witchcraft shops of hers."

Seth asked the question he'd never understood. "Why do you give her the money?"

"She messes with my mind," he said. "She makes me feel as though I owe it to her. But I didn't know about her. I didn't know that I'd had a daughter—with the witch. Just like her mother, she deserves to die. It's the only way I'll be free of her."

While the professor was distracted, Seth knocked off another rock. Maria shifted and moaned. But still she faced away from Seth. He had to see her, had to look into her eyes and assure her that she would be okay. He would keep his promise to protect her.

He wouldn't betray her trust again.

I love you…

Was it just his thought—his love for her—echoing inside his head? Or was that her voice he heard? Hell, he could smell her—the sandalwood and lavender that always filled the air whenever she was near.

Wouldn't her fragrance have washed away in the water that soaked her hair and clothes?

"She's your daughter," he repeated. "You can't want to hurt her like this. You can't want to kill her as you have the others."

"She's a witch," the professor said with disgust. "She has to die. All witches have to die! You know this—because of who your father was."

Seth shook his head and rose from his crouch, a rock clutched behind his back. "I'm not going to let you kill her. I love her."

"Then I guess you'll have to die for her."

Before he could react, before he could hurl the rock he clenched, a gunshot rang out, echoing off the cement walls of the cellar. Pain exploded inside him.

He couldn't die. Because if he died, Maria was dead, too.

Chapter 15

Pain pressed down on Stacia, squeezing the breath from her lungs, the blood from her heart. There was pain...

So much pain.

She couldn't stand it anymore. It was tearing her apart. She had to stop it before it destroyed her—before it destroyed them all. She had to stop everyone's pain...

She opened her palm and stared down at the charms. They had been so preoccupied—her mom and her aunts—that they hadn't noticed her slipping them off their bracelets. Aunt Irina had gone into labor, so she'd taken hers off so as not to scratch her babies. Mom and Aunt Ariel had done the same, leaving them all on the dresser just inside the master bedroom.

They would understand. Maybe...

That she'd had to take them. She had to save them and everyone else. But the evil man...

The charms protected the pure and vanquished the evil. They had destroyed the bad man who'd taken away the innocence of her childhood. He hadn't physically harmed her. But he'd shown her an evil that had stolen her innocence. She had had to grow up too fast.

But because she was older than her thirteen years, she knew what she had to do—just as that ancestor for whom her mom had been named had known what she'd had to do. Run. Stacia refused to run. She had to be strong. It helped that Grandma Myra's ghost was embracing her, wrapping the mist and smoke and her ghostly arms around her.

Stacia squeezed the charms tightly in her palm. Her skin warmed as the pewter heated and glowed, shining right through the skin and bones of her hand, illuminating them like an X-ray. This was how her mom and sisters had stopped the witch-hunter.

She hoped that it would work now. She hoped she would save her aunt Maria. And stop her aunt Irina's pain…

And her own…

Because all the pain was tearing Stacia apart.

And then it wasn't just her and Grandma. Her father was there, too, wrapping his arms around them both. He shivered, as if he felt her grandmother's ghost. But he held Stacia tightly; he held her together as the magic flowed through her…

Maria fought to still the trembling in her hand. She had never tried to kill anyone before, had never fired a weapon at a person. She was all about healing with her herbs, protecting with her amulets and crystals.

She wasn't about killing. But she would do whatever was necessary to defend the man she loved.

"Put down the gun!" she screamed at her father from where she stood behind him in the rickety stairwell. "Put it down, or my next shot will hit you."

The professor shook his head. "You didn't mean to hit me. You shot the right person. Agent Hughes—he's the one you hit. The one you should have hit…"

She gasped and ducked her head to see where Seth knelt next to a pile of rocks. He held his hand to his shoulder, where blood trickled down the sleeve of his jacket.

"Oh, my God…" She had done it, just like in his vision. She had shot the man she loved. The bullet she'd fired at the professor must have ricocheted off the stone walls or the stones piled beside Seth. Had her father been about to torture him?

"Maria?" Seth murmured, and his smoky blue eyes widened in shock—more over seeing her than her shooting him. He glanced from her to the pile of rocks. And then she noticed that the stones surrounded a body, one that had been tied down to stakes anchored in the floor.

Just as he had warned her that he'd seen in his visions. There was even the vat of water where a witch could be drowned.

She had been in this house before. But never in the cellar. Had this stuff always been down here?

"Who is that?" she asked, horrified that a body was beneath those stones. "Is it Ethan?"

"It's a woman," Seth replied. "I thought it was you."

"Of course he thought it was you," the professor

said. "That's why he's trying to kill her. That's why I have the gun. I'm trying to stop him."

Maria's gaze traveled from Seth to her father. Had the man moved closer? She tightened her grip on the gun. "He was trying to stop you."

"No, I found him down here," the professor blatantly lied. She could see the untruth in his gaze. "I thought that woman was you," he continued. "I'm so glad you're all right, honey. Hand me the gun."

"No!" She backed up a step and nearly stumbled.

"He's the one," the professor insisted. "You know who he is. A McGregor. He's the witch-hunter. His father killed your mother and would have killed your sisters if they hadn't banded together."

Maria glanced over his head to where Seth crept closer to the bottom of the stairs. He widened his eyes as if he was trying to send her a telepathic message. She had been sending him one ever since she'd left her sisters.

Had he heard her? Did he know that she loved him? She needed him to know that, needed to connect with him so that they could work together, as her sisters had, to vanquish this killer.

But she didn't have the charms. All she had was her locket. And Seth's gun. He should have had his gun. He would have saved her already. He would have saved whoever lay beneath those rocks, too.

"If he's the witch-hunter, why hasn't he killed me?" she asked. "We've been alone together many times. He had opportunity." And so had her father. "Why kill other people? Why not just kill me?"

"All the witches have to die," Dr. Chandler replied—

too quickly. Color rushed to his face as he hastened to add, "You know that's how the witch-hunter thinks."

And now she knew for certain who the witch-hunter was. Ethan O'Donnell hadn't had to say a name. She knew...

"If Seth was the killer, why wouldn't he have killed my sisters?" she asked. "He's known where they are longer than he's known where I was. And they're the ones who killed his father."

"But they're not real witches," the professor said with disdain. "They don't practice like you do, like those other witches wanted to learn from you—how to manipulate people. They had to be stopped." Madness glowed in his eyes. How had she not noticed it before?

Of course, she hadn't seen him very often in the years since she'd discovered who he was. She had never felt comfortable around him, and now she knew why.

He was evil.

"Who's that?" she asked, using her shoulder to gesture toward the rocks and the water-stained cement. "Who's being stopped right now?"

"That last witch's sister. She's a real witch, too. More powerful even than you, Maria," he said with begrudging respect. "She figured it out."

"That you killed her sister." He must have been the man who Raven had been staying with—that was why she'd been so private about him. She'd probably been embarrassed that he was so much older.

He shook his head, but the insanity flashing in his eyes belied his action.

"No, it was him," he insisted. "He's the McGregor heir. He's the one who killed her sister. He's the one trying to kill her." He lifted the gun. "I was just trying to stop him. Let me stop him…because he's going to kill you next. He just let you live so you could lure the others. The ones who wanted to be like you, with the potions and amulets, those were the real witches."

"They're not hurting people," she said. "I don't hurt people."

He jerked his head in a quick nod of agreement. "You're right. Of course. But he does. He hurts people. So let me stop him before he hurts you." He turned back, his gun drawn, but Seth was there with the rock. He swung it at the professor's hand, knocking his weapon to the floor. It skittered across the cement.

But Dr. Chandler was too crazy to stop killing now. He launched himself off the steps, his fists flying at Seth. Grunts and groans emanated from the two men as they locked in combat, grappling together on the floor.

Maria didn't just hear the pain in Seth's voice. She felt it, felt the burning in his shoulder from where her bullet had struck him. She lifted the gun again, but she dared not shoot yet. They moved too fast, rolling across the cement. One of them reached out toward the gun Seth had knocked from her father's hand.

She needed to fire; she needed to stop the professor before he killed the man she loved. But she hesitated, finger on the trigger. What if she shot the wrong one… just like his vision…?

That stray bullet had struck his shoulder. But what if the next one struck his heart—as they'd both envisioned?

Tears burned her eyes, blurring the men so that she couldn't discern one from the other. She couldn't shoot. Footsteps pounded overhead, drawing her attention to the top of the stairs as two men burst through the door. One blond, one dark haired. She didn't need their names to know who they were: her brothers-in-law.

"Help!" she pleaded. "Please help!"

But before they could even join her on the stairs, a shot rang out—echoing again off those stone walls so that she cringed at the noise. And the pain...

So much pain...

Images flashed through his mind: *those big hands holding Maria under water, her wet hair floating on the surface as the bubbles died. Then the rocks, piled atop her body, her hair dampening the cement on which it lay...*

He jolted awake, shouting her name. "Maria!"

"I'm here, I'm right here," she assured him, her fingers gently stroking his damp hair back from his forehead. "I'm here..."

He blinked, trying to focus on the blurry image leaning over him. "It's not you..."

"It is," she said. "It's me. Here—this will prove it." She pressed something into his palm, worn metal that was warm yet from her body.

"It's your locket," he murmured.

"It's yours," she replied. "The locket really belongs to you."

He reached up and cupped her cheek as she leaned over him. "It wasn't you...in my visions. It wasn't you."

"No, it wasn't me," she confirmed. "It was Raven's sister. Violet figured out who was responsible for her sister's death and confronted him."

He flinched as he remembered the torture he had seen so many times in his head and then in the professor's cellar. "And she got herself killed."

"No," Maria said. "You saved her. You got to her in time…before the rocks did more than bruise her and crack a few ribs. She's actually the one who shot the professor. She worked free of the ropes binding her wrists, and she grabbed the gun you knocked out of his hand and killed him."

He was glad that she hadn't been forced to kill her own father. He was also glad that he hadn't killed him. If she couldn't forgive what his father had done to her mother, she would have probably never been able to forgive him for killing her father—even if it had been self-defense.

"I'm sorry," he said, stroking his fingers along her jaw to soothe the pain she was probably feeling. "I'm sorry…"

"What are you sorry about?" she asked, her brow furrowing.

"He was your father."

"He was a monster," she said with a shudder of revulsion. "He killed all those people, and I still don't understand why…"

He shrugged, then groaned as pain gripped his shoulder.

"I'm sorry," she said, pressing her hands to his chest to gently push him down onto the pillows piled behind his back. "Let me get you something to ease your pain."

"No." He shook his head—just slightly, though, so as not to jar his shoulder again. "I must have had too many painkillers. There's so much that I don't remember."

Tears of regret glistened in her eyes. "I shot you."

"I remember *that*." Though at the time he'd had to

ignore the pain so that he would be able to save her from the professor.

But he hadn't saved her…

"I didn't mean to do it," she said. "I was shooting at my father."

"I thought you might have believed what he was saying about me," he admitted. "That I was the witch-hunter."

"I knew he was lying."

But she couldn't claim that she had never doubted him. His heart ached more than his shoulder as he remembered how devastated she had been when she'd learned who he was.

Instead of bringing all that up, he asked, "How did I get back home?"

She smiled. "Your stubbornness. After the doctors bandaged your shoulder, you refused to stay at the hospital. You insisted on coming home."

"I spent too much time in hospitals growing up— when my dad would hurt my mom or me. And he would find us there." He shuddered. And winced with pain. "He would always find us there."

She pressed something to his shoulder, some concoction of hers with the herbs and potions. And she chanted a prayer over him again.

And she healed him more than the doctor had been able to.

"I can take away your physical pain," she said. "But I wish that I could take away your emotional pain, too. That I could make you forget everything he did to you and your mother. He was a monster."

"He was," Seth agreed. "I can't help who my father was, Maria. Who I am…"

"You're a hero, Seth. My hero. I never should have doubted you. Never should have considered that you might be like your father." She leaned down and touched her lips to his, softly, as if she was afraid of hurting him.

He wrapped his uninjured arm around her back and pulled her down onto him. Cupping the back of her head in his hand, he held her mouth to his and deepened the kiss. Then, ignoring the pain in his injured shoulder, he lifted his other arm—and using both hands fastened the chain back around her neck.

She eased back and caught the locket in her palm. "You were right to take this," she said. "It belongs in your family."

"It belongs to you," he said. "All those centuries ago Thomas gave it to Elena to keep her safe. He loved her, like I love you. I would never hurt you. I may be a Mc-Gregor, but I'm not a killer."

"I know that," she said. "I never should have doubted you. I was just so hurt that you hadn't told me. And I grew up with my mama making me run all the time because she was convinced that all McGregors were killers. But you're not a killer. You're a hero, just like Thomas was Elena's hero."

"But I didn't save you," he reminded her, guilt and remorse gripping him. He should have known, should have suspected that the professor had been the killer.

"That's because I had your gun," she said miserably. "Because I stole it from you…"

He glanced around the bedroom. "I don't remember if you gave my gun back to me…"

"David took it," she said.

"David?" He dimly remembered some other men

coming down the stairs to that dungeon of witch-hunting horrors.

"Koster," Maria replied, "my sister Ariel's husband. Ty sent him and my sister Elena's husband, Joseph, with me."

"Where was Ty?" he wondered. The guy had been in Copper Creek when they needed him and had showed up when Waverly had been shooting at them.

"He needed to be with Irina," she replied. "She went into labor last night…when I was at their house."

"You went to your sisters when you left me?" he asked with surprise. She had been so adamant about staying away from them.

She nodded. "I felt as though I had to warn them about you."

He suspected that David Koster or Ty McIntyre had already figured out who he really was. "I'm sorry I didn't tell you sooner."

"I'm not," she said. "If I had known who you were, I wouldn't have let myself fall in love with you."

"You didn't really fall in love with me," he reminded her. "Because you didn't know who I was."

"I knew," she said with a smile full of confidence and certainty. "Your real name isn't who you are. You—the man who kept putting himself in danger to rescue me—are the real man. The man I love."

He expelled a ragged sigh. "Are you sure?"

"Irina was in labor," she reminded him, "but I left her and my other sisters because I was worried that you were in danger. I wanted to be with you."

"You can go now," he offered. "Chandler is dead. You should go—be with your sisters."

"I have the rest of my life to be with them," she said.

"To talk to my sisters and play with my nieces and nephews. I want to be with you instead."

"You can spend the rest of your life with me, too."

She broke into a wide smile. "What are you suggesting?"

He lifted his fingers to the locket. "That I find you a ring to go with this. And you and I make this connection between us legal."

She knit her brow. "I'm still not sure what you're suggesting…"

"If you'd let me up, I'd get down on one knee and ask for your hand…and your heart…and every wonderful part of you…" He leaned forward and pressed his lips to hers. "Marry me, Maria. Become my wife."

She stared at him, her teeth nibbling her bottom lip. She'd said she loved him. But…

"Can you marry a McGregor?" Seth asked, his breath catching at her hesitation. "Can you marry the son of the man who murdered your mother? Or is it all too much for you?"

She shook her head. "I'm the daughter of the man who murdered my friends, who would have murdered the man I love. Who would have murdered me…"

"I don't think he would have," Seth said, trying to offer her hope. "I don't think he would have been able to hurt you…"

"No matter how much he resented me, how much he felt manipulated by me and my mother?"

"I'm not sure that was his motive, either." Or if he'd just gone crazy. "I think he started writing that book, and he got all mixed up in the legend. That's my fault— my ancestor started that first witch hunt."

"And you ended it," she pointed out. "The curse ends with us."

"What about *us*?" He had to know even as his heart tensed with dread. "Are we ended, too?" Before they'd ever really begun?

A smile curved her lips and brightened her dark eyes. "We'll tell our children how they wouldn't have even been here if not for Thomas McGregor letting Elena Durikken go."

"I can't let you go, Maria." He shook his head, trying to clear it of the painkiller fog, and realized what she'd just said. "*Our* children? As in yours and mine?"

"Of course. I'm not having children with anyone else. I want a lot of them," she warned him.

Joy filled his heart. "Good. I never liked being an only child."

"Irina just delivered her second set of twins," she said. "I don't think we'll have to worry about having an only child."

He kicked his legs from under the blanket and planted his feet on the floor.

"Where are you going?" She laughed. "Are you going to run away now?"

"No, I'm going to bring you to your family. I promised them that I would." And instead he had been selfish and kept her all to himself.

She wrapped her arms around him. "I'm with my family. You're my family, Seth. We'll go see the rest of them in a little while. But first I want to celebrate our engagement…if you're not in too much pain."

"With you as my bride, I'll never feel pain again." He turned and wrapped both arms around her. "I love you…"

"Prove it," she challenged him as she tugged him back onto the bed.

She didn't let him prove it, though. She kept him flat on his back as she bewitched him with her lips and her caresses. When she finally eased down onto his straining erection, he was out of his mind, groaning, as tension gripped his every muscle.

"I thought you weren't going to feel any more pain," she taunted as she slid up, teasing him until he clutched her hips in his hands and sped up her ride. Pulling her up. Pushing her down...until his world exploded with pleasure.

She screamed his name as her muscles caught him tight, held him deep, and her orgasm spilled over him. "I love you!"

"I love you."

Maybe he had loved her forever. Or at least three and a half centuries. Their names were different now, but he had always felt the deepest connection with his ancestor Thomas McGregor, almost as if he had once been the man. But unlike Thomas, he would never let the love of his life go.

Pounding echoed throughout the shop as the man hammered in the nails to secure the sign above the door. Maria squeezed around the ladder and slipped out in the sunshine. He was up just high enough that she could admire his tight tush in his worn jeans. But staring at it wasn't enough; she had to reach up and squeeze.

"Maria..." a feminine voice admonished her. "Stop harassing the handyman."

She grinned at her sister Ariel as the redhead flitted around the store, helping her set out candles and crystals for the upcoming grand opening.

They'd already had an event at the new shop, though. They had held a séance to reunite Curtis Waverly with the woman he had loved and lost. Felicia had forgiven him and apologized for doubting him. And finally, Curtis had found relief and closure. That was what the shop was all about—helping and healing.

Elena, who worked at a computer on the counter, glanced up and tsked. "Maria can't keep her hands off that man."

"It's the hormones," Irina commiserated from where she nursed a baby on the couch. The other child slept in the bassinet next to her. There was a nursery in the back of the store, too, with a big playroom. The other kids were there—with Stacia babysitting.

They would be safe with her. At thirteen, Stacia was already the most powerful witch of all of them. Joseph had shared what she'd done with the charms; she had probably saved them all. Irina's difficult delivery might have taken her life if not for Stacia's interference.

And her magic with the charms had protected them from the evil in the professor's cellar—had stopped the bullet from hitting Seth's heart, as they had both envisioned.

"It's okay," Maria assured them with a wink. "My husband won't mind." She glanced down at the pewter wedding band, engraved with a sun, star and crescent moon. It matched the sign that the man nailed above the door of Charmed.

The last nail pounded in, he descended the ladder and wrapped his arms around her, pressing his palms over her protruding belly.

"Will your husband mind if I do this?" he asked as he lowered his head and kissed her lips.

She covered his hands with hers, and their baby kicked beneath their touch. "I don't know. Will you mind?" she asked him. "My wonderful husband…"

He kissed her again more deeply in response. When she pulled away, she was so flustered that she walked under the ladder when she waddled back into the store.

Her sisters all stared at her, their eyes—in shades of pale blue, turquoise green and dark brown—all widened with horror. "Maria, you just walked under a ladder."

She shrugged off the old superstition. "I spent too much of my life believing myself to be cursed. I'm not cursed." Or she wouldn't have found her sisters and developed deep relationships with them.

And if she were cursed, she most certainly wouldn't have met the man for whom she had unknowingly been waiting her whole life. The man fated to be her husband, the father to their children and her whole world.

"I'm not cursed," she repeated as he came up behind her and wrapped his strong arms around her again—offering support and protection even though she no longer needed it. She needed only him and her family. "I'm blessed."

* * * * *

MILLS & BOON®

Two superb collections!

40% OFF!

Would you rather spend the night with a seductive sheikh or be whisked away to a tropical Hawaiian island? Well, now you don't have to choose! Get your hands on both collections today and get 40% off the RRP!

Hurry, order yours today at
www.millsandboon.co.uk/TheOneCollection

15_INSHIP1

MILLS & BOON®

The Chatsfield Collection!

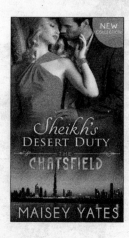

Style, spectacle, scandal…!

With the eight Chatsfield siblings happily married and settling down, it's time for a new generation of Chatsfields to shine, in this brand-new 8-book collection! The prospect of a merger with the Harrington family's boutique hotels will shape the future forever. But who will come out on top?

**Find out at
www.millsandboon.co.uk/TheChatsfield2**

CHATSFIELD_PROMO_BK

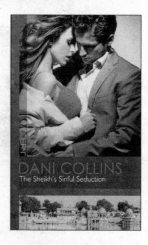

MILLS & BOON®

nocturne™

AN EXHILARATING UNDERWORLD OF DARK DESIRES

A sneak peek at next month's titles…

In stores from 20th March 2015:

- **Moonlight and Diamonds** – Michele Hauf
- **Possessing the Witch** – Elle James

Available at WHSmith, Tesco, Asda, Eason, Amazon and Apple

Just can't wait?
Buy our books online a month before they hit the shops!
visit www.millsandboon.co.uk

These books are also available in eBook format!